Mistress
No More

Also by Niobia Bryant

Heated
Hot Like Fire
Make You Mine
Give Me Fever
Live and Learn
Show and Tell
Message from a Mistress

Published by Kensington Publishing Corp.

Mistress
No More

NIOBIA BRYANT

KENSINGTON PUBLISHING CORP.
www.kensingtonbooks.com

DAFINA BOOKS are published by

Kensington Publishing Corp.
119 West 40th Street
New York, NY 10018

All Kensington Titles, Imprints, and Distributed Lines are available at special quantity discounts for bulk purchases for sales promotions, premiums, fund-raising, and educational or institutional use.

Special book excerpts or customized printings can also be created to fit specific needs. For details, write or phone the office of the Kensington special sales manager: Kensington Publishing Corp., 119 West 40th Street, New York, NY 10018, attn: Special Sales Department, Phone: 1-800-221-2647.

Dafina and the Dafina logo Reg. U.S. Pat & TM Off.

ISBN-13: 978-0-7582-3823-8
ISBN-10: 0-7582-3823-1

First Printing: June 2011

10 9 8 7 6 5 4 3 2 1

Printed in the United States of America

For all the friends in the world who, like me, are *always* the ear to listen and the shoulder to cry on in their friendships, but would never abuse or misuse the information to betray a friend.

Here's to *true* sist*ah*-hood.

Prologue

"hello, jessa bell"

I have played the fool, but no more. I swear it this time.

I made a choice. A scandalous choice. To have my friends or my man: the husband of a friend.

I chose to have my man.

I made a move. A bold move. I sent a message to three friends taunting them all that one of their husbands now belonged to me and only me. Only one truly had reason to worry.

And I made a mistake. An unforgivable mistake. The man I loved—or thought I loved—didn't love me. He didn't need me. He didn't keep his promises. He didn't leave his wife. He didn't come home to me.

And now? And now I have no choice. I lost so much going for the gold only to be left with nothing but the bitter dust of fool's gold in my hands. I risked it all for him. To have him, love him, fuck him on my terms . . . and I lost.

I put my house in Richmond Hills up for sale and leased a home that we were supposed to share. I sent a message that cut all ties with the three women who considered me a friend. My lover and I went from making plans to spend forever together to him telling me we had to slow things down because of my message. Bullshit. If he had stuck to our plan, my message shouldn't have mattered one damn bit.

My celebration and triumph have been replaced by bitter disappointment from his bullshit.

Now I have to make him pay.

I cut my eyes up to the rearview mirror and I could see the fat and flushed face of Lucky, the tubby security guard of the subdivision where I lived along with my three friends and their husbands. I had no doubts that the message I sent yesterday had shaken everyone to the rafters of their stately homes. Not my concern. Not one bit.

I revved the motor of my Jaguar, anxious as hell to get to the home of my lover. It was time for his wife to know the truth. No more guessing. No more games. I was putting his lying ass on blast. I was finally revealing which of the three husbands I had foolishly claimed as my own.

My silver BlackBerry rang inside my purse on the leather passenger seat. Steering with one hand, I dug in my purse and pulled it out. It was him. I pulled my car off the road onto the grass as I looked down at the PDA.

After ending things with a sorry-ass phone call this morning, I had threatened him before giving him the "click." His calls had been nonstop ever since. But was he calling to take back the words that ended things for us or was he just worried that his cover was blown?

I knew if I answered his calls, if I gave him half the chance to sweet-talk me . . .

Taking a deep breath, unable to fight the urge or deny my love, I answered the call and held my BlackBerry to my face. "What?" I snapped, not hiding the anger I still had for him.

I hated that I so badly wanted him to still want me. I couldn't resist him. Deny him. Leave him. I just . . . I just couldn't. Love never fades that quickly. And hope? Hope is eternal.

Yesterday I thought I had everything made. Today? Hmph. What a difference a day makes.

Chapter 1

One month later

Jaime Hall relished the feel of the cool cotton sheets against her naked skin. She stretched her long limbs before rolling over onto her side to clutch the pillow close to her body. With a soft moan that was filled with anticipation, she pressed her face into the softness and inhaled deeply of the lasting scent of her lover's cologne.

Just the thought of him in her bed and deep inside her walls made her wet as her heart raced.

She wouldn't have ever guessed she would spend her days and her nights lying nude in a bed waiting for a man to come sex her. Never.

All her life she'd played the role of being perfect. The perfect daughter, wife, parishioner, soror, and friend. All roles, as if her life wasn't shit but an ongoing play. None of it really gave her a chance to be herself or even know herself, for that matter.

Until Pleasure.

Jaime squeezed her thighs tightly, putting pressure on her throbbing clit as she craved that man. He was a stripper by night, her lover by day.

The things that man knew how to do were scandalously sinful and she couldn't get enough of him. It felt damn good, for once, to want something and to go for it. To get it. To have it. Damn good.

So good that Jaime could care less that a faux friend had sent a text to her and two other friends boasting about her affair with one of their husbands. Jaime's life did not revolve around figuring out the mystery or deciphering the puzzle of which of the men had betrayed their marriage with Jessa Bell. She'd left her husband and the months of verbal abuse and degrading sex behind. She was sure Aria and Renee gave way more of a fuck than she did about the guilty man. All she wanted that night was her freedom. That message had been just the right damn key to unlock the door to the prison of her marriage.

The old Jaime had spent the day pretending not to care on the outside but filled with fright on the inside that the bullshit in her marriage would be exposed for all to see. The old Jaime cared more about what other people thought, cared, or wanted.

"Not no more," she said aloud, closing her eyes as she tried not to count down the minutes until her lover would walk through the door and into her bed.

The new Jaime was ready to be fucked and fucked well. To hell with her marriage. Jessa. That stupid message. And Eric.

Brrrnnnggg.

Her heart raced as she rolled over to the other side of the bed and scooped up her cell phone. Disappointment flooded her like drowning waves. Flipping the phone open, she rolled her eyes. "What, Eric?" she sighed, sounding as bored as she truly was with his constant attempts at reconciliation. She reached for her monogrammed Louis Vuitton cigarette case and lighter.

"We need to talk, Jaime."

"Talk about what?" she asked, lighting a cigarette. She had given up cigarettes, but the day they'd received that message from Jessa, her fears over a flaw in her marriage being exposed had sent her back to her habit.

"I want my life back. I want my wife back. You know that."

Click.

Her eyes shifted at the sound of the bedroom door closing and a smile spread across her face as Pleasure took his hand from the closed bedroom door and reached for the hem of his T-shirt to pull it over his dreadlock-covered head. Tall. Muscled. Skin deeply bronzed caramel. Black tattoos scattered over his frame emphasized just how built he was to please.

Pleasure.

"I think we need to consider counseling, Jaime. We both have a lot to forgive . . . and forget."

Jaime barely heard her husband's pleas as she watched Pleasure unbuckle his belt and ease his denims and boxers over his narrow hips. She bit her bottom lip as each delicious inch of his long and thick curving dick was exposed to her hungry eyes. She was ad"dick"ted.

"Jaime . . . Jaime, you there?" Eric said into his phone.

As Pleasure walked the short distance to the bed with his dick swinging across his muscled thighs, Jaime licked her lips in anticipation. "Yeah, listen, I'll call you back," she said, her voice a whisper filled with nervous excitement.

She had to admit she got an extra thrill from having her soon-to-be-ex-husband on the phone begging her to reconcile while her new lover was flinging the covers away from her naked body.

"Jaime, Pastor Richardson still wants us to meet with him tomorrow before church."

Jaime shivered as Pleasure roughly pulled her by her ankles to the edge of the bed. "I'm not Catholic. You are. He's your priest. Not mine," she reminded him, spreading her legs wide as Pleasure dropped to his knees and buried his dreadlock-covered head between her thighs to lick the lips of her pussy.

"Aaah," Jaime cried out, arching her back and circling her hips as she pushed her free hands deep between the thin locks to grab the back of his head.

"Jaime, are you all right?" Eric asked.

Her eyes popped open as she pressed her lips closed. She remembered that her cell phone accidentally dialing Eric while Pleasure fucked her on the floor of the back room of the strip club was how her husband discovered her affair. Even though she and Eric were done as far as she was concerned, she snapped the phone closed, not wanting to give him a repeat of hearing another man give his wife the pleasure he *never* did.

Brrrnnnggg.

Jaime ignored the ringing phone, using her hand to push it off the bed to the floor to land with a soft thud. "I missed you," she whispered, her words floating up to the ceiling as Pleasure kissed a hot and moist trail up her thighs to her flat belly and then to the valley of her breasts. Her body shivered with each kiss. Her pussy ached. Her heart raced. A fine sheen of sweat coated her body.

Brrrnnnggg.

"I love your nipples," Pleasure moaned against the sides of her breasts before his tongue circled a brown peak twice.

Jaime cried out hoarsely, her hands coming up his strong back to dig her fingers into his broad shoulders. "Suck 'em," she begged.

Her wish, just like always, was his command.

"You like that?" he asked thickly, cutting his deep-set coal black eyes up at her as he dragged the tip of his tongue around her nipple before sucking it into his mouth.

Brrrnnnggg.

"Yes," she cried out, arching her back and not giving a damn that her expensive, bone-straight, jet black weave would be well sweated out by the end of the night.

Back and forth he went from one hard nipple to the

other until she was dizzy and high off his skills. Before Pleasure her husband had been her one and only lover, and even then she'd waited like a good girl for her wedding night—only to discover that they lacked chemistry. Fire. Passion.

She found more of it with Pleasure's dick inside of her for one hour than she had for many years of marriage. It wasn't just that Pleasure had one of those tree trunk kinda dicks while Eric was average. Ever since she first laid eyes on Pleasure at that bachelorette party all those years ago the man made her sizzle just from looking at him.

"What do you want from me, Jaime?" he whispered in the back of his throat, the faint sounds of a wrapper tearing in the background.

Jaime locked eyes with him as she brought her hands up to ball his thin dreads within her fist. "I want you to fuck me," she admitted, spreading her legs wide as he settled his muscled frame atop hers.

"Right now?" he asked, his breath breezing against her mouth before he licked her quivering bottom lip.

"Please."

He smiled and it was filled with his confidence. His sexiness. His boldness.

Pleasure growled a little as he used nothing but his strong hips to ease the tip of his dick inside her. Her pussy lips closed around him. Her juices caused her flesh to smack lightly in the air.

"No massage tonight?" he asked before nibbling the side of her mouth.

"No."

He gave her another delicious inch, her body spreading to accommodate the width of his dick.

"No edible body paint?"

Jaime tugged his dreads bringing his head down closer to hers. She sucked his mouth. "No," she stressed.

Pleasure offered her his tongue to suck as he slid another inch of dick inside her.

"Just dick?" he asked.

Jaime sucked his tongue deeply with a purr, still amazed that this man could make her feel so free. So wild. So freaky. "Just. Dick."

"What's my name?"

"Pleasure."

"And what do I give?"

"Pleasure," Jaime sighed in anticipation.

He growled as he pushed the rest of his dick deeply inside of her until the soft and curly hairs of his dick tickled the clean-shaven mound of her pussy.

"Fuck back, Jaime. Shit, give me that pussy, girl."

Just like he'd taught her, Jaime worked her hips, meeting him stroke for stroke until he took over again and worked her body and her walls until she was exhausted and excited all at once.

Pleasure fucked her like there was nothing else in the world he'd rather do. He stroked her pussy with his dick and spoiled her body with his hands and lips and tongue.

Lord, this man was made for sex, she thought, crying out roughly as he made her come again . . . and again . . . and again.

Hmph. He was worth every red cent.

Although Aria Livewell was sitting next to her husband, Kingston, on the leather love seat, she had never felt so distant from him. Never. That hurt like hell. Their marriage had been the kind that most people dream about. Great chemistry. Explosive sex. Communication. Teamwork. All of it. The whole nine. Not an unreal perfection but a good solid marriage that was destined to last fifty years or more.

And then came the message that day, exposing the betrayal of a husband and a supposed friend.

Aria felt anger burn in her stomach at the thought of Jessa Bell the Jezebel having sex with her husband. Planning to steal him away. Taunting her, Renee, and Jaime with that damn message.

Aria hadn't seen the bitch since, but first chance she got, Jessa's ass was grass. Point blank. Period.

The door to the office opened and both Aria and Kingston looked up as their marriage counselor, Dr. Matheson, strolled in. Aria eyed him. Tall, wide, and balding with a beard, the man looked more like a lumberjack or hunter. Still, after three sessions, she felt comfortable around the man and she especially loved that after calling him about a nasty, down and dirty fight last night, he'd volunteered to meet them for an emergency session on a Sunday. Aria was more than ready to get to the bottom of their shit.

"How did things go last week?" he asked, folding his broad frame in the black leather club chair positioned in front of them.

"The sex was awful," Kingston blurted out, shifting in his seat and holding his hands out there like "There it is."

Aria's eyes got round as saucers as she turned on the sofa to look at him. *No, this Negro didn't.* "Well, it's a little hard to be enthusiastic about having sex when all I can see is you in bed with Jessa's no-good behind," she snapped.

Kingston jumped to his feet. "I did not cheat on you with Jessa or anybody else and I am sick and tired of explaining myself in my marriage over some other man's bullshit."

Aria jumped to her feet and pointed her finger at him. "Mr. Perfect cursing. Oh my Lord, hell is about to freeze over!" she exclaimed emphatically, damn well meaning to be sarcastic.

Kingston eyed her, his handsome face tight with anger.

"Why do you feel Kingston is Mr. Perfect?"

They both turned their heads to look down at Dr. Matheson calmly sitting there but watching them with eyes like a hawk.

Aria sighed as she plopped back down on her end of the sofa. Kingston adjusted his pants before he settled down on his end.

She could hardly believe how badly Jessa's message had fucked with her marriage. She couldn't believe any of the shit that went down.

She could see and remember that text clear as day. Word for word.

LIFE HAS MANY FORKS IN THE ROAD AND TODAY I'VE DECIDED TO TRAVEL DOWN THE PATH LEADING YOUR HUSBAND STRAIGHT TO MY WAITING AND OPEN ARMS. I CAN'T LIE AND SAY I HAVE REGRETS. I LOVE HIM MORE THAN YOU AND I NEED HIM MORE. YOU SAW HIM FOR THE LAST TIME THIS MORNING. TONIGHT HE COMES HOME TO ME. HE'S MY MAN NOW. THANKS FOR NOT BEING WOMAN ENOUGH 4 HIM.

XOXO

How in the hot hell she could forget it? Especially when all three husbands had come home that night, all three denying Jessa's words. All three claiming it wasn't them.

That bitch was supposed to be their friend—especially *her* friend—since their college days. Straight bullshit. No chaser.

"Aria?"

She shifted her eyes to Dr. Matheson.

"Why do you feel Kingston is Mr. Perfect?"

Aria bit the IMAN gloss from her lips as she closed her eyes and spoke the truth about how she felt. "He is *too* good to be true," she admitted softly, feeling emotional.

She felt Kingston stiffen beside her. "I am sick of this—"

"Let her finish, Kingston."

Blinking away tears, Aria wrung her hands. "I always feel like I am waiting for the other shoe to drop. I feel like this marriage is what everyone dreams of but no one has—no one I know anyway. And so I was waiting for something to pop off, something to prove that . . . that . . . that . . ."

"That what, Aria?" Dr. Matheson nudged.

"I don't know. I . . . I . . . don't . . . I don't know." Aria shrugged.

"You're right, you don't know," Kingston muttered under his breath.

Aria side-eyed him. "No, what I don't know is if my husband fucked my friend. I don't know if my husband was planning on leaving me to be with my friend. That's what the hell I don't know."

"Because I'm too good to be true," he drawled.

"Damn right," she flung back.

"So if I beat on you, cuss at you, cheat on you, lie to you, and disrespect you, then what?" he asked, turning in heat to face her, his expression incredulous. "Why is it so hard to believe that there are good men—good black men. That's crazy!"

"Because I know men can't be trusted. As soon as you give them a foot of space they no good ass is off cheating and tricking and doing shit they got no business. I know," she stressed with emotion. "I. Know."

Dr. Matheson jotted something on his notepad. "And how do you know that, Aria?"

She froze, hating that her eyes shifted. She hated that

the fear she carried with her was just as strong as ever. Secrets had a way of revealing themselves. Secrets that filled her with guilt every day. Secrets that could— would—ruin her marriage.

Wild teen years filled with lots of partying, weed, and even more men—most married. Trying to be grown way too soon. Abortions. Liquors. Scheming. Lying.

And now she couldn't have children.

That was the secret she'd confided to a friend and she'd been afraid Jessa would tell Kingston about it. But she hadn't. She couldn't have because he would have confronted her about it. Having children was the next step in his plan for their happily ever after.

Kingston didn't know.

"I just know," was all that she finally answered.

"This myth that there are no good black men is just that: a myth," Kingston said. "I've done nothing to make my wife suspect me. Nothing but do what I'm supposed to do as man—as a husband: love my wife. That's it. I love my wife. I'm good to my wife. And I'm being punished for that. A brotha can't win for losing."

Aria's eyes were troubled as she shifted them out the window to the late summer scene. All of her doubts plagued her. Was it possible that Kingston was not the guilty husband? Was she punishing her husband for nothing and ruining her marriage?

Was the fact that a little ghetto girl from Newark with brains enough for a full scholarship to Columbia had actually snagged an upper-middle-class man who seemed to step right out of a romance book so hard to believe?

"And do you love Kingston, Aria?"

"With all my heart, Dr. Matheson," she stated, without hesitation, question, or second thought.

"And Kingston, do you love Aria?"

"I love her. I love the hell out of her. . . ."

Aria felt waves of relief flood over her.

"But if she doesn't appreciate me and trust me . . . then I don't know if we'll make it."

Aria turned to face him. She knew her husband very well. There was no doubt that the words he spoke were not an idle threat.

Another woman is pregnant with my husband's child.
Another woman is pregnant with my husband's child.
Another woman is pregnant with my husband's child.
Anotherwomanispregnantwithmyhusbandschild.

Renee Clinton dropped her head into her hands and fought the urge to scream at the top of her lungs. To release all the pain, the frustration, and the disappointment. "Maybe if I get it out it'll stop eating me up inside," she muttered, her eyes closed as she leaned back heavily in her office chair.

Another woman is pregnant with my husband's child.
Another woman is pregnant with my husband's child.
Another woman is pregnant with my husband's child.
Anotherwomanispregnantwithmyhusbandschild.

"I hate my life."

She folded her feet beneath her in the chair as she looked at the framed pictures of her family. Snapshots of a better time—not the best of times but definitely better than now. She laughed bitterly at the thought that she'd spent a full day worrying about whether Jessa Bell had fucked her husband when she'd been completely blindsided by the news that her husband had cheated and his mistress was pregnant with his child. "Talk about not seeing the forest for the trees," she muttered sarcastically.

Jessa was the least of her damn worries.

Brrrnnnggg.

She cut her eyes over to the cordless phone ringing on the base. Who could it be?

Her husband with his new responsibilities and obligations to another woman? Or her kids off enjoying their young lives without a real care in the world? Or her friends who were caught up in the drama of their own marriages?

Beep . . . beep . . . beep.

"Hi, this is Jackson . . . Renee . . . Aaron . . . and Kieran. The Clintons. We're not available to take your message. After the beep, do your thing."

"Hmph. I need to change *that* shit." After the gun she'd pulled on him the night of his big "revelation" Jackson didn't have any choice but to move the hell out. Jackson's no-good cheating ass was now the proud renter of a two-bedroom town house downtown.

Beep.

"Renee, this is Darren. You really need to show up at the luncheon for the upcoming CancerWalk. All the head figures are looking for you to be there. Call me back so I know what to say."

That shit went right out of her head. It was Sunday. How many weekends had she been off at work while her husband had been fucking another woman? No. She couldn't handle it anyway. Her assistant was a handy little thing and she knew he would handle things. "Tomorrow, I will go to work. Tomorrow," she promised, her words sounding hollow to her own ears.

The job she'd once loved was now a reminder of her failed marriage. Her need for a career had caused such a wedge in her marriage. These days she couldn't muster the passion and love she'd had for working for a nonprofit benefiting cancer. These days she was too busy nursing a shattered heart.

"Love don't live here anymore," Renee sang, completely off-key as she reached for the bottle of Patrón and poured herself a hefty shot.

Beep . . . beep . . . beep.

Straight tequila was an acquired taste, especially for a causal drinker, but for the last month she had come to love everything about the liquor. Every single thing. The look of it as it poured into a clear glass. The smell of it filling her nose as she held the glass to her lip and prepared to take a sip. Even the slight burn in her throat as she swallowed. And finally . . . finally . . . the way the liquor made her numb.

Her husband's outside baby. Her job. Her marriage. Her stress. Her kids. Her secrets. Her husband's secret. Her bullshit.

The bullshit.

All of it went away when she was deep into her Patrón. All of it.

"Fuck that shit," she muttered, swiveling in her chair to turn away from the photo of her two children, smiling and happy without a true care in the world.

And how would they feel when they discovered their father had a child on the way with another woman? How do you explain *that* to children? Especially teenagers.

She couldn't even grasp all of the emotions that flittered through her in the course of a day. How was she supposed to be ready to take on their feelings, their reactions, and their questions as well?

"I shouldn't be dealing with this shit." Sighing, Renee lifted her glass, took a deep inhale that filled her chest, and then sipped intensely, letting the tequila float over her tongue before she swallowed it with only a slight wince.

This last month of her life had been the absolute worst. She never dreamed shit could be so damn bad.

Never.

And she needed her friends. Although she was confident that Jackson was too busy fucking some other woman to slut around with Jessa Bell, just the fact that the scandalous bitch had sent the text was enough for Renee to cut her ass loose. Plus, if she was dirty enough to fuck either Aria's or Jaime's husband then Renee figured the slut could have just as well have stabbed her in the back, too.

"So fuck you, Jessa Bell," Renee said aloud, wiping a bit of spittle from the corner of her mouth.

Since Jaime had walked away from Eric and their marriage, Renee hadn't seen her and they'd spoken on the phone only briefly. Whatever new life she was carving for herself didn't seem to include her husband or her friends.

"C'est la fucking vie, Jaime."

And Aria.

"Hmph." Renee shook her head, running her trembling free hand through her short, ebony curls.

She couldn't believe that Aria had had the nerve to judge her. Yes, her marriage had been so shaky and she had felt so neglected by Jackson that she'd almost given in to a fleeting attraction to her assistant, Darren. Only his homosexuality had kept them from sealing the deal on the most awkward foreplay ever.

In a moment of weakness she'd admitted her near infidelity to a friend and she'd felt Aria's cold shoulder ever since. No lunches. No random phone calls throughout the day. No dropping by each other's house to gossip or catch up. Just bullshit waves or head nods usually shared by strangers.

"To hell with you, too, Aria."

She really needed her friends more than ever. In truth they all had shit to deal with, but it would be a helluva lot easier if they toughed the bullshit out together.

They hadn't even discussed the message or Jessa Bell since that day.

Another woman is pregnant with my husband's child. Another woman is pregnant with my husband's child. Another woman is pregnant with my husband's child.

Pain that was becoming as familiar as well-worn slippers clutched at her chest and refused to let go . . . until she swallowed down another drink. And another. And another.

"Ma! We're home."

Renee lifted her head from the desk, using her hand to wipe the drool connecting the side of her face to the executive desk mat. Her head suddenly pounded and her heart raced like crazy. Sweat matted her short, ebony curls to her head.

"Ma! Where you at?"

"When the hell did I fall asleep?" she asked herself, as her eyes shot to the door of the office she used to share with her husband. Her kids were home from their weekend visit to their father's new bachelorhood.

Renee grabbed the bottle of Patrón and hid it beneath the papers and discarded bills in her wastepaper basket.

"Ma! You home?"

Their voices were getting closer. That innocent teenage chatter about crushes, the newest sneakers, or the hottest videos. Lives that shouldn't be filled with lies and pain.

"Shit," she swore, yanking open the drawer to her desk to frantically push stuff aside to find gum or a breath mint.

Nothing.

The office door swung open and Renee looked up with red-rimmed eyes as her seventeen-year-old son and fifteen-year-old daughter came to a stop. The expression on their faces went from happy to completely devoid of emotion.

Kieran eyed her with clear and present anger. "Is that what you did all weekend, Ma? Drink?"

So they know, Renee thought, wiping her face with her hands as she struggled to sit up straight in her chair. "Excuse me, but I'm your mother. Not the other way around."

"You don't act like a mother anymore," Aaron snapped, his broad face a junior replica of his father.

Inwardly, Renee couldn't handle it. The truth of their words was just another problem. Another wrong. Another damn stressor. She couldn't handle it. Not now. She wanted to shut the door, close the curtains, and turn off the lights. It was a struggle to maintain any semblance of composure.

"So I'm the bad parent, huh?" she asked them, welcoming the anger she felt rising as the alcohol still in her system fueled her emotions.

"Is your drinking the reason Daddy left?" Aaron asked.

Ain't that a bitch?

Renee laughed bitterly as she rose to her bare feet and stumbled around the desk to stand in front of her children. "So I'm the reason your daddy and I broke up? You two think that, huh? You had to find somebody to blame for this . . . and you two picked *me?*"

They both stepped back from her, their eyes widening. "Ma, why are you drinking so much!" Kieran yelled, crossing her slender arms over her chest.

"I'm just toasting your father's new baby that's on the way," she snapped, closing her eyes and tilting her head back as soon as the words left her mouth.

"You're lying!" Kieran screamed.

WHAP!

It wasn't until her hand landed on her daughter's cheek that Renee even realized she'd swung at her. Kieran gasped and held her own hand to her cheek.

"Dayum, Ma," Aaron said in obvious disbelief.

Renee reached out for her daughter, who turned and ran from the room, the sound of her sneakered feet tearing up the stairs echoing.

BAM!

Renee felt the slam of her daughter's door reverberate through her body. She craved a drink.

"Is what you said true, Ma?" Aaron asked. "Does Daddy have a baby on the way?"

Renee just dropped into a nearby armchair, putting her head in her hands. "I don't want to talk about this right now, Aaron. Just go to your room and I'll be up in a minute. Okay?"

Aaron stepped close to her and lightly placed his hand on her shoulder. "Are you okay, Ma?" he asked.

She kept her face—with its tears and embarrassment—in her hands and nodded her head. And she felt relief when her son finally turned and left the room.

Renee knew without a doubt that she had just made a bad-enough mess horribly worse. She reached over and grabbed the wastepaper basket, quickly snatching the bottle from beneath the paper camouflage. For the first time ever, she didn't even bother with a glass, just popped the top and took a swig.

She just wanted to forget. Fuck it.

Chapter 2

Jaime released a heavy breath filled with every bit of the emotions she was feeling. The nervousness. The anxiety. The fear and the triumph.

For so long she had been the woman scorned in her marriage. She had to admit to herself—and anybody else that would listen—that she got a thrill from Eric chasing behind her.

When he had me, he didn't want me, she thought, easing out of her silver Volvo C70 in a strapless gray dress by Tracy Reese.

The valet drove off in her car just as one of the heavy wooden double doors of the restaurant opened. She eased her long slender clutch under her arm as Eric left the restaurant and walked up to her. With deep-set feline eyes that hinted at her mother's Asian legacy, Jaime watched the handsome man she had once loved and cherished. The hard lines of his clean-cut bronzed face with those soft and full lips that she'd thought she would kiss forever. The broadness of his shoulders. The cocky strut of his walk. The way his clothes hung off of his frame. She couldn't ever deny that he was a handsome man, but now she knew there'd been an evil streak deep within him all that time.

Her affair had brought it to the surface.

"Thanks for agreeing to meet me, Jaime," Eric said, stepping forward to wrap his arms around her. "You look so different but still beautiful as ever."

Jaime stepped back, thinking of the harsh words and sexual cruelty he'd put her through in the past. "It was time," was all that she said, stiffening her spine. A memory of his hand around her throat the night she left him came back to her. She reached in her purse for a cigarette and lighter.

"It's time, Jaime. Go hard or go back home . . . to Eric."

Eric let his arms drop back to his side with a lick of his lips. "You always loved the food here," he said, saying nothing about her smoking even though his eyes dipped down to her filled hands.

Rolling her eyes, Jaime said nothing as she shoved the items back into her purse as she walked beside him back to Ma Belle's, the upscale soul food restaurant in Maplewood, New Jersey. Every year Eric and she had come to the spot to celebrate all of their events: anniversaries, birthdays, and holidays. So many different milestones in the life of Eric and Jaime Hall. And eventually so many occasions of pretending to be happy in public.

As soon as they walked into the brick building, the flamboyant host's smile became brighter than a thousand lit bulbs. "Our favorite couple. How are you, Mr. and Mrs. Hall?" he asked, already reaching for two leather-bound menus.

Jaime froze when Eric slid his arm around her waist and snuggled her close to his side. "Thanks, Antoine. We're doing real good."

Jaime smiled even though she was busy thinking: *No, this Negro is not about to front?*

"Right this way." Antoine turned away from them.

No. No. Hell no.

Jaime jutted her elbow back hard enough to knock Eric's arm from her body. "Um, Antoine," she called out softly.

He turned. "Yes, Mrs. Hall."

"Actually, I'd like for you to address me as Ms. Pine. That's the name I'll be using when our divorce is final," she said with ease.

Antoine's lips pursed as his eyes widened just a bit at her words. "Um . . . okay. Right. Yes. Then, um . . . um . . . Mr. Hall and Ms. Pine, right this way."

Antoine was polite but his eyes said "DRA-MA!" before he turned again, avoiding Eric's eyes.

Jaime followed behind him, feeling free of the bullshit. Eric's hand tightly gripped her upper am, stopping her. She turned enough to look down at his hand and then up into his eyes. He released her and smoothed his double-knotted silk tie.

"Was that necessary, Jaime?" he asked.

She nodded. "Yes, Eric. It was *very* necessary and *very* true," she said, before turning to follow Antoine.

The smell of the Southern-food-with-a-twist cuisine made her stomach growl like crazy. *I guess my diet of Pleasure's dick isn't very filling.*

That made Jaime smile. Pleasure's dick was like a chocolate-dipped banana built to please. She laughed a little to herself. Soon she didn't find shit funny when she spied the table Antoine led them to. Both her parents and Eric's decked out in their Sunday finest, along with Father Richardson, were sitting there waiting for them with serious expressions. Her steps slowed but the anger she felt shot through her body with a quickness.

Eric stepped past her to pull out one of the two empty chairs directly between her mother, Virginia Osten-Pine, and his mother, Kittie Hall. "Here you go, baby," he said.

Jaime's eyes met his. He knew damn well the position

he was putting her in, blindsiding her with their parents and his clergy, knowing they all wanted nothing more than to see them reunite. She hadn't seen any of them since she left Eric.

To her it looked like Eric's eyes dared her not to give in.

Lord knows it wasn't the time or the place. "What is this, an intervention?" she said lightly. Jokingly but truthful to her actual thoughts.

"It is a family dinner," her mother said, her hand crossed primly in her lap. "We are a family joined together by your marriage to your Eric."

Translation: Your marriage to Eric is not over.

Eric pulled the chair back some more.

Jaime noticed that the caramel skin over his knuckles was stretched thin from his gripping the back of the chair so tightly. But she stayed rooted in her spot as she felt the pressure and the tension and the expectations. It was too much. It was just too damn much. She felt nauseous.

She felt everybody's damn eyes on her.

Her mother's disapproval.

Her father's forgiveness.

Mrs. Hall's nervousness.

Mr. Hall's contempt.

Father Richardson's assessment.

And Eric's pleading.

It was all too damn much.

I wasn't prepared for this bullshit today.

There was no way she could get out of this easily. It was too many voices, and opinions, and reprimands against her. Just her. The shit wasn't fair.

I can't beat 'em, so I'll join 'em . . . for now. With a cold stare into Eric's eyes Jaime forced herself forward to finally take the seat he offered.

When his hands landed lightly on her shoulder she fought the urge to snatch up a fork and dig it deep into his flesh. *Slick bastard.*

He took the seat next to her at the round table and Jaime felt her dislike for him go up a big notch. As they all chitchatted like this wasn't the most awkward situation, Jaime tuned them all out.

She thought about rolling over in her bed this afternoon, not at all surprised to find she was alone. Pleasure had left while she slept off a sexual explosion from their last go-round in the shower. It had been a day filled with Pleasure. Her body, particularly her pussy, had felt turned inside out.

"What are you ordering, baby. Your usual?"

Jaime side-eyed Eric. "I'm tired of the usual," she said to him, clearly speaking between the lines even as she ignored the hunger grumbles of her stomach.

Eric was relentless in his desire to reconcile, but Jaime could no way in hell fathom going back into the prison of her marriage. The role of the perfect wife smiling on the outside while slowly dying on the inside awaited, but she couldn't play the part anymore.

Besides she found it bizarre that he wanted to reconcile. For the last six months of their marriage he pretended to love her in public, tolerated her in private, and humiliated her in bed.

Her annoyance went up yet another notch when he ordered for her.

Bzzzzzz.

Jaime opened her clutch and removed her cell phone, not missing Eric's eyes on her movements. A text. She left her cell hidden by her purse flap and opened the message.

> I feel like eating UR pussy. U Home?
> This 1s on me.

Her heart raced. Pleasure. She wasted no time texting him back, not really giving a damn if Eric snatched the phone and read the messages.

NOT HOME. WILL CALL WHEN YOU
CAN CUM. ☺

That made Jaime's clit swell with life. As she pushed the cell phone back deep into her clutch, a smile smooth as butter spread across her face. Long night ahead, she thought, as the servers began to bring out the steaming hot plates.

"Let's bless the food," Father Richardson said, his round and bald head beaming beneath the track lighting of the restaurant.

Eric forced Jaime's left hand out of her lap and into his own hand. Her mother reached for her right hand and then pulled Jaime over toward her. "I forgive you," she whispered in Jaime's ear. That made her mouth drop open.

Remembering the harsh words and lack of support her mother had for her, Jaime didn't want her forgiveness. She felt her mother should ask for hers.

Jaime focused back on the prayer.

". . . and we thank you for the reuniting of your children Jaime and Eric," Father Richardson said.

Jaime's head jerked up. *The what?!*

"With their love, my guidance, and most important Your presence in their marriage I know this union will succeed."

She eased her hand out of Eric's and then slid it beneath the white tablecloth to tightly grab his dick and balls.

He grunted in pain and shock.

Jaime leaned in close to his ear, whispering, "If you ever pull a stunt like this again I will castrate you and then feed it to you. Understand?"

He nodded once.

Jaime released him and then stood. Everyone looked up at her. "I'm sorry, but Eric has lied to you all. He lied to get me here. We are not getting back together. We are getting a divorce. Please, please respect that this is what *I* want and . . . it is what *we* need. Please."

Before they could throw holy water on her and begin the tirades, Jaime tucked her clutch under her arm and got the hell away from them and the charade.

As soon as they got home, Kingston was called into the hospital and the last thing Aria wanted to do was sit home alone with her thoughts, her regrets, and her doubts. She grabbed her monogrammed Coach duffel and her keys, and headed out of their spacious Mediterranean-styled home to climb into her silver Range Rover. As she reversed down the paved driveway, she paused and turned her head to look up the street at Jessa Bell's brick and stone French country-styled structure.

The bitch hadn't been back to her house in Richmond Hills since her coward-ass message. And Aria had spent many a day and night waiting for the bold bitch to return. "Hmph," Aria grunted, imagining the Brick City beatdown she so badly wanted to lay on Jessa.

"Dumb bitch," Aria drawled, checking for traffic before she reversed onto the street.

She *needed* to confront Jessa. She needed to find out who the tramp had slept with and planned to run away and start a new life with. Aria felt like she needed it more than she needed air and water. She needed to know if all her fears about Kingston were true. Had her friend put him in the corner and forced him to come out?

Aria pounded the wheel in frustration as she cruised at fifteen miles per hour through the winding streets of the cul-de-sac. Richmond Hills was the very epitome of suburban upper-middle-class living, but she saw none of the well-manicured lawns, perfectly maintained homes, and

clean streets. For all outward appearances it was the epitome of nothing but happy homes.

"A bunch of bullshit," Aria muttered, cruising past the
security station and through the electronic wrought-iron
gates to the world outside of Richmond Hills.

She listened to some classic R&B as she made the forty-
minute drive to her mother's house in her hometown of
Newark. Although she didn't get home weekly like she
used to, Aria always felt a different energy as soon as she
got into her hometown and began to reminisce on the days
growing up in the city. She'd gotten her street smarts from
growing up on Sixteenth Avenue, her book smarts from
her full scholarship to Columbia University, and her common sense from her mama. All that equaled one bad chica
not taking no shit.

She floated easily between the roles of the doctor's wife
and the inner-city girl willing to deliver a cussout and a
beat-down.

Aria knew she had come a long way from her past to
being an award-winning journalist and writer married to a
prominent surgeon. She was proud to be a ghetto girl who
had fought hard for her dreams. And that's why it was damn
hard to think of life without Kingston. Or a life where she
had to swallow him cheating on her.

She didn't want her happily ever after fucked with.

But if she discovered Kingston had cheated with Jessa—
or any other woman—could she forgive and forget?

Sighing, Aria turned the Range Rover off Springfield
Avenue onto Seventeenth Street. She smiled a little as she
passed her old school, South Seventeenth Street Elemen-
tary, on her left and Westside Park on her right. Eighteen
years of her life were spent in this part of the Central Ward.
There were so many memories she would never forget . . .
and many she wished she could.

She parked in front of the three-family apartment

building where she'd grown up. Aria grabbed her purse and made sure to lock and alarm the Rover before she stepped up onto the sidewalk.

Aria was headed up the brick steps but paused at the sounds of laughter and music coming down the alleyway in between the two apartment buildings. She headed that way, knowing her crazy, tell-it-like-it-is family was in the backyard.

Sure enough her family was scattered about the small yard. Her mother and three aunts were in the middle of the paved backyard laughing and doing the Electric slide.

"All right now," Aria said loudly, raising both her hands in the air as she rushed over in her Guiseppe heels to join them.

Her uncle and cousins, scattered around the yard sitting in chairs, cheered her on. Heather Goines, an older, slightly shorter, and far curvier version of Aria, winked at her daughter as she rocked her hips down to the floor and then brought her body up with a sassy little kick and a big laugh that echoed from deep within her.

Aria loved her mother endlessly.

Heather was a no-nonsense, tell-it-like-it-is woman who loved to laugh, to dance, and to help everyone.

Just laughing, dancing, and chilling with her family, Aria was almost able to forget about the troubles in her marriage. Almost.

"I didn't know you was coming down," Heather said as they all left the makeshift dance floor.

"And I didn't know y'all was chillin' and grillin'," Aria countered as she hitched her purse up higher on her shoulder before taking a seat next to Uncle One-Eye.

He turned and peered at her through the oversized shades his optometrist had given him thirty years ago when he had surgery on his left eye, a casualty of a car accident during his young and running wild days. "Ain't seen you in a while," he said, the smell of his AXE body spray heavy in the air around him.

Aria blinked as her eyes filled with tears. She leaned back from him. "I've been busy with work, Uncle One-Eye."

He leaned over and nudged her with his shoulder. "Your mama brag on you all the time, making all that money and married to that doctor."

Aria reached in her purse, not at all missing the hint, and folded a couple hundred dollar bills in her palm to slide to him. While in college, it had been her mother and her uncle scraping to send their last so that she had money in her pocket. Now that she made a good living, Aria made sure to take care of them.

"Hot dayum. That's my niece. Heh-heh-heh!" Uncle One-Eye laughed like he'd won the lottery as he slid the bills into his shirt pocket and stood up to shuffle onto the dance floor.

"Aria, you want something to eat?" her mother called over from the smoking grill positioned by the rear door leading into the apartment building.

"Yeah, Mama." Aria reached for her cell and dialed Kingston's cell number and office number. Both went straight to voice mail. That made her stomach nervous as hell.

Was he really at the hospital or was he locked away with Jessa Bell?

Aria closed her eyes at a vision of Kingston's dark and strong buttocks clenching as he stroked between Jessa's thighs. His mouth on her breasts. His hands on her body. His words of love whispering in her ear. His seed filling her womb.

Heat filled her chest. It was a mix of anger, mistrust, pain, and complete frustration.

Aria kept calling Kingston's phone, unable to explain

her need to keep trying to reach him. Knowing with each failure to reach him that her emotions were running high and she was likely to go off on her husband, Aria stood up and headed for the alleyway.

"You leaving?" someone hollered out after her.

Aria shook her head and kept it moving up the long alley. Kingston's voice mail came on again.

Beep.

"Kingston. I don't know where you are or what the fuck your sneaky ass is up to, but I am not the one to fuck with . . . and you know that. You better call me ASAP or shit 'bout to get real motherfuckin' hectic—"

"Hey, cuz, can I talk to you for a sec?"

She paused, turning to find her cousin P-Nut standing behind her. *Did she ear hustle my damn conversation? What the hell?*

"What, P-Nut?" Aria snapped, her face filled with the frustration she felt.

P-Nut pushed her hands into the back pocket of her jeans. "I hate to bother you but—"

Aria ended her call and rammed her cell inside her purse. "I don't have no money."

"What?" P-Nut snapped, her round and pretty face filling with anger. "I wasn't gon' ask you for no fucking money, Aria. I wanted to use you as a reference on a job application. Damn, why you come at me like that?"

Oh shit. "P-Nut, I'm sor—"

"You get on my damn nerves, Miss High and Mighty Ass, acting like everybody need you and your money."

Aria went from apologetic to pissed. "P-Nut, don't front like your ass don't borrow money. Matter fact you been in my pocket for five hundred dollars for the last five years. Since you took it there . . . hello, here the fuck I am, too."

"Ooooh my God. Lord help me pay her back that five hundred damn dollars." P-Nut stomped her foot.

Aria raised her hand. "Amen to that."

"Hey, hey, hey. What the hell going on?" Uncle One-Eye hollered from the end of the alley.

"Nothing but your niece acting like she better than somebody with her nasty-ass past," P-Nut snapped, eyeing Aria with a head roll that screamed, "Now what?"

And *that* brought out the old Aria from the early nineties and not the doctor's wife living in a home worth a quarter of a million dollars. She swung quick as shit but P-Nut stepped back to avoid Aria knocking her the hell out.

Her mother raced up the alley and squeezed past P-Nut to jump in between them. "Oh hell to the no. We don't play this fighting bullshit. Two grown women in the alley like a couple of drunks. What the *hell*?!"

"I'm sorry, Auntie," P-Nut said.

"I don't have time for this." Aria just turned and stalked to her Range Rover. Her mind was on finding out just where the hell her husband was. Not family drama.

"Aria Monique Livewell!"

Aria heard her mother but she kept moving until she was behind the wheel of her Range Rover and headed toward home. *I'll worry about that shit later*, she thought, pushing her past and her family behind her as she drove as fast as she could. If she came to a red light, she turned and made her way up another street. She laid on her horn at any cars driving slowly or pedestrians taking their time crossing the street.

She was beyond road rage. She was on a mission to catch her husband in a lie.

Images of Kingston and Jessa laughing it up together pushed her. Kingston denied cheating just as strongly as she accused him. The last thing she wanted was to actually catch the love of her life cheating, but she damn sure didn't want to be made a fool of by him either.

Pulling up outside Kingston's brick and stone office building, it was hard to miss the emptiness of the large parking lot. Aria snatched her cell phone up from the console. Her heart was pounding and the anger she felt was becoming too familiar to her lately.

His cell phone rang once.

"Hey, baby."

Aria pressed the phone to her ear with one hand and banged on the steering with the other. "Don't 'hey baby' me. I'm at your office . . . where you at—"

"Aria, are you kidding me!"

She raised a threaded and shaped brow at the anger in his voice. She fought the urge to throw her cell phone out the window and then crush it under one of her tires. "Where are you, Kingston?" she snapped.

"Home," he said, his voice hard and cold.

Negro, please. "Hold on." Aria clicked over to her other line and dialed their landline house number.

It rang once before it was picked up.

Aria felt relief.

"I'm your husband, not your child . . . and if you don't cut out all this craziness I don't know how much longer I'll be that."

Click.

BAM! BAM! BAM!

Renee's head was pounding harder than whoever was beating down the door to her . . . to her . . .

She winced as she lifted her head from the carpet and looked around from where she lay sprawled on her stomach. "I'm in my bedroom," she said, her mouth dry as a cotton field as she came out of her drunken stupor.

Renee remembered grabbing her bottle of tequila and fighting like hell to make it up the stairs to the solitude of her bedroom. In between sitting on the edge of the bed sipping her way to the bottom of the bottle and waking up on the floor was a huge indistinguishable blur.

BAM!

"Open up, Renee!"

She frowned at the sound of Jackson's voice. Taking a huge breath and mistakenly inhaling a small dust ball into her open mouth, Renee struggled and worked her way up to stand on her bare feet. She pulled the dust ball from the back of her tongue, thinking it still didn't taste worse than the combo of bad breath and stale liquor.

BAM! BAM!

"Go away," Renee hollered over her shoulder, sounding more like a drag queen than herself.

"I'm not leaving until we talk, Renee!"

The nap had sobered her up, but she still didn't want Jackson to see her with carpet dust and sleep creases on the side of her face. Her short and naturally curly hair was either matted down or sticking off her head like she was a descendant of Buckwheat.

Dragging herself into the bathroom, she rinsed her face with cool water and brushed the hell out of her tongue, teeth, and gums.

BAM!

Renee stood and eyed her reflection in the large wooden oval mirror over the pedestal sink. She shook her head. She was far from crazy. Obviously the kids had called Jackson and he was pissed.

"Hmph. Daddy Dearest ain't so perfect anymore, huh?" she said smugly to her reflection as she fluffed her short curls out with her fingertips.

BAM! BAM! BAM!

"Stop banging on my damn door, Jackson," she screamed at the top of her lungs, moving over to stand outside her bathroom.

"Great example you're making for the kids, Renee," he hollered back through the solid wood of the door.

That insult—and that's how Renee took his comment—was like flashing a red blanket in front of a raging bull.

"You motherfucker, you," she roared, racing across the spacious and disheveled bedroom suite to unlock and snatch open one of the double doors.

Her quick reaction must have surprised him because it showed on his square and handsome face.

Renee pushed him square in his large chest. "Are you and the shit you're putting this family through a great example, Jackson? Huh? Huh? Don't you fuck with me, Jackson. How dare you judge me! How *dare* you judge me, Jackson. *You* ruined this family. No one but you."

He was a tall and solid man. With pure ease he picked Renee up into his arms and crossed the room with long strides to abruptly dump her onto the middle of the unmade king-sized bed.

Renee rolled over just as Jackson turned to walk back across the room to slam the bedroom door closed.

WHAM!

"You have lost your right to touch me in any way. You've lost your right to enter this house as you please. You chose to start a new family," she told him in quiet anger.

Jackson crossed his arms over his chest, looking at her like a parent chastising a child. "I cannot believe you would handle breaking the news to our children about the baby that way."

Renee laughed bitterly, feeling her pain deep in her chest. "What the hell you want me to do, throw a fucking party? Huh? Should I smile and shoot fireworks out my ass for you and your whore?"

"Your thoughtless words hurt the kids, Renee," he said, his voice almost incredulous, as if she should understand his point of view.

"No! What *you* did hurt the kids." Renee's long and strong legs carried her across the room to stand before him. "*You* got the new baby on the way. *You* have your new home. *You* have the new life separate from this family. You."

"And you put me out, Renee. What was I supposed to do, live on the goddamn lawn?" he yelled back, bending down to put his face in hers.

"You damn right I put your whoring ass out. What else was I supposed to do? Huh? What other choice did I have? What other choice did you give me . . . besides putting a bullet in your ass."

Jackson made a face as he straightened his frame. "So you have been drinking, Renee?" he asked in disbelief.

Renee paused in surprise, but recovered quickly. "If you don't know the difference between alcohol and Listerine, then that's your concern. Worry about not being here for your son."

Jackson's jaw tightened. "I'm there for both of my kids. I'm a damn good father and you know it."

Renee laughed and applauded sarcastically. "Whoopdie damn do. I'm sure you'll be a good one to your new one, too."

"Go to hell, Renee."

She locked her fiery eyes with his. "You already put me there, Jackson."

The bedroom doors burst open. Aaron and Kieran stepped into the room. Both were tall like their father, with Renee's bright eyes. They were of the age to fully understand the serious nature of their parents' breakup.

"Stop arguing," Kieran said, her eyes filled with tears as her gloss-covered bottom lip trembled. "I'm sick of this."

At the sight of her daughter in tears and her son's handsome and thin face filled with questions, Renee lost all her will to fight. She slumped down onto the bed, feeling helpless and hopeless tears rise. She swallowed them back, not wanting to break down in front of her children. She felt like all of her emotions were drowning her. She'd give anything to rewind time and make all the bad shit that had destroyed their family go the hell away. All of it. Even her desire to have a career. That was the beginning of the end.

Looking up, she fought her desire to drink as she eyed her husband and her children. In truth, she wanted her family, but visions of the future chased her all the time.

Her husband in the delivery room holding the hand and caressing the scalp of another woman having his child.

Some faceless woman making demands on her husband.

A child not born of her womb running around her home yelling for daddy. Or her husband going to the woman's home to visit their child.

Any way it played out it spelled pain, embarrassment, and disappointment for her. Renee just couldn't swallow that.

Pain radiated from deep in her soul and across her entire body. A pain that she wanted to numb with drinks. Lots of them.

"So it's true, Daddy? What Mommy told us was true?" Kieran asked, sounding more young and immature than her fifteen years.

Renee said nothing. She wished her drunken tongue hadn't dropped the news to them the way it had. But it was true that a drunken person speaks with a sober mind. The truth had to be told . . . one way or the other.

"Is that why y'all broke up?" Aaron asked, his voice deep and filled with his flourishing manhood.

Renee craved a drink.

"Your mother and I love you both very—"

Kieran gasped dramatically. Her eyes got big and wide. "Oh. My. God. It's true?! Onmygod, Daddy. Seriously. SE-RIOUSLY?"

She pushed past Aaron to run from the room.

"Damn, Daddy, how could you?" Aaron said, his eyes filled with disappointment before he made a noise with his mouth that was filled with his disgust and then left the room.

Jackson wiped his hands over his close-cropped hair that was lightly sprinkled with silver. "Renee, I am so sorry that I hurt you and the kids and if I could fix this I would. I've tried, but she wants to have the baby—"

"No!" Renee held up her hands and shook her head vehemently as tears filled her eyes like a flood. "I will not sit here and converse with you about this shit. I. WILL. NOT. No, Jackson. No."

She whimpered as his strong arms surrounded her and pulled her close to his chest. Renee inhaled deeply of his familiar scent and for just a second allowed herself the comfort and security of his embrace. She had thought it would be available to her for the rest of their lives.

"Oh God why. Why, Jackson? Why did you do this to me?" she whispered, all strength and all resolve gone from her body as she wept like a child. "Why . . . why . . . did you do this to me?"

He rocked her. "I'm sorry. I'm so sorry. I swear."

"It hurts . . . it hurts so bad. Oh God. It hurts so bad," she said, her voice husky with pain. She felt the weight of her world crumbling around her.

Jackson placed kisses on her brow and Renee found the last bit of her strength to free herself of his embrace. "Just go, Jackson. Just, please, please, leave me alone," she begged, closing her eyes as she lay back on the bed on her side and then pulled her knees to her chest.

Eventually he did leave the room. Renee knew she should go after her children. Soothe them. Tell them it would be okay.

Renee didn't feel like lying . . . to herself or to anyone else.

Chapter 3

One week later

Aria drove through the winding streets of Richmond Hills, pausing at the intersection at the top of the small hill and looking down at the cul-de-sac. She could see the houses. Jaime and Eric's house, Renee and Jackson's, and that of Jessa Bell.

"Who was she fuck-*ing*?" Aria asked herself out loud, her eyes going from house to house to house.

Jaime had said that Eric denied being the one but then she left him anyway. Was she just too ashamed to admit that her husband was Jessa's lover? In the first couple of weeks after that day, Aria had tried calling Jaime, but she either never answered or short-talked her like she was too busy with something to talk for very long.

Renee said that it wasn't Jackson, but then the rumors being spread over the picket fences and morning cups of coffee was no one had seen Jackson Clinton in a long while. Had Renee discovered in time that he was Jessa's lover? Aria didn't have the clit to call Renee and question her. Not after the anger she had for Renee once she found out that her older friend had come so close to cheating. Their relationship had been cool and distant ever since.

After the dust had settled only she and Kingston were still together, but no one knew better than her how tenuous things were between them.

She let her eyes fall on Jessa's grand house at the end of the cul-de-sac. It sat empty, almost a mocking tribute to the affair their friend had so flippantly announced via text message. Sometimes her anger for her college friend burned so deeply that Aria could easily imagine soaking the entire three thousand square feet with gasoline and lighting the motherfucker with a match, then standing and watching it burn.

Her eyes focused on two tall male figures stepping out the front door of Eric and Jaime's house. Her eyes squinted as she leaned forward.

"Kingston?"

As far as she knew the men's friendship had slacked off as well. She couldn't remember Kingston mentioning them meeting for any golf games or fishing expeditions. She pulled up in front of the house and lowered her window. They both looked over at her.

"Hey, baby. Hi, Eric."

"How you been, Aria?" Eric asked as Kingston stepped down off the porch and walked over to her vehicle.

"Busy working. Just trying to make it. You?" she called back.

"Just doing the same."

It was odd not asking him about Jaime. The brief silence felt so awkward.

"All right, man, I'll talk to you later," Kingston said, before climbing into the passenger seat.

Eric waved and turned to walk back into the house.

"Have you talked to Jaime?" Kingston asked as soon as Aria pulled off for the very short drive to their own home.

She frowned. "I called her last week, but she rushed off the phone talking about a pleasure session or something or 'nother. Why?"

"It's just that their marriage seemed to be doing fine and Jaime left the same night you all got the message from Jessa."

Aria glanced over at him before she slowed down and turned left onto their paved driveway. "And?"

"It's time to get to the bottom of this Jessa Bell mess."

Aria said nothing as she climbed out of the vehicle and grabbed the canvas shopping bag of groceries she'd just purchased. "You think it's Eric?" she asked, coming around the front of the SUV.

Kingston took the bag from her hand. He shrugged. "The only thing I know for sure is that it's not me but I'm catching all kinds of hell because you think there's a chance it is."

"So you asked Eric?"

"Damn right. And I called Jackson."

Aria stopped in her tracks. Kingston unlocked the side entrance and then looked over his shoulder at her. "Eric got offended that I asked and Jackson hasn't called me back yet."

Aria pushed her asymmetrical bangs back from her bronzed face, choosing her words carefully. In their last therapy session, Dr. Matheson had taught her to take a five-second pause to breathe and think before she spoke out. "Do you think either would admit it to you?" she said calmly, proud of herself for not screeching: "Mother-fucker, puh-leeze."

He shrugged a broad shoulder before he walked inside the house into their sleek contemporary kitchen. "It's time one of them fessed up to the affair because our marriage is suffering because of one of them."

Five, four, three, two, one. "Because it's not you, right?"

Kingston sat the bag atop the granite top of the island, his dark mocha eyes locking on her. "That's right, it's not me, but you're around here playing Inspector Gadget, sneaking and snooping through my things trying to catch me. Basically wasting your time and making my life—our life—a living hell."

Aria's eyes searched his face as he spoke. "So life with

me is hell?" she asked, her voice low and the five count forgotten.

Kingston nodded. "It's hell being accused daily of doing something I know damn well I'm not doing."

"What do you want from me, Kingston?" Aria asked, looking away from him as she rubbed her palms on the back pocket of the cutoff shorts she wore.

At his silence she looked up. She gasped a little in surprise and sharp awareness to find him standing in front of her. "I want to come home from work and find you naked in my office. I want to make love to you damn near every night like we used to. I want to be able to talk to you without it becoming an argument. I want to feel like there is nothing more important than our marriage. And I want to tear those damn shorts off you and fuck the shit out of you."

Aria shivered. Her heart pounded wildly. Her pulse raced crazily. Her clit throbbed. "Ooh, you're, uh, talking dirty, huh?" she asked, her voice breathless as her eyes fell to his mouth.

Kingston stepped closer to her, closing the distance between them to less than an inch. "You like it when I talk dirty, don't you?" he asked low in his throat as he brought his hands up to unbutton the shorts.

"You know I do," she admitted, just as the shorts slid down her thighs with a slight *whoosh*.

"You know how long it's been since I slid this dick into you?" he asked against her mouth, before blessing her with a dozen tiny but tantalizing kisses.

"A week," Aria answered in a hot whisper, letting her head fall back as her husband pulled her hot pink thong to the side to palm her clean-shaven pussy.

She brought her hands up to clutch at his broad shoulders as he plunged his tongue into her open mouth and his finger deep inside her pussy. He twirled them both.

Aria kissed him back, releasing all the passion and love she had stored up for him. "I need you, Kingston," she whispered into his mouth as she spread her legs wider.

Kingston leaned back a bit, breaking their kiss, as he looked down into her glazed eyed with intensity. "Do you love me, Aria?"

She nodded without hesitation. "I love you. I love you so much."

Kingston quickly dropped his pants and boxers, his hard, lengthy dick curved away from his body. Aria gasped hotly when Kingston grabbed her waist and easily lifted her frame to sit her on the edge of the island. "Get in the middle," he told her, climbing up onto the island.

Aria shifted back, hurried out of her thongs, and flung them away from her carelessly as she spread her legs wide like propellers. She eyed Kingston's strong body crawling onto the cool granite to settle atop her.

He eased his hands under her bare ass, lifting her up just enough to slide each delicious hard inch deep inside her pussy with one thrust of his hips.

Tears filled Aria's eyes because of how complete she felt with Kingston atop her, his dick buried deep within her walls. They always fit together like two puzzle pieces.

"Aw, baby, don't cry. I swear I love you. I don't need anybody but you. Don't you know I love you, Aria," he told her fiercely as he kissed away her tears between each hard stroke that pushed his dick so deeply inside her that his dick hairs tickled the lips of her pussy.

He rode Aria long and hard until both of their bodies were covered in sweat and their hearts beat furiously in their chests. The sounds of their sex juices echoed in the air along with their moans and grunts of pleasure.

Aria pulled downward with her hips as she sucked the tip of Kingston's tongue. "Mmmmm," she moaned as the base of his dick slid against her swollen and throbbing clit.

"Aw shit, you gon' make this dick come. Pull that nut. Pull it, baby. Pull it."

Aria looked up into his eyes, raising her arms above her head to grasp the edge of the granite. "Like this?" she asked, biting the bottom of her lip as she rocked her hips slow and steady, squeezing the thick tip with her tight walls.

Kingston raised up on his arms and looked down at her pussy lips kissing his shiny wet dick. Up and down. Up and down. "Look at you. Fuck me. *Fuck* me."

Aria's nipples tingled as the tiny explosions began. She locked her eyes on Kingston's face as his body stiffened and she felt each jolt of his dick as he filled her with his cum. As he grunted with each spasm, and she let her eyes drift closed as her pussy walls clutched him tightly with her own release, she wished like hell that her body could use his seed to give them a child.

Renee looked up from the marketing report she was reviewing as her office door opened. Her assistant, Darren, walked in carrying a white cardboard box with the logo of CancerCure, the nonprofit foundation where Renee served as the vice president of marketing.

She used to love developing partnerships with major corporations to garner donations and coming up with innovative ideas to increase national visibility for the foundation work toward cancer research and awareness across the country. Now that her marriage was quickly sliding down a one-way shithole, Renee found herself struggling to give a damn.

"I have your messages and the address labels for the CancerWalk," he said, setting the box and the pink slips of paper on the end of her oval-shaped glass desk.

"Have the registration forms come in?" she asked, removing her bright red, square-shaped reading glasses to look up at him.

Darren made a face. "They came in this morning, remember?"

No. "I meant the posters," she said, smoothing the lapels of the dark navy Ann Taylor blazer.

Darren frowned as he sat down in one of the two club chairs in front of her desk. He steepled his fingers under his chin and looked at her intently.

Renee eyed him in return, patiently awaiting his next words. Darren was an excellent executive assistant who had turned his senior internship into a paid position through his hard work and dedication. For the last month he had pulled her ass from the fire on many occasions while she failed in her personal life.

"If I can be frank, Mrs. Clinton, you have got to get your shit together," he said. "People are noticing and talking."

Renee shifted her eyes away from him and picked up the stack of messages. There was truth in his words and she knew it. Of course, most assistants didn't address their superiors so frankly, but they had skidded past normal protocol when they almost slept together a few months ago. Knowing about Jackson's infidelity the normal guilt she felt was completely gone. Now she wished like hell her "in the closet" homosexual assistant's dick had worked and got the job done. *Thank God I didn't suck his dick because the thought of where he puts it woulda really pissed me off.*

"I got a lot going on at home. It's a fucking mess, but thanks for the heads-up," she told him, shifting her eyes back to his filled with concern.

"No problem," Darren said. "Anything you can—or want—to talk about?"

Besides foolishly blurting it out to her children, Renee hadn't talked about the situation with anyone. Maybe it would help to get it off her chest, but what should she say: My husband knocked up some bitch? No, too embarrassing.

Something like this you talked about with your friends— not your gay assistant you almost slept with.

"No, it'll blow over," she lied, finally reading each message.

Jackson called?

She hated that her heart raced.

"Just let me know if you need to talk," he offered, rising to his Gucci-clad feet.

Renee's eyes shifted from the slip in her hand to his hard and tight buttocks in the impeccably tailored pinstripe slacks he wore. A hint of his warm and spicy cologne still clung to the air. Although he lacked classically handsome features, his dark coloring, strong angular features, and lean muscular build were hard to ignore. On top of all that, Darren's wardrobe was always well tailored and stylishly on point. All of it equaled one sexy-ass black man.

"Maybe I should come by your house tonight and we can work on getting these mailers out," Darren suggested.

Renee genuinely smiled. "Thanks, Darren, I appreciate that."

"No problem," he said over his shoulder, before walking out of her office.

She leaned back in her chair, looking down at Jackson's message in her hands. *What does he want,* she wondered. Her entire body felt tired, her brain felt fried, and her soul was long past weary.

Another woman is pregnant with my husband's child.
Another woman is pregnant with my husband's child.
Another woman is pregnant with my husband's child.

Anotherwomanispregnantwithmyhusbandschild.

It hurt too much to even talk to Jackson, hear his voice, or even hear his name called. Anything and everything involving him was like a sharp dagger to her heart. Balling the message up in her hand, she dropped it into her leather wastepaper basket.

Renee took a deep breath to try and beat down the emotions she felt rising from the pit of her stomach. She fought hard to focus on her work, but in the back of her mind she couldn't forget.

Another woman is pregnant with my husband's child. Another woman is pregnant with my husband's child. Another woman is pregnant with my husband's child.

Anotherwomanispregnantwithmyhusbandschild.

She felt a strong pull within her to drink, but she fought it hard.

"I gotta get my shit together," she whispered to herself, sliding on her reading glasses and picking up her Mont Blanc pen. "I can't let this shit—*his* shit—beat me."

The night he'd told her about his one-night stand and the baby, Renee had only wanted Jackson out of her sight. Thinking of the gun she'd held on him, she was glad he'd obeyed her command to just leave. She couldn't swear that she wouldn't have shot his ass. In the days after, she'd offered him nothing but her anger and her silence. She avoided his calls. She made sure not to be in his sight when he picked up or dropped off the kids. She created a world where Jackson didn't exist. At least she tried to. But they had children. They still had a huge mortgage and so many ties that even his adultery couldn't break.

Still, a million questions flitted into and out of her mind throughout each and every day. Questions that a wife deserved to have answered. Questions only Jackson could answer.

Renee eyed her phone, biting at her bottom lip. *Do I*

really want to know the who, what, when, where, and why? Do I?

"No, not yet. Not while I'm sober," she admitted even as she reached for her phone and dialed Jackson's office number.

"Kilton Enterprises. How may I help you?"

"Hello. May I speak to Jackson Clinton, please?" Renee leaned down to open her Coach briefcase with her index finger.

"Yes, ma'am. Who may I say is calling?" the female voice said politely.

"His wife." Renee cringed, hating that the words had slipped out of her mouth with ease.

It took her a minute to notice that the line was quiet. She assumed she was being transferred.

"His wife?"

Renee's back stiffened at the sound of annoyance . . . anger . . . or shock in the woman's tone. "Yes, his *wife*," she stressed, her eyebrows drawn together.

Click.

The line disconnected.

Renee's mouth fell open as she looked at the phone like she held a deadly cobra in her hands. "What the . . . hell?"

And she sat there for a very long time, trying to make sense of the odd exchange. Trying not to draw conclusions. Trying not to get answers to questions she wasn't ready to have answered.

She felt the dread deep in her bones. Weighing her down. Angering her. Disappointing her. Stunning her.

Fucking with her.

Bzzz . . . bzzz . . . bzzz . . .

Renee's eyes quickly shifted to her BlackBerry vibrating where it sat on the corner of her desk.

She knew it was Jackson. She just knew it was him.

She hung up her office phone and picked up her cell.

His office number showed on her caller ID. She answered the call with one hand and pulled her little silver flask of Firefly Sweet Tea from her briefcase to pour a hefty shot into her cup of tea. She'd learned the alcohol blended well with real tea and was a perfect camouflage at work. "Jackson, I have just one question for you and if you are half the man I *thought* you were you will tell me the truth," she said, slowly and almost methodically as she fought hard not to scream.

"Renee—"

"Does your pregnant whore work there with you?" Her voice was cold, but her heart was prepared to turn completely frigid where he was concerned.

"Renee—"

"Yes or fucking no, Jackson."

He sighed heavily. "Yes, Renee, but . . ."

Renee laughed bitterly as she skipped the cup and took a hefty swig from the flask. "One-night stand, my ass, you lying motherfucker you. I'm sorry that me calling there upset her so much that the bitch had to hang up on me and then I assume she called you to . . . what . . . ask you why your *wife* is calling you and then you hopped your happy ass on the phone to call me, worried about what she said to me. Am I right?"

"Renee, meet me for dinner. Let's sit down and talk about this—"

"Wow, Jackson, the gut punches just keep coming," she said softly but sarcastically, ending the call as she looked up to the high ceilings before she closed her eyes.

Jaime bit the gloss from her bottom lip as she logged into her online banking account. "Ooh," she said with a slight wince as she looked at the balance in her checking account. She had just a little over five grand left.

But the money would not last. Plus, she had to define her new life outside of Pleasure's dick. Hell, outside of the town house. *What's my next step?*

Alimony would be great, but she knew Eric would use her affair to make sure she didn't get one red cent—even if Jaime had relied on Eric to take care of her financially during their marriage. She had ignored her own college degree and made being the perfect wife her career—just the way her mother taught her and just the way her husband wanted.

But an angry and hurt husband wielding a checkbook over his adulterous wife was too shaky a position for Jaime. Particularly when she was used to designer clothing, expensive weaves, and a very comfortable life. She was used to her husband taking care of her.

She would have been a fool not to fear how she would take care of herself if he left her or made her leave. And her fears of being booted to the curb without a nickel to her name had led to her siphoning money from her husband into her own secret account. When she left him that night, she left with a little over eight thousand dollars.

That money had come in handy for the lease on her town house, her upkeep, and her rendezvous with Pleasure.

"Two tears in a bucket . . . fuck it," she said, exiting out of her account and closing her laptop where it sat on the counter in her kitchen.

The sex during the first years of their marriage was humdrum—quite a disappointment after waiting for their wedding night. No fireworks. No explosions. Just a few pumps between her thighs and it was over. Their sex had been . . . safe, comfortable, predictable, and very anticlimactic. And then the last six months of their marriage had been centered on living as strangers during the day, with the weirdest, most degrading sexual torture and humiliation during random nights of his choosing. "That bastard deserves to pay for me to get some good dick," she muttered under her breath, reaching in the fridge for a bottle of apple juice.

The first step was leaving the security and seclusion of her town house. It was beyond time. And next? Lawyer time. Her marriage was over and no matter how much Eric fought it, it was time to finalize everything. Hate it or love it, the happily ever after for Eric and Jaime Hall was—in the words of Aria—a done dada.

In the meanwhile she needed to focus on a career and making her own money.

She'd acquired her bachelor degree in interior design, but she was caught up in planning her wedding and she never obtained the required work experience to even sit for the exam to obtain her certification from the National Council for Interior Design Qualification (NCIDQ). In college, she and Eric had dreams of opening a business together. With his degree in architecture, they'd planned to design, build, and then decorate residential, commercial, and retail properties. The total package. Once she strolled her happy-to-be-getting-married behind down the aisle, all talk of a career just disappeared. She gladly stepped into the role of wife, socialite, and volunteer.

A fucking Stepford wife dipped in chocolate.

Maybe she could start her own interior design firm, but first she had to get in the hundred hours of work experience to get her certification. The skill was there, but she had to get her level of professionalism up to par. She'd decorated her own home and the majority of Aria's and Renee's homes as well. They had loved the way she mixed textiles and did unexpected small things to take their wishes to the next level. She did it out of love, but maybe it was time to start charging.

Jaime shook her head as she looked around at the decor of her town house. It was clear the sparsely furnished space had yet to become home for her. The little furniture she had came with the rental. A large sofa. A table. A lamp. A few nondescript paintings. Very hotel like. Very cute, but mostly just functional as hell.

Nothing at all like the design showcase of the home she'd shared with Eric. Not much of her life was, for that matter.

She brought her hand up to run through the chin-length soft waves of her natural hair. No more eight-hundred-dollar weaves by celebrity hairstylists. Her closet was no longer filled with the newest designer clothes. The eight grand was going fast and for now the days of thousand-dollar outfits were over.

She'd wanted a new life and a new life was what she'd gotten.

Finishing her drink, Jaime hurried into the adjoining bathroom to shower and get dressed. She had been summoned to her parents' for another wonderful night of scolding and dinner. They'd promised her that Eric, the minister, or any other part of the cheering squad for an Eric and Jaime reunion would not be in attendance. Supposedly they just wanted her back in their lives. "Fun, fun, fun," she said sarcastically as she undressed.

Jaime enjoyed a steamy hot shower and then massaged her shapely figure with her favorite lotion and a few precious sprays of perfume.

She chose a pair of skinny jeans, heels, and a short-sleeved ruffled blouse of the finest linen in a bright fuchsia that really was more Aria's style than Jaime's usual slacks, suits, and dresses. She was trying something new.

Jaime slid her feet into her heels just as someone rang the doorbell. Frowning, she grabbed her cell phone from her nightstand before she made her way to the door. Her parents were home waiting for her and no one, besides Pleasure, knew where she stayed.

Stepping up onto her toes she looked out the peephole.

Her eyebrow arched at the sight of the broad-shouldered bearded man standing there. Jaime recognized him from the town house next door. Still . . .

"Who is it?" she asked, lowering her slender frame back down onto her heels.

"It's your next-door neighbor, Lucas Neal. I have some of your mail."

She stepped back enough to open the lightweight fiberglass door. "Hi," she greeted him with a smile, looking at him. He was the same height as she was, with one of those round, boyishly cute faces and a round belly that spoke of his love of food.

"I hope I wasn't interrupting you, but some of your mail was in my box," he said, his voice kind of raspy like he could sing the hell out of a smooth slow jam.

"No, no problem. Thanks," Jaime said, taking the mail from him with one hand and extending the other. "Jaime Hall—well, soon to be again Jaime Pine."

He engulfed her slender hand in his as he smiled, two huge dimples filling his round cheeks. "Divorce?"

Jaime nodded. "Soon. Hopefully very soon."

"Me, too," he said, holding up his left hand to show his bare ring finger with just a lightened area where his wedding ring used to sit.

They fell silent.

"Thanks for the mail," Jaime said, sifting through the stack of mainly advertisements and credit card offers.

"No problem. Glad to be a good neighbor."

Jaime looked up, her eyes shifting past him to the silver pickup truck parking behind her Volvo. Her face showed her surprise and Lucas turned to look over his shoulder.

Pleasure climbed the brick steps with ease, dressed in a black shirt and black slacks, his thin dreads pulled back from his face, looking sexy as shit on his tall muscular frame. Jaime lost her breath as she eyed him with a smile. The stance of her body changed as she leaned in the doorway and she arched her breasts forward just a bit more.

"I see you have company," Lucas said.

Jaime barely heard him as Pleasure breezed right past the man, his height dwarfing her neighbor easily. "I wasn't expecting you," she said, looking up at Pleasure in all his handsome glory.

"I couldn't get you off my mind," Pleasure said. "Busy?"

Jaime shook her head. "Not anymore," she told him, her body already reacting to him in just pure anticipation of the dicking down he was about to deliver.

"So I'll just be going," Lucas added.

Pleasure picked her up with one arm and held her body close to his, pressing his smooth lips to her neck. "Damn, you smell good," he moaned against her pulse, pulling her into the house to solidly close the front door in Lucas's face.

"Was the dough boy trying to take my spot?" he asked, carrying her into the living room.

"Who?" Jaime asked, sliding down his body to drop to her feet and kick off her heels.

"Fat boy at the door," he said.

Jaime waved her hand dismissively, dropping to her knees in front of him. "Jealous?"

He chuckled. "You love this dick too much," he said, all cocky and bold.

"Oh really?"

Pleasure unzipped his pants and worked to free his dick. "Really," he said, tapping the thick tip against her chin and mouth.

Jaime moaned in pleasure, opening her mouth wide to unroll her tongue.

Pleasure stroked her tongue with his dick.

Jaime felt it growing hard inch by inch in her mouth.

"You the best at this shit," he moaned.

Jaime laughed. "You taught me well," she said, her voice muffled from her mouthful.

Jaime had already forgotten her neighbor, dinner at her parents', and everything else as she got caught up in Pleasure's heat.

Jessa Bell

I may be many things to many people, but a fool isn't one of them.

One advantage I've always had over other people is how observant and attentive I am. I miss nothing and hear everything. I listen. I see. I pay attention. I've been that way since I was a child. Really didn't have much choice with a mother like mine, who meant it when she said to be seen and not heard.

And so I learned to pay attention and to listen well.

In fact, I knew that my lover was open to cheating on his wife—my friend—long before I knew he was open to having an affair with me.

And it was hard for me to miss that my lover was either still with his wife, still trying to get back with her, or had yet another mistress in his life. For damn sure, I wasn't getting any extra time, or words, or dick play. Not at all.

Not once had he spent the night with me here in this house that was supposed to be our home.

My dinners? Eaten alone.

My bed? Slept in alone.

My house? Lived in alone.

My life? Alone. Alone. Alone.

The sigh I released was filled with the weight of the bullshit I was letting this man put me through. Enough was fucking enough and this time there was no turning back. No changing my mind. No more of the bullshit.

I laid my heart and my pussy on the line and it was time to deal with the fact that I lost. My message failed because my man was not here with me. He was no more my man than he was before.

He stayed in my bed a little longer and fucked me a little harder. He was filling me up with nothing but dick and empty promises. For the first time during our entire affair I felt like I was being used. That was a no-no.

I finally got it. There would be no divorce. There would be no he and I for all eternity. I was a mistress. His mistress. And nothing more. Well, not anymore.

I'm done with my lover and ready to reclaim my old life . . . in Richmond Hills. It was costing me a pretty penny to break my one-year lease on the new home, but my beautiful home in Richmond Hills was off the market.

I was going home.

Bold move? Of course.

Still, I knew I had some loose ends to tie up once and for all. It's time for my ex-friends to know just which one of their men had made me look just as foolish as them. I knew the shit would hit the fan but I was ready.

Picking up my BlackBerry I entered the cell numbers of Aria, Jaime, and Renee. Next my message. I already knew what I was sending; I'd written it weeks ago.

Without one moment of hesitation I hit SEND.

There was no way I would just sit back and let him have his happily ever after—the one he'd promised me. Oh no. My ex-lover was going to pay for my broken heart.

Chapter 4

Aria stirred awake, hugging her plush pillows to her side as she stretched her curvaceous frame. The sun was just beginning to rise and peep through the sheer summer curtains hanging on the glass patio doors.

She rolled over in bed, looking at the peacefully sleeping face of her husband. She could easily envision him as a handsome young boy, tall and lean in his preppy private-school uniforms, living a life of privilege. Probably never figuring he would marry a ghetto girl from Newark whose smarts got her onto the campus of Columbia University. Probably dreaming of the days he would start his own family.

He shifted in his sleep and let out a little grunt. Aria's hand literally itched to stroke the side of his face as guilt covered her like a blanket.

Aria had been just fourteen when her Uncle Freddie's daughter, Jontae, came from down south to spend the summer with her father. A whole new world was introduced to her: partying in the clubs, dressing sexy, staying out late, just staying in trouble. It was shameful enough all the stress and drama she brought to her mama's life.

But her family still didn't know the half of it and her husband knew even less.

Jontae had taught her this "fuck and pluck" scheme

they ran, luring men to hotel rooms, sexing them, and then robbing them while they slept. Just straight wildin'.

Abortions. STDs. Even getting slapped around by strange men once or twice. It took her last abortion to get straight. She focused on school, got good grades, and graduated high school with honors.

The repercussions of her past on her present life were always there mocking her, making her feel like she was being punished, making the weight of the secrets she kept from her husband heavy as hell on her shoulders.

Kingston had no clue that Aria was unable to have children. After a year of trying, Aria began to suspect her infertility, and a visit to her gynecologist confirmed her fears. Knowing how badly her husband wanted children and knowing that her scandalous past left her with almost no chance of giving him a baby, Aria didn't have the heart or the clit to tell him the truth. A sucker-ass move for sure, but with each passing day the omission of her infertility became an even bigger cross to bear.

Aria jumped a little in surprise when Kingston's eyes popped open and he was looking at her. Lying there. Waiting.

She knew what he wanted, but she couldn't give it to him. Aria refused to pretend that him going out of town wasn't a problem. "You all packed for your trip?" she asked, flinging the covers back to roll out of bed before she felt even remotely tempted to straddle his hips and plant his dick deep within her walls until she drained him.

"It's only one night, Aria," Kingston said.

"Hmph," she grunted, reaching into the top of her dresser drawer for clean lingerie. She felt soft ebony hairs on the back of her neck stand on end and she knew before he even touched her that Kingston was near. Even with the Jessa Bell bullshit that chemistry and awareness between them had never faded. Never.

"I'm gonna miss you. It's been a long time since I've slept without you, Aria." He wrapped his strong arms around her waist and pulled her body back close to him, his long and hard dick snuggling between her round buttocks.

Aria shivered as he pressed kisses to the base of her neck. "Then don't go."

Kingston sighed. "Because you will miss me or because you don't trust me?" he asked, the softness leaving his voice.

Aria stepped out of his embrace, saying nothing. It had been an ongoing argument since he'd told her about the lecture he was giving at the hospital where he used to work in Pennsylvania. She'd sulked, argued, bitched and moaned. He still was going.

Aria was a journalist and far from a fool. She'd called the hospital and confirmed his part in the lecture series.

But was Jessa going, too?

Aria walked into the bathroom. Before she could close the door, Kingston stepped in behind her. "I asked you to go with me, Aria," he said, his eyes locked on her.

"And you know I have the big exclusive interview with Nona Richards today," she said, sitting down on the edge of their black Jacuzzi tub. "Just forget it. Just . . . whatever, Kingston. Enjoy your trip and your trick."

"Man, to hell with this shit."

WHAM!

The bedroom door slammed behind him.

"Damn!"

Aria didn't emerge from the bathroom until after she'd showered and gotten through her morning ritual, including making up her face. As soon as she stepped into their bedroom, she knew Kingston was gone. The house was empty. His presence was gone.

In the past they'd never left each other angry. Never.

But fuck that. Aria didn't like feeling like she was being played for a fool especially by the man she loved and a woman she'd considered to be a lifelong friend.

Bzzzzzzzz.

Her eyes shifted to her vibrating cell phone on the dresser. Her heart hammered to think Kingston had called to say good-bye, to say he loved her, to say he wasn't going.

Aria crossed the room to snatch up her cell phone. Seeing her mother's number she felt a mix of disappointment and happiness all at once.

"Hey," Aria said into the phone, walking back across the room to spray her pulse points with her favorite Armani perfume, Diamonds.

"Whatcha doing?"

"I snagged an interview with Nona Richards. It's today. No, it's this morning. Matter of fact, it's in an hour or so." Aria shoved the phone between her ear and shoulder as she pulled on the Tracy Reese white cotton wrap dress she'd picked out last night. It looked great against her deep complexion and emphasized her small waist and wide hips.

"Nona Richards!" her mother exclaimed. "Girl, I used to love me some Nona Richards . . . pre-crack, of course."

"Well, she's making a big comeback and your baby girl has the exclusive first interview. Say what, what?" Aria did a little booty dance before she stepped into the bronzed sandals.

"When is the new album dropping? Is her voice the same? Did she really run around her front yard ass naked, and singing? How many husbands she had again?"

Aria paused in checking out her reflection in the mirror. "Mama, you got more questions than me."

Heather laughed. "Well, I'm proud of you, baby."

Aria knew that she was. Her mother had several photo albums filled with clippings of all her interviews and articles with the corresponding cover of the magazine. Bump the baby pictures, Heather Goines was whipping out those albums to show anyone new who strolled through her door.

"Where's Kingston? Working?"

"He went out of town. Deuces." Aria rushed down the hall to her office, barely taking in the chocolate and hot pink decor as she grabbed her Coach briefcase sitting by the door. It was packed and ready.

"You still worried Kingston messin' 'round with Jessa?"

Aria shrugged as if her mother could see her. "I don't know, Ma . . . but I do know that since that stupid-ass message she sent my marriage is in so much trouble. I'm scared because I love Kingston so much."

"Trusting him is a part of loving him, Aria."

Aria closed her eyes, her head falling back a little bit as she stood at the top of the stairs. "Mama, you always make things seem so simple, so cut and dried, so black and white, and they're not. There are a million shades of gray."

"And sometimes you young girls make shit way more complicated than it needs to be. The advice I gave you before still stands. You remember it?"

How could she forget it?

Either he's a no-good dog and don't deserve one tear shed over his corpse far less because some other woman got to try and keep him chained . . . or it's not him and you crying for nothing.

Aria rushed down the stairs and out the front door. "Ma, I'll call you back. I'm jumping in the car and you know you hate for me to be on the cell and driving," she said, pulling her keys from inside her briefcase to unlock the Rover.

"Okay, call me as soon as your interview is over. I just gots to know if Nona is still thin and smoked out as a burnt match. Loving you."

Aria smiled. Her mother was funny as hell when she wanted to be. "Loving you back, Ma."

She put her briefcase on the backseat and hopped into the driver's seat. The hotel where Nona was staying was just a twenty-minute ride away, but Aria was not chancing traffic or anything else making her late.

Not worrying about Kingston.

Not being overly concerned with her outfit.

Not even chitchatting with her mother on the phone.

Nothing. Nada.

Aria drove the winding curves out of the cul-de-sac, eventually cruising out through the gate of Richmond Hills. She forced herself not to think about Kingston. This interview was a huge deal for her career and she didn't want the moment soured because she didn't trust her husband as far as she could see his ass. *And put my foot so far up Jessa's ass that I don't see it.*

Ding-ding.

Aria wrinkled her brows as she reached over to dig her cell phone out of her book bag. "A text," she mumbled, keeping her foot pressed on the brake pedal as she looked down at her cell phone.

19735550666

She didn't recognize the number. Aria opened the text message. She gasped in surprise to see the message. Shock. Horror. And pure indignation.

"Jessa!"

Someone laid on the horn behind her and Aria's rush of adrenaline caused her to jump and slam her foot on the accelerator. She screeched as the Rover sped forward. She dropped the phone as her heart pounded and she grabbed the steering wheel to keep the Rover from running up onto the curb and slamming into the light pole.

Aria slammed on the brakes, causing her body to slam

forward against the steering wheel. Cars from all points of the intersection laid on the horns, but she didn't give a shit that she was blocking the flow of traffic.

She was too shocked to do anything else.

———— ∞∞∞ ————

Jaime made sure to breathe in and out of her mouth as she jogged around the block. It was one of the first times she'd actually spent time in the area where she now lived. With its small town houses, mini-malls, and apartment buildings, the vibe was more young urban professional just starting out than the settled, more accomplished feel of Richmond Hills.

In truth? Jaime longed for the quiet elegance of her old neighborhood. In Richmond Hills the most noise you heard was the steady whir of the sprinkler systems and certainly not the thump thump of nearby restaurants and bars or the roars and hollers of those enjoying the late-night vibe of the trendy neighborhood.

Would Eric consider letting me have the house in the divorce? she wondered, continuing her jog past a brick apartment building.

When she'd left Eric that night, she'd been glad to be free of the memories of the house, but in hindsight she knew she could redecorate and get past all of that to be back in her home. Four thousand square feet of luxury beat the hell out of nineteen hundred square feet of functionality.

And it would be a great showcase for clients of my interior decorating business . . . especially with a home office.

Jaime would move back to Richmond Hills in a heartbeat if Eric would vacate the premises. She'd spent nearly four months decorating the entire house. She'd made sure it was a home he could be proud to live and entertain in.

He's not giving it up, she thought, slowing down from a jog to a brisk walk as she neared her town house.

Jaime patted the sweat from her forehead with her forearm. She remembered when she would have never run outside or dared to show herself with a sweaty hairdo. *Change is good,* she thought, turning up the short walkway to the front door of her brick-faced town house rental.

As soon as she locked the front door behind her she began to strip out of the crisp white tank and running shorts. Jaime left a trail of clothing, sneakers, socks, and undergarments as she made her way to her bedroom. The jog had done her good. She had a lot on her mind and it was good to get away from her distractions.

"You back?"

Jaime eyed Pleasure sitting up in the middle of her bed. Naked. Muscled. Strong. Leg bent. Dick laying across his thigh like a snake.

Sexy as shit.

Jaime nodded, wishing her cheeks didn't feel hot and that her heart and clit weren't fluttering like butterfly wings.

Jaime had many decisions to make about her life and she knew Pleasure was one of them. "Don't you want more out of life than selling your dick?" she asked, leaning her bare ass back against her dresser.

He locked his intense ebony eyes on her as he used one strong hand to lazily stroke the long and thick length of his dick. "Don't you want more out of life than paying for my dick?" he countered, said dick stretching and hardening in his hand.

Jaime's eyes locked on his erotic movement. Her nipples tingled. "Yes," she answered, forcing her voice to be as bold.

"Liar." His eyes and his tone were serious as he massaged the tip.

Jaime felt a little offended. "You don't think I want a better relationship than . . . *whatever* this is that we have?" she asked, pushing off the dresser to step closer to the foot of the bed.

"I like to fuck and you like for me to fuck you. It is what it is, Jaime. You knew that. You know that." Pleasure inched his body down on the bed so that he was lying flat, spreading his legs wide as his grip on his dick tightened.

She forced her eyes to stay locked on his, ignoring the way he bit his bottom lip as the stroke of his hands quickened. "So you plan to sell yourself until when? Until you lose your looks and your dick needs Viagra or some shit?"

Pleasure laughed, never once taking his eyes from hers, as he rose to stand in the center of her bed, his deeply dark and delicious dick still in his caramel bronzed hands. "Until women like you no longer need my . . . *services*."

"So there are more than me?" she asked, hating that his dick was now level with her gaze and she missed not one moment of him shaking his dick at her. Like it was a joke. Like her need for him was a joke.

"You know that and you couldn't care less," Pleasure told her boldly, walking down the length of the bed to stand precariously on the edge. He raised one strong arm upward until his hand was pressed to the ceiling and steadying him.

His dick was just inches from her mouth and Jaime could smell that addictive mix of his warm and spicy cologne and the natural scent of him. She cut her eyes up to look at his face. The look of bold conquering was in the ebony depths of his eyes as he tapped his dick lightly against her closed mouth.

Jaime opened her mouth and easily captured his dick between her lips. "Am I the only one you fuck for free?" she asked around her mouthful, feeling it throb like a racing pulse against her tongue.

Pleasure put both hands on the ceiling and arched his hips forward sending a few more inches into her mouth. "Yes."

It was Jaime's turn to feel cocky. She jerked her head back and freed his dick from her mouth with a *pop*. "Maybe *I* need to charge *you*?"

Pleasure just laughed.

Ding-dong.

Jaime looked over her shoulder out the door and down the hall at the front door. "Be right back," she told him, reaching behind the bedroom door for her red satin robe before she left the room.

Bzzzzzzzzz.

Before she could reach the door her cell phone vibrated on the countertop. Jaime grabbed it, looking down at it as she continued on to the door.

A text from a number she didn't recognize.

"Who is it?" Jaime said loudly through the door, using her manicured thumbs to open the text.

"Your mother, dear."

And the sound of Virginia Osten-Pine's voice weakened Jaime to no end. She bit her bottom lip as she glanced back at her open bedroom door. The last thing she needed was her mother finding a sexy stripper, butt naked with a hard dick and a smile, in her bedroom. Jaime just wasn't up for the histrionics.

"One second, Mother." She turned and rushed down the hall to her bedroom. Pleasure was back in the middle of the bed, propped up, dick still in hand, sexy smile in place, and ready to fuck and be fucked.

Jaime had to shake herself from the dick trance as she motioned for him to be quiet before she pulled the room door closed. Cell phone still in hand, she tied her robe closer around her body as she rushed back to the front door to pull it open with the biggest and fakest smile. "Good morning."

Virginia's critical eyes went from Jaime's still damp and lifeless curls to her robe. Her disapproval was clear as she strolled past her daughter, dressed in her signature Kasper suit and Evan Picone low-heeled pumps. Her graying curls were pulled back in a low chignon. The café au lait of her complexion—a result of her Korean and African-American heritage—only accentuated by neutral makeup. The perfect socialite wife.

And she'd groomed Jaime to be her clone. Her own Mini-Me.

"You're not out of bed, Jaime?" she asked.

"Where's Dad?" Jaime asked, looking out the door and hoping to see her burly father making his way toward the house. Instead, she saw nothing but her parents' black Lexus LS400 parked behind her Volvo.

"At home."

Jaime fought hard not to roll her eyes. Her dad was the buffer between them, and now that she had claimed her own life and independence, Jaime needed him more than ever.

"So what are your plans, Jaime?" Virginia asked, sitting down on the sofa and placing her patent leather tote in her lap.

To get fucked before you dropped in, she thought, crossing her arms over her chest as she walked into the living room. She nearly dropped her cell phone and had to move fast to catch it.

Remembering the text—and looking for a diversion—Jaime used her manicured thumbs to open it. Her eyes widened as she read the entire message. She frowned. Deeply. "Jessa? What the hell?"

"Jaime, it's rude to play with your cell phone while I'm talking to you."

But Jaime barely heard her mother. Jessa Bell was up to her games again and frankly, Jaime wanted no part of it.

Her marriage to Eric was over and everything before the moment she'd decided to leave his sadistic ass just didn't matter anymore.

"Sorry, Mother," she said, deleting the message from her phone and Jessa Bell from her thoughts. "Um, actually I'm planning to start my own business doing interior decorating."

Virginia Osten-Pine sighed. "What about your marriage?"

"Seriously, Mother, you have to know when to stop beating a dead horse," Jaime countered, thinking it felt damn good to finally say the words that came to her mind. The words she usually swallowed back in her haste to agree to her mother's every demand and wish.

"You have to understand Eric's position with this. I thought it was clear when you two married that he is Catholic and doesn't believe in divorce."

"I'm not Catholic and neither are you, Mother. Besides, Eric is suddenly clutching on to his faith to keep me when he wasn't man enough to do it himself."

Virginia clutched at her pearls. "But you had the *affair.*"

Jaime almost giggled at the way her mother said "affair" as if just pronouncing the word would send her straight to hell . . . still clutching at those damn pearls. "You ever think he wasn't man enough to keep me from doing that either?"

Her mother's mouth dropped open.

"For goodness sake, Mother, the man had me thinking a leprechaun and a pot of gold were easier to get than an orgasm."

Her mother gasped so deeply Jaime thought she'd choked on a hair ball. She knew she was wrong to enjoy shocking her mother.

"Listen, I'm sorry, but I deserved to feel like a desirable

woman and not some clinical, passionless, robotic lay that left me waiting for more all the time."

Virginia arched a brow as she sat forward to level her eyes on Jaime. "Listen, I don't know what or who you think you are, but I raised a young, respectable lady and not a—"

Jaime's face hardened. "Not what, Mother, A slut? A whore? Go ahead. Say it. It won't be your first time . . . remember?" she asked, her voice cold as she flung back the harsh words her mother had called her when she'd learned of Jaime's affair.

Her mother shifted uncomfortably before she rose to her feet, her hands tightly gripping the handle of her tote. "Your father and I are tired of being the victims of whispers and stares and gossip about our daughter. Get your act together, Jaime," she said, briskly walking to the door and snatching it open.

"Or what?" Jaime asked, her voice cold. Bitter. Hurt.

WHAM!

She turned, surprised to see her mother still standing there after hearing the door slam shut.

Virginia pointed her clear coated nail at her. "Or we will—"

"Come on get this dick."

It was Jaime's turn to gasp in horror as she turned. Pleasure stood at the end of the hall, still naked, still sculptured, still holding his hard dick in his hand. *Oh Lawd, whhhyyyy?*

Jaime closed her eyes and dropped her head into her hands.

"You see, Daughter, I call it as I see it."

WHAM!

This time Jaime knew her mother was gone . . . .maybe even for good.

"You look like you have a lot on your mind?"

Renee shifted her eyes from some unknown spot on the textured wall of her spacious living room to look at Darren and her son, Aaron, looking at her. "Huh?" she said, setting down the box of brochures she was supposed to be folding before she rubbed her eyes with her fingertips.

"You okay, Ma?" Aaron asked, his face filled with concern.

Neither of the children was taking the news of their father having another child very well. Most days both stayed closed up in their rooms, refusing to have a casual conversation with him, although neither showed any disrespect. Renee hated that they were hurting just like she was.

"I'm good, just ready to get this event all done and over," she assured him, reaching over to smooth the fine waves of his low-cut hair. "Nothing a long nap won't help."

And a stiff drink.

She ignored Darren's intense eyes on her as he edged forward on the suede sofa to press his elbows to his knees in the distressed jeans he wore with a white collar shirt and a deep navy V-neck sweater. "Your mom does have a lot of work stuff on her plate," he said, his voice deep and masculine as he gave Aaron a reassuring smile. "It's all a part of being a busy marketing executive."

Aaron turned his attention back to the brochures he was helping her fold.

Renee ran her hands through her short ebony curls. "Thank you," she mouthed to Darren.

In his efforts to help Renee get her shit back together at work—especially for the upcoming fund-raising event—Darren had put in so many hours outside of work. She couldn't thank him enough.

His presence around her had forced her to cut back on

the drinking, but the craving, the thirst, the need for how it made her feel hadn't let up one damn bit.

When she lay alone in bed at night and remembered the days that she had had the warm body of her husband by her side . . . she drank.

When she gave in to the torture of putting a face to the woman who had fucked her husband . . . she drank.

When she thought of the end of her marriage of over twenty years . . . she damn near swam in the liquor bottle.

Fighting the urge to go into her office for a quick sip, Renee rose to her feet and walked to the front door to step outside. The sprawling homes with landscaped yards looked the same, but absolutely nothing about Richmond Hills felt the same.

Her marriage had changed.

Her friendships had changed.

Her life had changed.

Renee had honestly thought she and Jackson would spend the rest of their lives together in this house in Richmond Hills. She closed her eyes as a sharp and intense pain radiated across her chest.

"Shit," she swore, inhaling deeply and seeking an inner calm that was completely lost to her these days.

Jackson wanted her forgiveness and love.

Renee was empty of both.

"Ma, your phone is ringing."

Renee turned as her son stood behind her and pushed her BlackBerry into her hand. "Thanks," she said, frowning as she looked down at the flashing text message icon. Renee hated texts. She found them juvenile.

As a matter of fact the last text message she'd gotten was from . . .

"Jessa?" Renee said in a soft voice filled with her confusion and surprise as she read the text again . . . and again . . . and again.

"Why is she sending *me* this?" she asked aloud, her face troubled.

"Something wrong, Ma?" Aaron asked from behind her.

"No, nothing," she lied, lifting her eyes to look at Jessa Bell's empty home at the end of the cul-de-sac.

Was there a chance that Jackson had cheated with Jessa *and* fathered a child with another woman?

Renee felt her nerves react to just the idea of it. She felt as if her bowels were loose. This was more than she could handle.

Enough was fucking enough.

Renee turned and breezed past her tall and slender son. "Darren, I have to go run an errand real quick. Will you be okay here 'til I get back?" she asked, grabbing her keys and her purse from the end table even as her heart pounded loudly enough to sound like the pounding hoofs of a dozen horses.

Darren rose to his Gucci-covered feet. "No problem. Is everything okay?"

Renee nodded as she turned and sailed out of the house.

Racing to the car, getting in and cranking it, even the drive to Jackson's town house was all a blur.

Jackson and Jessa? Was there a chance he was fucking Jessa, too? Was Jackson a sex addict or some weird shit? Just where all did that motherfucker have his dick?

"Like the fucking baby ain't enough shit on me," Renee snapped, slamming on the brakes so hard her tires squealed against the streets outside Jackson's house. She threw the Benz into PARK wishing her thoughts would stop racing.

Another woman is pregnant with my *husband's child. My husband fucked my friend. Another woman is pregnant with* my *husband's child. My husband is a man-whore. Another woman is pregnant with* my *husband's child. My husband ain't shit. Anotherwomanispregnant-*

withmyhusbandschild. Jessa and Jackson? That crusty dick bastard.

Renee fought the urge to scream as she hopped out of the car and charged up the concrete walkway to the black front door. She made a fist and knocked on it like she was the police.

It was time to get all her questions out. The answers would hurt like hell, but the uncertainty was hurting worse. Way worse.

As the door swung open, Renee felt her mouth water for a drink. She fought it off, but it kept nudging her, poking at her, calling her name. Renee licked the beads of sweat from her upper lip as she looked up at Jackson's square handsome face shaped with surprise . . . and some other emotion she couldn't quite put her finger on.

"Hey, Renee," he said, stepping down to pull the door behind him.

Renee studied the eyes of the man she had lived with for well over twenty years. Although she'd completely missed his affair, she knew him well. The look in the dark depths of his eyes was guilt.

Renee reached past his broad frame and opened the front door, pushing it open wide. He moved to shut the door and step in front of her. Using one of her son's tackling moves, Renee crossed her arms and pushed Jackson square in his gut. He fell back against the door, pushing it open wide and sending him crashing to the floor with an "umph."

Renee stepped right over his dazed and amazed ass, but it was her turn to be shocked as she locked her eyes on the white woman sitting on the leather sofa of her husband's living room. Her eyes missed nothing. Not one detail. The straight blond hair she flipped over her shoulder, the coldness of her blue eyes, or the pale whiteness of her hand as she stroked her belly.

"Renee," Jackson said from behind her, touching her arm.

Renee slapped his hand away. Hard. "Are you the bitch pregnant from my husband?" she asked in a low voice.

"My name is Inga . . . not bitch," the blonde said with a slight accent.

Renee laughed bitterly as she raced across the room quick as shit. "No, bitch, your name is mud," she said, reaching out to connect her palm with the other woman's face.

WHAP-BAP-DAP.

She landed three good slaps before she felt Jackson's strong arm around her waist. As the woman gasped and pressed her own hand to her reddened cheeks, Renee turned in Jackson's embrace and began delivering blow after blow to his head and shoulders.

"You no-good bastard.

"You slick son of a bitch.

"You sellout.

"You fucking coon.

"Get off me!

"Let me go."

"Jackson, she is acting like an animal!" Inga screeched.

Renee saw all shades of red. All of them. She bit down on Jackson's shoulder.

"Ow! Damn, Renee," he hollered.

Renee jumped down to her feet and raced at the blonde bitch. The woman's blue eyes got big before she turned and ran. Renee reached out for a handful of blond hair and tugged hard with her fist, feeling a clump of the strands break free of her scalp.

"Help me. Please help me," Inga screamed.

"Shut up," Renee snapped, tugging some more on her hair.

Jackson recovered and grabbed Renee's wrists. "Let me go, Jackson," she warned.

"She's pregnant, Renee," he stressed, tightening his grip on her wrists.

She looked up at him with eyes filled with the anger and—in that moment—hatred that burned deep inside her chest. "Who gives a fuck?" she said coldly, her chest heaving like she'd just run a marathon.

"Oh my God, she pulled out my hair," Inga wailed from behind them.

"So you're begging for me to forgive you and you're still fucking this trash?" Renee jerked her head toward the other woman.

"Trash!" Inga snapped with indignation.

"Be quiet, Inga!" Jackson snapped. He focused his eyes back on Renee. "I didn't ask her over here, Renee. It's over—it's been over—between us."

Renee hated the tears and sadness that threatened to overwhelm her. "This is your drama. Your mess. Your life. I'm done. I. AM. DONE."

"I messed up, but I love—"

Renee shook her head. "Save your lies for someone else. Barbie can have you. Now *release* me."

Jackson hesitated. "Renee, don't—"

"Now!"

He unwrapped his hands from around her wrists.

Renee turned and jumped at Inga. She smiled coldly when the woman jumped back. Taking little joy in that, she turned and walked to the door. Hand on knob, she looked over her shoulder at him. "An affair I could have forgiven because our twenty years is so much more than some sexual slip-up . . . some worthless fuck . . . some worthless woman," she told him, looking at the man and hating that she felt like she didn't know him at all. Like the last twenty years—their marriage, their life—had all been some dream.

Renee pointed to Inga. "That I can forgive."

Renee pointed to Inga's belly. "That *bastard* I cannot."

She left the house, closing the door behind her and thanking God that he let her be. Every step away from his door felt like one heavy weight after another was placed on her shoulders. She felt like breaking down, crying, having a fit, but she refused to let him or his bitch see her fall.

Renee barely made it inside her vehicle before her body trembled and the tears fell.

Should it matter that her husband's mistress was a white woman? Did it matter?

Renee reached into her purse for her flask and took a deep swallow of the gin and cranberry juice inside. She felt hopeless. Images of her husband's beautiful brown ass clutching and releasing as he stroked between Inga's pale thighs taunted her. She took another sip, licking her lips at the familiar warmth of the liquor as she swallowed it down.

She picked up her cell phone atop her purse. The text message from Jessa was still open.

> Importance: High
> To: 19735558932
> From: 19735550666
> Subject: Let's talk . . . ASAP
>
> I'm woman enough to admit I was
> wrong. Your man is not the man for me.
> Not at all. Want the truth? Meet me at
> the Terrace Room at noon.

Renee honestly didn't know if she could take much more truth.

She texted Jessa back quickly.

> FUCK A MEETING. JUST TELL ME
> NOW.

She hit SEND and then dialed Jackson's phone number.

"Tell her to get the hell out," she told him as soon as he picked up. "That's your house and your mess, Jackson, but you're still *my* husband and I'm not leaving here with another bitch in your house. Now either she comes out or I'm coming the fuck back in."

Renee ended the call and carelessly tossed the Black-Berry onto the butter-soft leather of the backseat. Her show of bravado ended.

The door opened and Inga walked out, being sure to rub her belly as she passed Renee's vehicle to climb into some nondescript royal blue four door. Renee watched her in the rearview mirror until she pulled off and drove away. She had to fight the urge to ram her car into the rear of her.

She jumped, turning to the passenger window to see Jackson leaning down to peer in. Renee pushed the flask down in between the door and the car seat. She lowered the window an inch as she eyed her husband through the clear glass. "A white woman? How fucking cliché, Jackson," she drawled. "If I were you, *mandingo*, I would give me fifty feet. Seriously."

She pulled off, not giving a damn if she ran over his feet as she sped away. But she made it no farther than the corner before she pulled over and let her tears rise and her head fall to the steering wheel.

Chapter 5

As soon as Aria finished up her interview, she hopped into her Range Rover and headed to the Terrace Room. The joy and excitement she'd had about her exclusive interview with a pop icon was squelched by the Jessa Bell bullshit. She'd gotten all the questions out. She'd even thought of a few more as they talked in the living room of her penthouse suite at The Plaza. But the whole time her mind was on Jessa Bell.

Was this another game?

Would she even show?

Did Renee and Jaime get the message, too?

Was she going to find out that her husband was having an affair?

Aria had made it from New York to New Jersey in record time. As soon as she pulled up to the valet station of the Terrace Room, a château-styled home of the 1930s that had been converted into a restaurant, Aria grabbed her cell phone and purse before she hopped out.

"Good afternoon, Mrs. Livewell," Andre, the valet, said politely before climbing into the seat of her Range Rover.

Aria gave him a polite smile, nothing like her usual chatty and friendly demeanor. Coming from Newark and having plenty of family work in the service industry, Aria never looked down her nose at those most of her Richmond Hills neighbors considered "help."

She didn't give a damn how many celebrities she interviewed, how many million-dollar homes she lived in, there was no sign of bougie in her.

Aria started to call Kingston, but she decided against it. *No, I'll let this shit play out first,* she thought, pulling her bronze leather Fendi tote up on her shoulder.

What if Jessa is laying up with Kingston and playing me for the fool sitting at the restaurant?

As she walked across the drive to the brick steps of the restaurant, Aria pulled up the text and dialed the number Jessa used to send it. She had tried it twice before and it was never answered.

"Hello, Aria."

Her steps froze at the sound of Jessa's husky voice.

"Where are you?" Aria asked coldly.

"Nice dress. White always looked great on you. Come on in."

Click.

Aria's heart hammered as her cinnamon eyes shifted over the windows of the restaurant, looking for a sign of her. Clutching her cell phone, Aria slid her shades down from the top of her head to cover her eyes. Jessa didn't need to know shit about what she was feeling or thinking.

"Welcome back to the Terrace Room, Mrs. Livewell," Kilpatrick, the maître d', greeted her with a slight bow of his balding head.

"Thank you, Mr. Kilpatrick," she said absentmindedly as she looked past his shoulder into the restaurant. *Where is that bitch?*

"Right this way, ma'am. Ms. Bell is awaiting you."

Aria stiffened her spine as she followed him through the elegant restaurant with its French country decor. She eyed the very same table Renee, Jaime, and she had sat at when they'd first received Jessa's text. Aria came to a stop next to the empty table. "Mr. Kilpatrick," she called out softly.

He turned. "I'll be sitting here. Please ask Ms. Bell and the rest of her party to join me here," she said. *Might as well end this bullshit in the same spot where it all began for Renee, Jaime, and me.*

Kilpatrick moved his tall and slender figure to pull out one of the parson chairs for her. "I'll be right back with Ms. Bell," he said, after she was seated.

Aria didn't like that her back was to a portion of the restaurant so she shifted over to the next seat, putting her back to the beautiful wood paned windows directly overlooking the gardens surrounding the restaurant.

And when Kilpatrick emerged from the rear of the restaurant and Aria laid eyes on Jessa Bell walking behind him, it took everything Aria had to remain seated. From behind her shades, she missed not one detail about the scandalous bitch. The full waves of her shoulder-length ebony hair. The bright redness of her matte lipstick against the creamy mocha complexion of her skin. The tailored black dress she wore like a second skin on her curves. The arrogant tilt of her head and the sultry nature of her walk.

Aria had never wanted to slap the taste out of someone's mouth so badly. Taking a deep breath, she licked her glossy lips and pushed her chair back a bit to cross her legs.

As Kilpatrick held Jessa's chair, Aria promised herself that there was no way on God's green earth that she was letting Jessa Bell leave without getting some answers.

Enough was enough.

"That will be all," Jessa ordered him, setting her clutch on the table beside her silverware.

"Thank you, *Mister* Kilpatrick," Aria said with emphasis, taking her eyes away from Jessa Bell long enough to smile up at him.

"How have you been, Aria?" Jessa asked, removing her own shades to expose her eyes.

"Don't play any more games with me, Jessa. We go a long way back and you know I ain't never in the mood for bullshit," Aria told her in a low voice that was brimming with anger. She sat up on the edge of her chair, removing her shades to lock her eyes with Jessa's. "Are you fucking my husband?"

Jessa's eyes shifted to the left and to the right like she was concerned someone had overhead Aria. "I thought doing this in a public place would erase the opportunity to be vulgar and loud, Aria."

Aria jumped to her feet.

Jessa held up her hands. "Sit down, Aria," she said calmly. "Kingston is not—was not—my lover."

Aria absolutely hated the waves of relief she felt cascade over her body as she sat back down in her chair. "So who is it, then, Jessa?"

Jessa shifted her eyes to the entrance of the restaurant. "I really wanted all of you here, but Renee didn't want to meet and Jaime never answered me," she said, sounding disappointed.

"And I wish Mark could be here," Aria spit out. "I'm sure he'd be so proud of his wife for fucking one of his friends."

Pain flashed in Jessa's eyes. "Mark would understand that I fell in love, plain and simple."

Aria's brows furrowed as she pierced Jessa with her eyes. "In love? In lust, must be. If you're so in love then why didn't your shit work out? Renee and Jaime are not with Jackson and Eric. So if he *loved* you, if he *chose* you, if he *couldn't get enough* of you . . . then why the hell ain't he *with you.*"

The look of surprise on Jessa's face was hard to miss.

"Oh, you didn't know that. Recognize when you're

nothing but a sideline ho, a bust-it baby, a hit-it-and-quit-it bitch, a nut buster."

Jessa's face shaped with anger.

"I had no idea that you were . . . so childish, sneaky, manipulative, and cruel," Aria continued. "Did you have any idea the effect that stupid motherfuckin' message of yours had on all of our lives or didn't you give a shit?"

Jessa eyed Aria with defiance. "You all deserved it."

"What?" Aria snapped.

Jessa smirked. "My friends. None of you trusted me anyway. Once Mark died the ladies in the neighborhood all began to clutch their husband's arms a little tighter when I walked by or would innocently stroll up while I was simply having a conversation with their man. Everyone began to treat me like a whore on the prowl for a new pimp. Including the three of you."

Aria waved her hand dismissively. "Bullshit."

"Puh-leeze. I noticed little things you all did . . . just like every other scared and insecure housewife. Little comments, little side-eyes. Obvious questions that double-checked the who, what, when, where, and why of me being in one of the men's company." Jessa's short laughter was filled with bitterness. "I never expected that bullshit from the three of you."

Aria balled up her fist and brought it down on the table so hard that the silverware clanged. "So you prove that you're to be trusted by sleeping with one of our husbands and then planning to run the fuck away from him?" Aria asked her bluntly. "Bitch, you are crazy out your ass."

Jessa's eyes flashed. "Crazy is lying to your husband about being able to have children, or almost having an affair with your gay assistant, or stealing money from the husband who busted his ass to give you everything—after you're caught cheating."

Aria thought of the hell she'd put Kingston through, accusing him, arguing with him, searching through his dirty clothes and his cell phone while he slept, following him or at least double-checking to make sure he was where he said he was. As if the guilt of keeping her infertility from him wasn't enough, she damn near ruined her marriage because of this delusional bitch.

"I cannot believe you tryna be a big and bad bold bitch. I ought to slap the shit out your *cra-zy* ass. *Bitch*."

Jessa smirked as she reached into her clutch and pulled out her cell phone. "I'm moving back to my home in Richmond Hills and I'd advise you all to get ready."

Aria frowned as she watched Jessa typing away on the keypad of the black and silver BlackBerry as she spoke. "Are you serious?"

Jessa set the cell phone down on top of her clutch. "Very."

"Still playing games, huh, Jessa?"

"Excuse me?"

"Which husband?" Aria asked, amazed that she could sit here so calmly.

"I already told you: not yours. Don't worry, you still have Kingston's nose wide open. I guess all those tricks you learned in your teens paid off."

Aria bit back her words as the waiter sat two goblets of iced water on the table. Jessa waved her hand dismissively, sending him on his way.

Aria shifted her eyes to the BlackBerry. She reached across the table to snatch it up so quickly that she knocked over the glasses of water.

Jessa reached across the table and Aria roughly slapped her hand away. "Touch me or this phone again and I will lay your ass out . . . and you know I will," she warned.

Aria scrolled through the recent calls. Her eyes widened at the sight of the cell phone number. She recognized it and it was in Jessa's phone. Again and again and again.

She opened a text and her mouth fell open at the picture

of a man's dick. It was way more of her friend's husband than she needed to see. Aria stood up and threw the BlackBerry like a fastball pitch. It struck Jessa square in the center of her forehead, sending her head flying back from the impact.

"Ow!" Jessa cried out, all sophisticated composure gone as she fell backward in the chair.

A collective gasp of shock came from everyone in the restaurant.

Aria stepped forward, but Kilpatrick quietly and calmly appeared to step in her path.

"Mrs. Livewell and Ms. Bell, our manager has asked me to escort both of you from the premises. You are more than welcome to return at another time . . . *separately*."

Aria looked around and saw all eyes were on them. Kingston was well known in the community and a scene like this would embarrass him. *Especially if I drag that bitch around the restaurant.*

She shifted her eyes back to Jessa as the woman clutched at the chair and struggled to climb up to her knees. Aria squatted down and leveled her eyes with Jessa's. "You know, I really thought I would beat your ass wherever I caught you, but now I know you ain't even worth it. You're a miserable, lonely bitch who couldn't stand to see her friends happy because your husband passed away."

Aria rose up and reached to grab her pocketbook. "I apologize for the commotion, Mr. Kilpatrick," she said, before turning to strut out of the restaurant with her head held high—like she didn't just chunk Jessa in the head with a BlackBerry à la Naomi Campbell.

As soon as she stepped out of the door, she called Kingston's cell phone. She wanted to—had to—apologize for the craziness she'd put him through. Her marriage was in therapy and her husband had threatened divorce because she'd believed Jessa over him.

His phone went straight to voice mail. She didn't leave a message.

Besides groveling, she wanted his advice on breaking the news to a friend that her husband was the culprit. Taking to his voice mail wasn't going to offer any suggestions.

Aria pressed a ten-dollar tip into the valet's hand and climbed into her Rover. She was just pulling out when she saw Jessa step out of the restaurant clutching the arm of a busboy and looking around like she was worried Aria would jump out of the bushes and teardatassup.

"Punk bitch," Aria muttered with anger.

She pulled out of the driveway and came to a red light. She had no time for Jessa . . . for now. She cleared her throat as she dialed her cell. It rang three times and went to voice mail.

"Hey, it's Aria. Listen, um, give me a call back. I really need to talk to you about something."

Aria released a heavy breath as she tossed the Black-Berry onto the seat and drove away.

"Ma, why are you sleeping in the car?"

Renee opened one eye and looked up at her son and Darren peering through the driver's-side window at her. For a few seconds she struggled between that sleep and wake zone as she wiped the sweat from her face and neck. She avoided their eyes as she sat up straight and then opened the car door.

"I just felt sick at the store and fought my way home. I couldn't even get out of the car," she lied.

"How long have you been out here?" Darren asked, setting the box he held onto the driveway.

"Not long," she lied again. "But I feel better."

In truth she didn't remember even driving home from Jackson's apartment. Her head was pounding and she felt nauseous.

"We finished the brochures, Ma."

Darren nodded before he picked up the box. "I'm heading home. See you Monday."

"Where's your sister?" Renee asked, watching Darren as he carried the box to put into the trunk of his late-model black Lexus.

"She went bowling with her friend Gina. She called to ask permission, but you weren't answering your phone, so I told her to go, to get out of her room."

Renee smiled at her son as she rose to her feet, trying her best not to wobble on her feet. "Thank you, Aaron."

He stepped forward. "You want me to help you into the house, Ma?"

Renee slammed her mouth shut and shook her head no, knowing if it tasted like shit—and it did—that it had to smell twice as bad.

Darren blew his horn briefly before pulling off.

Aaron waved him off and then turned to head into the house.

Renee tilted her head back, enjoying the feel of the summer rays on her face. She smiled softly when she thought of barbeque and the get-togethers she and Jackson used to host all through the summer season. They both loved the heat and would lay in the yard, in hammocks—back before she went to work. Back before their marriage was over and her husband began playing buck to some white woman.

"Hey, Renee."

She opened her eyes and looked at Aria walking up from her Range Rover parked on the street. She couldn't keep the surprise from her face. "Hey, hi, Aria. Something I can help you with?"

"I left you a message to call me back and when I got home I saw you outside so I decided to drive down," Aria explained, crossing her arms over her chest.

"Yeah, I didn't hear my phone ringing," Renee stumbled to explain.

Aria came to stand beside Renee and leaned back against the Benz. "You're probably wondering why I'm here."

"Considering you hate my guts because I'm the whore of Richmond Hills . . . uh, yeah, I did kinda wonder," Renee drawled sarcastically.

"I don't hate your guts, Renee, I just—"

Renee laughed. "No, you just judged me and threw our friendship in the trash like a rotten banana when I needed you most," she admitted, ending with her voice barely above a whisper as tears rolled down her cheeks. "You and Jaime just pulled away."

Aria eyes widened in surprise. "Is that about Jessa—"

Renee waved her hand. Slashing the air. "Jessa. I fucking wish the only problem Jackson and I had was Jessa's dry behind. My husband has a baby on the way with another woman—"

"Oh my God," Aria gasped, reaching out to wrap her arms around Renee's shoulders. "Are you okay, Renee?"

"No," she admitted, dropping her head in her hands. "Ain't a damn thing about me all right."

She hadn't shared even twenty words with Aria since that day, but it felt easy, natural, and damn good to finally have someone to talk to. Never underestimate the value of friends.

"I'm sorry, Renee, I didn't know. I shouldn't have judged you, just you almost had an affair and Jessa's stupid message and all the shit I was going through. I overreacted. And then I was so caught up in falsely accusing Kingston and couples therapy and . . . and—"

Renee looked over at Aria with red eyes. "Falsely?" she asked.

Aria nodded. "Did you get Jessa's invite to lunch today?"

Renee nodded. "I was so busy trying to tear all the blond hair out of my husband's baby mama's head that I told Jessa to just tell me."

Aria arched an eyebrow. "Blond hair?"

"All pussy is the same color in the dark," Renee said, sliding her hands into the pocket of the cotton peasant skirt she wore.

"True."

"Did you go?" Renee asked, thinking maybe it would have been good to lay a little ass whupping on Jessa, too.

"I did and the bitch is moving back to Richmond Hills. Now you tell me she doesn't have a clit on her big as a set of balls on an old man."

Renee shifted her eyes to Jessa's house with a snort. She thought back to the day they'd gotten the message and then used her alarm code to break into her house to snoop for clues on the guilty husband. It was that day that Renee had learned to use alcohol to numb the pain.

"It's crazy, but I spent that whole damn day thinking it was my husband, wishing it wasn't my husband sleeping with my friend, and he comes home to tell me another woman is pregnant with his child." Renee closed her eyes against a wave of pain. "I never thought I could actually hurt Jackson but that night I knew that if he didn't leave my eyesight I would have shot him."

"What are you going to do?"

Renee looked down at her bare left ring finger. She'd stopped wearing her wedding rings the morning after Jackson's announcement. Everything the rings stood for felt like a mockery anytime she looked at them. "He wants me to forgive and forget but I can't see it. I can't envision it. I can't do it . . . as much as I love him I can't forgive this. I won't."

"Just even thinking Kingston was cheating drove me crazy so I cannot even imagine what you are going through," Aria admitted.

"It is horrible. It is the worst feeling. It is my worst nightmare. And I wish like hell that I could just wake up and all of this shit was a bad dream or movie or some shit, you know." Renee looked down at her toes bared in the flip-flops she wore. A tear fell from her eye and landed on her big toe like a raindrop.

"You yanked her a bald spot, huh?" Aria asked, nudging her with her shoulder.

Renee actually laughed a little, before looking up at her younger and usually feistier friend. "I had enough to make a blond ponytail. O-*kay*?" she joked, thinking it felt good to laugh.

Aria smiled. "You shoulda kept it. I coulda made me some highlights."

Renee flung her head back and laughed.

"And how about Jessa and I were asked to leave the Terrace Room after I bounced that bitch's BlackBerry off her forehead. Put a lot on her mind, you know what I'm saying," Aria said with her normal sass and spunk as she did a two-step. "I know she 'bout deep as hell in a Tylenol bottle."

Renee shook her head as she smiled. "I missed you, girl," she admitted, completely honest.

Aria turned and hugged Renee close. "Me, too, friend. Me, too."

Renee cut her eyes up to the blue sky, wishing her life felt more like a clear summer day than an April shower downpour. "It wasn't Kingston, was it?" Renee asked softly, wishing like hell that she knew it wasn't Jackson. Her mental plate was full.

"No, it isn't. Wasn't. Whatever."

Renee pulled away from Aria's embrace, stepping back

to look at her. "What did you need to talk to me about?" she asked, finally feeling ready to hear the truth.

If Jessa and Jackson were lovers it would just be the crappy icing on top of a shitty cake.

She studied Aria's expression.

"Renee, you not gon' believe *this* shit. . . ."

Some things you never forget.

For all her bravado and stance that her new life was all her own, Jaime had been raised a certain way to live life a *certain* way.

She made concessions to the rules over the years: her affair, her professional-sexual relationship with Pleasure, and leaving her husband—but most of her mother's training on what was and was not appropriate was as deeply ingrained in her as her own DNA.

Standing in a living room with your mother when your lover-for-hire walks in with his dick swinging like a bat was just the utmost level of impropriety. In the hours since her mother had stormed out, Jaime had tried calling her, but Virginia Osten-Pine wasn't having it. Jaime shook her head knowing that was the only other dick her mother had laid eyes on in over forty years. "Lawd," she sighed, still feeling embarrassed and anxious about the whole incident.

She released a stream of smoke, watching it fan out against the window from where she sat in the club chair beside the front bay of windows. She looked out through the sheer curtains at the children in the neighborhood playing double dutch, running, playing tag, or sitting on the porch with their heads bent down over portable video games.

Enjoying life. No worries. No concerns.

"Hmph." Jaime picked up her tall glass of white wine and took a deep sip.

The grocery-store brand was a long way from her days of spending a hundred dollars or better a bottle, but it was working just fine to settle her nerves.

Everything had changed in just a little over a month. Everything. Most for the better. Some for the worse.

Like marriage, she thought, *but less stressful.*

"Hey, Jaime, I gotta go."

She looked up at Pleasure dressed in a black sleeveless tee and basketball shorts, his dreads pulled back at the base of his strong neck. He was texting away on his cell phone, his eyes not on her. "Busy, busy, busy," she said sarcastically, flicking the ashes from the tip of her cigarette into the ashtray on the windowsill.

Pleasure cut his eyes up at her before he squatted down beside her chair. "Can you handle this?" he asked, the deepness of his voice seeming to vibrate within the strong confines of his chest.

Jaime allowed herself to take a deep inhale of his spicy and warm cologne. "What is *this*?"

"Listen, I met you stripping and slinging my dick for dollars. Harsh but real . . . and that's what I am." He locked his eyes with hers. "I mean, we ain't in no relationship so why you been actin' up?" he asked.

Because I want more.

Pleasure reached up and took the cigarette from her hands. "You shouldn't smoke. It's not good for you."

She laughed sardonically. "Neither are you."

He broke the cigarette in half and dropped it into the ashtray. "You control this, Jaime. It's all on your demand. Turn it loose," he said, finally looking up to lock his eyes with hers.

"I can't," she admitted softly, her heart pounding fast and hard as hell in her chest. She was ad"dick"ted and knew it.

Ding-dong.

She looked out the window and her eyes widened.
"What the hell?" she said, jumping to her feet and rushing
to the front door to fling it open.

Aria and Renee both smiled at her as she stepped forward. She couldn't help but feel and show surprise.

"Don't look crazy. We called your mother and she gave
up the address," Aria said, stepping past Jaime into the
foyer. "And she said something strange about it being a
whorehouse over here. I was telling Renee what in the
devil's drawers is Mama Pine talkin' about."

Renee stepped into the foyer. "Whatever it is your
Mama is fired up. . . ."

Jaime gave what had to be her thousandth heavy breath
that day as Aria and Renee eyed Pleasure as he rose to his
full height. Both of their heads tilted back a bit to take him
all in.

"Oh," they both said in sudden understanding.

Jaime watched Pleasure smile and give them his intense
stripper eyes as he walked up to them with his large and
very able hand outstretched.

"Um . . . ah . . . well, hey now. Say what, say who?"
Aria stumbled softly as she eyed him.

Jaime's stomach clenched as he kissed the back of both
of their hands.

Renee looked over her shoulder at Jaime with a questioning look.

"I am Pleasure and please remember me, ladies, because
I am here for all of your wants, desires, and of course,
pleasures," he said, reaching into his pocket for business
cards to hand them.

Jaime's mouth fell open. *No, he is not soliciting business in my face . . . from my friends!*

She stepped between Aria and Renee, turning to snatch
the cards from Aria and Renee's grasp, tearing them in
half. "Okay, you tripping," she snapped, grabbing Plea-

sure's strong arm and pulling him past Aria toward the door. "It's my *pleasure* to show you the door," she snapped.

Pleasure moved forward but turned to wave. " 'Bye, ladies."

Jaime moved behind him to push him to the door, motivated by anger, embarrassment, and jealousy. She hadn't been that jealous when she'd thought Eric and Jessa Bell's friendship was a cover for their affair—and that was way before that damn message. *What the . . . ?*

Pleasure turned on the doorstep and bent down to kiss her cheek. Jaime leaned back like she was in *The Matrix* and tossed the torn pieces of his business cards against his face before she stepped back and slammed the door hard enough to rattle the doorframe.

Knowing their eyes were on her and their questions had long since formed in their heads, Jaime allowed herself a moment to compose herself—a trick from her days of being Mrs. Perfection.

When she turned to face them, she had a smile on her face. "Haven't seen you two in a while. What've you been up to?"

Renee and Aria shared a long look before turning to face her again.

"What?" Jaime asked innocently, raising her hand to smooth her new shorter tresses.

"If he's not a walking 'fuck me' sign I don't know who is," Renee drawled.

"And *soooo* . . . are y'all fucking?" Aria asked with a comic expression as she took in Jaime's obvious nakedness under her clinging silk robe.

"Stay focused," Renee cut in before Jaime could say yay or nay.

"Focused on what?" Jaime asked, her anger at Pleasure still nipping at her even as she tried to hide it.

Renee and Aria shared another look.

"What?" Jaime snapped in irritation.

"Aria saw Jessa today," Renee began, biting her bottom lip.

Jaime arched a brow as she waved her hand dismissively. "I ignored it. I was . . . busy at the time and I've moved on from it. Calling divorce lawyers. Ending the marriage. Eric and I are done. . . ."

The rest of her words faded as she zoned in on the faces of her friends. Jaime's heart felt like it dropped to her stomach. Jaime frowned so deeply she swore she could see her eyebrows lowered in front of her eyes. She felt like someone had kicked her square in the gut.

Oh. Hell. No.

"Are you kidding me?" she asked. "Are you . . . are you . . . here to tell me . . . *me* . . . that it was Eric? Seriously? Seriously."

Aria stepped up and took Jaime's hand in hers as she nodded. "I snatched her phone and his numbers—house, cell, all of them—were in her phone. There was a picture text from his cell number and I saw way more of Eric than I needed to see ever. E-*ver*. Okay?"

"Aria," Renee snapped, stepping up to wrap an arm around Jaime's shoulders.

"I'm sorry, Jaime," Aria added.

Jaime shifted and freed herself of their touch and embrace. She closed her eyes as anger nearly consumed her like fire from the very gates of hell.

"Jaime, I know you loved Eric very much," Renee began.

Jaime whirled on them. They both stepped back at the look on her face. "Love him? I used to, but having your husband treat you like a hired sex slave while calling you every disgusting and degrading name in the book killed that love a long time ago."

"What?" Renee and Aria gasped in unison.

Jaime felt like she was standing deep in the midst of an emotional tornado. "I can't care less that Eric carried his dead-ass fucking to Jessa or that he lied about their friendship. No, no, no, I am furious that he treated me like shit on his shoes for fucking Pleasure one time—"

"So y'all was fucking?" Aria asked.

Jaime ignored her. "One time. One time," she stressed, tears filling her eyes, "Y'all don't know what I went through. What he put me through. What I put myself through to make my marriage work and the whole time I was fighting and dealing and pretending for . . . *for nothing?*"

Jaime felt her entire body shake and tears of anger and frustration raced down her cheek. She'd thought she didn't care. She'd thought it didn't matter. "I fought hard, I begged, I pleaded, I felt so guilty, I let myself be degraded for his forgiveness and . . . and . . . and—and the whole time he's fucking Jessa. Like, are you fucking kidding me right now?"

This was wrong. Seriously wrong.

Jaime grabbed her keys from the small table in the foyer and yanked the front door open wide with so much force it slammed against the adjacent wall. She flew down the walkway.

"Jaime, where are you going in your robe?" Renee called behind her.

Jaime didn't answer them and barely noticed her next-door neighbor, Lucas Neal, waving from his front yard. She hopped into her car and had just one thing on her mind. To hell with everything and everyone else.

Chapter 6

As soon as the front door of the house opened, Jaime swung and landed a hard punch to Eric's jaw. He stumbled back, more in surprise than from the actual weight of her blow. "After everything degrading and disgusting thing you put me through, punishing me for *my* affair, you were the bastard fucking Jessa Bell?" she roared.

"Jaime, no, don't," Renee said from behind her, running up the stairs to try and catch her.

Jaime whirled on Renee as Aria parked the car and raced up the driveway to rush up onto the porch. "Thanks for the backup, but I got this. I'll be with you in just a second," she said, before stepping back and firmly closing the door in their faces.

Her eyes blazed like the fiery bowels of hell as she turned to face him. "After all the shit you put me through you were the bastard cheating with Jessa? After all of your lies that you two were just friends? After your bullshit that you would never fuck your dead friend's widow?" she roared. "You were the low-down, deceiving, conniving, underhanded son of a bitch?"

Eric shook his head calmly as he watched her closely. "That's a lie, Jaime, and you know it."

"No, our bullshit marriage was a lie. From the beginning it was a lie. Everything about it was a lie." Jaime crossed her arms over her chest to keep from striking out at him again as she eyed this man she'd once thought she loved.

Eric slid his hands into the pocket of his tailored slacks. "There's no way Jessa told you that and if she did she's a liar," he said, his voice and stance hardening. "I don't have time for this foolishness. Our marriage doesn't have time for it. Why are you running around the city in a damn robe anyway? It's not appropriate."

Jaime's chest began to fill with hysterical laughter that she couldn't hold back. As it spilled from her mouth she began to wonder if she was losing her mind. The way he strangely eyed her, she knew he wondered the same thing. "Inappropriate? *I'm* inappropriate? No, motherfucker. No. I'm not a damn thing but free of your ass."

"You knew I didn't believe in divorce going in and nothing has changed. I'm not getting a divorce. I don't want one. My faith does not allow for one. If it did I would have divorced you after your affair . . . but I didn't," Eric said plainly, turning to walk out of the living room and toward the kitchen.

Jaime's anger soared. "If I knew the sex was going to be as dry as dust I wouldn't have married you," she yelled behind him. "And I wouldn't have cheated on your ass."

He froze.

She steeled herself. She wanted to hurt him, anger him, and get more of the truth from him.

He turned to look at her. His square and handsome face was cold and hard, cloaked by that hate-filled mask that she had come to find familiar in the days after her affair. "Don't make excuses for being a slut, Jaime."

Jaime felt that familiar uneasiness in her soul whenever she was alone with him and all semblance of their charade gone. She pushed it aside. That Jaime was gone and like a caterpillar turned butterfly or phoenix rising from the ashes, someone new stood before him. "And don't make excuses for the sadistic sex freak that you are, pervert."

Eric nodded as if they dueled and he acknowledged her strike. "Our marital bed was not your problem, it was your fault."

That stung, but Jaime literally shrugged off the insult. "I was a virgin. A clean slate for you to teach and to mold. You failed. You didn't step up to the challenge. You didn't get the job done."

Jaime arched a brow, chuckling as she thought of the passion Pleasure gave and received. "I thought it was my fault, too . . . until another man with more skill made me come . . . for the *very* first time in my life."

Eric nodded again. Another acknowledgement. "It's funny, but the pussy didn't get interesting *until* I fucked you like the whore you are."

The gloves were off.

"I think I owe Jessa thanks actually because I thought your ass was a closet homosexual looking for a woman to be your mustache as your cover." Jaime arched her brow and eyed him from head to toe. "Maybe one of them high and holy Catholic priests brought the little fag out of you."

Quicker than the snap of a finger, Eric took two large steps and grabbed Jaime by the throat, slamming her back against the door so hard that it jarred the mirror from the adjacent wall, sending it crashing to the floor. "Don't say that. You don't know what the hell you're talking about," he ground out through clenched teeth.

As she struggled to kick at him and free his hands from her neck, Jaime flashed back to the night she'd left him. Same shit. Different day.

Boom-boom-boom.

"Jaime, open this door. What's going on in there?"

Jaime brought her hands up and scratched at his face as she fought to get out the words, "Let me go, bitch."

"Take it back," he demanded, not even flinching from the long scratch down the side of his face. "Take it back."

Boom-boom-boom.

"Open this damn door or I'm calling the police."

Suddenly she was free and she shoved his chest hard. "If you ever put your hands on me again I will have you thrown in jail," she told him, her throat hoarse from the pressure of his hands.

Eric sneered. "I gave as good as I got."

"And so Jessa got better?" she snapped at him.

"She gave better!" he shot back, instantly looking like he regretted his words.

Jaime clapped sarcastically. "Thank you for your honesty," she said, opening the door. "You'll be hearing from my attorney."

He grabbed at her arm. "Jaime."

Renee and Aria turned to look at them.

"Jaime, are you okay?" Renee asked, her eyes dropping down to Eric's hand tightly grasping her upper arm and then up to the dark bruises already forming on her throat.

"Let her arm go, Eric," Aria warned, her eyes hardening.

Jaime whirled on him, pulling her arm free and slapping him across the cheek in one fluid, anger-filled motion.

WHAP!

Aria and Renee both gasped sharply.

"How long, huh? How long were you screwing Jessa Bell behind my back? Huh? How long?" she asked him coldly, her eyes blazing as her fists clenched and unclenched.

Eric just slid his hands into the pocket of his slacks, his expression blank. "I love you, Jaime. I am going to prove that to you."

Jaime's anger dissipated and her confusion and disbelief reigned at how quickly he'd slipped into the charade in front of Renee and Aria. Standing there like a stream of blood wasn't running down the side of his face and dripping onto his Polo shirt. Who was this man she'd married? Tears filled her eyes. "You are crazy and I thank God that I am free of you."

She turned and welcomed the arms of her friends as they walked her off the porch and away from a man that she knew was a stranger to her.

Renee accepted the glass of red sangria Aria handed her and Jaime. Truly she wanted—needed—something more. Something stronger that would numb the pain and not just serve as a cute summer refreshment for three friends reconnecting.

"Aria, do you have a mirror?" Jaime asked, gently touching the tender bruises on her neck with her fingertips.

"Sure do. I'll go get it." Aria walked into the kitchen from where they sat on the deck at the rear of the house.

Renee eyed Jaime over the rim of her wine goblet. "Why didn't you tell us the truth?"

Jaime shrugged. "Pride. Stupidity. Trying to please everybody but myself," she admitted, smoothing the cotton maxi dress Aria had given her to wear.

"I thought you and Eric had the perfect marriage," Renee said.

Jaime shook her head. "We gave the perfect performance."

Aria walked out onto the deck with the mirror in one hand and the pitcher of sangria in the other. She handed Jaime the mirror and refreshed Renee's glass. "I've been trying to call Kingston, but his phone is off," she said.

"No worries now, huh?" Jaime said.

Aria did a double take. "I will never sleep, trust and believe that, but I do owe him an apology for this Jessa bull-shit. Hell, I'm still not sure he'll forgive me when he believes I should have trusted him."

"That is lightweight compared to me and Eric," Jaime said, studying the bruises on her neck in the mirror.

Renee took the whole goblet to the head in one gulp, drawing Aria's and Jaime's questioning stares. "What? Walk in these size tens and then judge me," she drawled, closing her eyes and leaning back against the wicker chaise lounge.

"Jackson still bitching about you working?" Jamie asked.

Renee opened one eye. "I wish. Hmph, I spent that whole day worrying about Jessa Bell only to have my husband come home to tell me he'd had a one night-stand—"

Jaime grimaced.

"And she's pregnant," Renee added.

"Oooh." Jaime looked to Aria, who solemnly nodded in confirmation.

Renee shook her head as she tapped a fingernail against her empty goblet, signaling she needed a refill. "And she's white. Blond hair, blue-eyed white."

Aria shook her head. "Not the olive-skinned brunette who might pass for a mixed sistah or a Latina?"

Renee scoffed. "*Hell* to the no."

"Wow. I know it's 2011 and it shouldn't matter and the world should be color-blind and all that good shit, but that is insult on top of injury right there." Aria sat up in her chair.

"Why? Pussy is pussy," Jaime said. "The fact is Jackson had an affair with another woman and who cares if she's blue, black, green, or white. It doesn't make it more wrong because she's white. It's just wrong period."

"Yes, but I would feel like is she offering him something he's always coveted and how can you compete with this myth of the freaky white chicks who swallow, butt fuck, and the whole nine."

"So there are no freaky *black* women?" Jaime asked in disbelief.

"Listen, there's not a damn thing me and Kingston haven't done and I mean nothing, even down to golden showers . . . but there is this idea white chicks are complacent and giving and serving and we're just the angry black bitches who don't let a man be a man and ya-ya-ya and all that dumb shit. It's more than another woman, it's competing with a myth. That's all I'm saying."

Renee sighed. "So maybe I was that stereotypical strong black woman who pushed my husband into the arms of this white woman?"

Aria just held up her hands. "But that's not your fault or your issue, it's Jackson's. You did nothing wrong and he shoulda dealt with whatever issues y'all had better and gotten to the root of why he is so afraid of you having a career."

Renee smiled. "That therapy is something, huh?"

Aria shrugged. "Now that the mystery is solved I'm ready to throw up a deuce to the therapy, but I did learn that there's a reason for everything."

Renee looked off into the distance. "Sometimes I feel like my life is a movie and I'm just somebody waiting along with all the moviegoers to see how it all turns out."

She thought about the bottle of tequila stashed away under her mattress. She licked her lips as she craved a drink. The sangria just wasn't cutting it. "My life went from this romantic love story to a fucking horror show."

"Are *you* going to file for divorce?" Jaime asked.

Renee shrugged. "Honestly, my mind hasn't gotten that far yet."

Aria sat up in the chair and looked at Renee like she was crazy. "You're thinking about taking Jackson back, Renee? Hell to the no."

The thirst for the tequila grew.

"You're wrong, Aria. Don't ever say what you will or

will not take or do or say because you never know until you're in the position to decide." Jaime reached over and patted Renee's hand. "It's your marriage, your pain, your decision."

"Wow. I know you are not coming with the holier-than-thou, forgive-and-forget, marriage-is-'til-death crap?"

"And I know you're not sitting on your high horse pushing your opinion on other people like she doesn't have a mind of her own?" Jaime snapped back.

Renee held up her hands. "Ladies, we just rediscovered our friendship. Please don't ruin it, because we need each other more than ever," she admitted, her voice hoarse with emotion.

Aria and Jaime nodded in agreement.

Renee rose to her feet, unable to fight the desire brewing in her. "Bathroom break," she said, moving across the deck to enter the house.

She didn't go through the kitchen and down the hall to the half a bathroom. Instead, she made her way to the living room and grabbed a bottle of gin from the built-in bar. Renee had barely unscrewed the cap before she tilted the bottle up and took a deep swig from it. Once, twice, three times. Wincing at the burn of the liquor down her throat, she quickly screwed the cap back on as she welcomed the familiar warmth of the liquor.

"Take the edge off a little bit," she whispered into the room as she set the bottle back.

Renee made her way to the bathroom, securely closing the door before she plopped down onto the commode. She didn't bother with turning on the light, welcoming the cool darkness and the quiet as she waited for the effects of the liquor to kick in.

She didn't want to hear her friends analyzing why her husband had fucked another woman. She didn't want to hear that she was a fool because she hadn't already run to a divorce attorney. She wanted to get drunk. Fucked up.

High off some liquor. And then go home and sleep. In her dreams Jackson hadn't fucked her over. In her dreams she was happy. In her dreams all her drama was forgotten.

Renee bent over, pressing her elbows into her knees, as she rubbed her eyes with her fingertips.

One thing kept fucking with her though. Why did the concept of her working threaten Jackson so much? Was Aria right? Was there a reason for everything? And did it really even matter?

———❦———

Aria turned as Renee stumbled through the doors onto the deck. She frowned. "Are you okay?" she asked her.

Renee fanned herself. "Girl, that sangria sneaks up on you," she said airily, before dropping down onto the chaise lounge.

"Well, no more for you," Aria teased.

"No, no, I'm good. No more for me."

Aria picked up her cell phone and dialed Kingston again. It went straight to voice mail. She wanted to talk to him. The storm in their marriage was over. It was time to get back to their lives.

She eyed both Renee and Jaime, both lost in their thoughts, and she was grateful that the abundance of marital drama hadn't hit her marriage. Yet.

Tomorrow when he walked through the door she planned to meet him butt naked as the day she was born, on her knees, mouth open and tongue ready to suck the life from his dick where he stood.

Maybe it's time to tell Kingston the truth.

Aria shook her head slightly as she watched the chunks of fruit circle in her sangria. *At least let him know having children may be a challenge. . . .*

She took a deep sip of the drink. *But what if his desire for children is greater than his desire for me?*

"My marriage was a lie," Jaime admitted softly, shaking her head as she lowered it. "My life was a lie."

Renee yawned, her eyelids drooping lazily, as she looked at Jaime. "Secrets and lies are the kryptonite of a healthy marriage."

Aria shifted uncomfortably in her seat, the weight of her own secrets and lies weighing her down. *Tell him, Aria. Tell Kingston.*

"If the secrets and the lies are part of the foundation of your marriage . . . Hmph. Just how solid is it?" Renee asked, her words slurring a bit.

"Especially when the secrets are used by an undercover slut on the prowl for your man," Aria added, thinking of Jessa's earlier taunt.

Crazy is lying to your husband about being able to have children, or almost having an affair with your gay assistant, or stealing money from the husband who busted his ass to give you everything—after you're caught cheating.

Jessa had all of their secrets ready and aimed like an arsenal. Aria already knew about Renee's near affair, but she decided not to mention the money Jaime must have taken from Eric when she left him. *No need adding fuel to the fire.*

It was obvious that she wasn't the only one who'd fucked up and trusted Jessa Bell as not just a friend but a confidant.

The sound of a gentle snore caused Aria to eye Renee, who was stretched out on the lounge, head tilted back and mouth slightly ajar.

"She gon' fuck around and inhale a fly," Aria joked, glad for a diversion from her thoughts.

Jaime chuckled. "That would be *so* wrong."

"But *sooooo* funny."

Renee mumbled something in her sleep as she shifted onto her side.

"I'm real sorry that y'all are going through these storms in your marriages," Aria said with honesty.

Jaime shrugged. "I—we—had no right getting married," she admitted. "We weren't ready. We didn't even know each other. Thank God we never had kids. More of a clean break, you know."

Aria squinted her eyes as she took a sip of her sangria. She had to bat her eyelashes to fight back the swell of sudden tears. It struck a nerve deep within her to hear Jaime be thankful for not having a child when she would give up anything and everything to have her body filled with Kingston's child. Anything. Everything.

"Excuse me, girl," Aria said awkwardly, rising to her feet and rushing into the house just a second before the tears fell and her body shook.

Most of the time she was able to bury that longing deep. Push it aside. Pretend she didn't care. Make like it was all right.

She wished she could have children, but not every wish was granted. She would never be a mother and that fact left a hole in her that nothing could fill. "Oh God," she wailed, bringing her hands up to wipe some of the free-flowing tears from her face. She hugged and rocked herself but none of it could fill that void.

"Aria?"

At the sound of Jaime's voice, Aria took deep calming breaths and quickly wiped away her tears. She turned just as Jaime stepped through the patio doors into the kitchen.

"I'm gonna hit the road because Eric keeps calling me and I'm headed back to my side of town before he decides to stroll his silly ass over here," she said, setting her wine goblet in the sink.

"So he doesn't know where your new house is?" Aria asked, keeping her back to Jaime as she pretended to look through the refrigerator.

"No, thank God."

Feeling like her tears had dried up enough, Aria pulled out a colander of rinsed grapes and closed the refrigerator door. "I think you're handling this Jessa Bell thing—affair, mess, whatever—really well," Aria told her.

Jaime picked up the paper shopping bag sitting on one of the stools surrounding the massive island. It held the infamous robe. "With trying to focus on getting back into interior design and taking a little time to find out just who the fuck I am, I can't let it sidetrack me. You know? I mean, I'm hurt, I'm angry, I'm disappointed, but I'm moving on. I got to get my shit together ASAP."

Aria smiled in genuine pleasure. "Wow. You are so different now. Jaime Hall working?"

She nodded with a smile that was the most genuine Aria had ever seen. "I gotta be happy, you know."

Aria leaned forward against the edge of the island. "And does Pleasure make you happy?" she asked teasingly.

Jaime flushed. "He's just a friend."

Hmph. "Well, then, you wouldn't mind me referring your friend . . . who *strips* . . . to my cousin for her bachelorette party?" Aria asked, her eyes locked on Jaime's face for the slightest hint of her giving a fuck.

She wasn't disappointed.

Jaime's expression instantly switched to annoyed. She quickly tried to cover it. "I don't care," she said nonchalantly.

"Bitch puh-*leeze*," Aria said, laughing. "That Negro got you sprung."

Jaime hid a smile behind her goblet.

"That dick good, ain't it?" Aria stretched her leg and tapped Jaime's thigh with her French-manicured toes. "Huh? Ain't it, girl? Tell me. Tell me. Tell me."

"Okay, yes," Jaime roared at Aria's insistence. "It's damn good—"

Aria raised her glass in a toast to Pleasure's dick.

"But he's not my man. It's not like that at all," Jaime stressed.

"Even better. Twice the dick with half the headache. Sounds like a fucking plan to me, boo-boo." Aria took a big gulp of sangria on that.

"It wasn't that Eric was like extra small or deformed," Jaime admitted, sounding slightly bashful. "Just compared to Pleasure he . . . you know . . . comes up a little short." But hell Pleasure got the dick of a horse.

Aria leaned forward, wishing she wasn't visualizing Eric naked. "Well, we could hear y'all arguing through the door and, well, you know, I uh, I just, uh, you know, *assumed* that was the . . . you know . . . problem."

Jaime rolled her eyes. " 'It's not the size of the boat, it's the motion of the ocean' can go two ways, you know."

Aria nodded in agreement. "Yes, girl, Hector Sanchez. That's all I have to say. Hector Sanchez."

Jaime laughed as Aria shivered in mock disgust.

"Damn shame for eleven inches of pure hard dick to be so boring. Oh my goodness. Lawd have mercy. No way. Hell no. Hell. To. The. No."

Jaime sat her glass down and pointed at Aria. "Yes! Yeessss! That's how IT was with Eric! It wasn't even wham bam. There's was no wham and to hell with the bam."

Aria shook her head and held up her hand. "Just a dead dick."

"And no chemistry. No sparks. Just going through the motions. . . ." Jaime looked off into the distance as she frowned and then shrugged helplessly.

Aria watched her. She couldn't imagine not having that intense connection with Kingston. Just his touch made her shiver and the right look in his eyes made her wet. Chemistry was everything. Everything.

"I guess he had that spark, the excitement, the passion or whatever with Jessa and Lord knows I got it with

Pleasure," she admitted, a smile spreading across her face like sunshine after a hard rain.

Aria licked the last remnants of her IMAN gloss from her lips. "Jessa is moving back to Richmond Hills," she said, knowing that of the three, Jaime might find that the hardest to swallow. Aria decided to drop the bomb just like pulling off a Band-Aid.

Jaime's mouth fell open a bit and her eyes widened. "No. She wouldn't," she said, more in disbelief and disapproval than question.

Aria snorted in derision. "That bitch is going to make me catch a case. Straight up."

Jaime bit her bottom lip as she shook her head. "She's not worth it," she said softly but firmly. "All she did was finally expose the cancer that she was in our clique and we don't need that. We don't need her. Fuck her."

"I don't travel the high road too often, Jaime, and this shit—fucking Eric, sending that message, betraying all of us—deserves a beatdown and she really thinks she just gon' stroll around Richmond Hills and be at all the same functions and events like she don't know she need her ass whipped!" Aria's hand slashed the air. "Bullshit. Complete and total bullshit, Jaime."

Jaime reached over and grabbed Aria's hand, squeezing it. "It's okay. I don't live here anymore. Remember?"

Aria winked. "It ain't over 'til it's over."

Jaime just shook her head.

As Renee released another snort in her sleep, Aria reached for her vibrating cell phone. Hoping it was Kingston her heart raced as she eyed the caller ID. "Hey, baby," she sighed, standing up from the chair to walk into the kitchen.

Kingston laughed. "You sound like you're in a better mood," he said.

Aria closed her eyes and just absorbed the vibrant energy he gave her. Just the sound of his voice made her pulse race. That was the chemistry Jaime had spoken of.

"I am. I can't wait for you to get home, but I am so sorry, Kingston, for how crazy I've been acting lately," she said, pressing the phone so tightly to her face that she swore she felt the keypad against her cheek.

"What happened?" he asked.

Aria pulled the phone away from her face to look at it before she frowned and pressed it back to her face. "Why did something have to happen? And how do *you* know something happened?" she asked, instantly suspicious and on her guard.

"There is no way you would apologize for no reason. Not Mrs. 'Ride-or-Die' Aria Livewell," he insisted.

She eyed Jaime through the window before she turned and sucked air between her teeth. "Okay, you're right, but we'll talk about it after you get home."

He laughed. "Turn around."

Aria whirled and dropped her cell phone in surprise at Kingston standing at the front door. "What are you doing here?" she asked, rushing across the tiled floor toward him.

"I'm pulling one of your 'incognegro' moves, doubling back to catch your lover up in here," he said, a smile on his handsome face as he reached out and pulled her body close to his muscular frame.

Aria smiled softly and allowed her curves to melt against him, loving him and needing him. "Ha, ha, ha," she said, pressing her mouth to his to kiss him passionately as she began to undress him.

"Whoa," Kingston said as a button from his shirt flew and hit the wall.

"Oh, it's on," she promised into his open mouth, grabbing his shirt front before she jerked it down his arms to fling behind her.

Kingston's eyes flashed hotly before he rushed out of his slacks and boxers.

Aria eyed him, her hands easing down his flat abdomen to grasp his dick possessively. "I'm ready to milk this with my hand, my titties, my pussy . . . my mouth," she whispered to him, loving how it hardened in her hand.

"Damn," Kingston swore.

"Aria," Jaime called out from the kitchen.

Both Aria and Kingston's eyes widened as Jaime strolled into the foyer. Kingston quickly snatched up his discarded pants to hide his dick as Aria turned, standing in front of him.

Jaime's expression was priceless as she diverted her eyes up to the ceiling. "Um, hello, Kingston."

"Hi, Jaime. It's good to see you," he said politely.

Jaime cleared her throat. "I wish I could say the same in this moment—"

Aria giggled.

"Okay, so I'll wake Renee up on my way out," she said, turning with a brief wave to walk back into the kitchen and out the patio door.

Aria turned and faced her husband, her heart filled with love for him as he easily swung her up over his shoulder and carried her up the stairs to their bedroom.

The sounds of their laughter and loving soon echoed throughout their home.

Jessa Bell

For me, my face is everything. It represents me. So the fact that I wasn't pleased at the kiwi-sized lump on my forehead is a fucking understatement. In the few hours since that bitch attacked me, it had only gotten worse.

I brushed back my soft bangs to lightly stroke the lump with my fingertips. "Stupid trick," I swore, thinking of the embarrassing scene Aria had caused in the restaurant.

I understood their anger; I just didn't give a fuck about it. Still, Aria was an intelligent woman, but that street edge was there and I knew it. I should have expected nothing less and had my guard up.

Click.

At the sound of the front door latch, I looked up in the mirror just as my lover walked into my bedroom. "My guard up and my locks changed," I thought as he walked over to stand behind me. I was naked and fresh from a shower, but I didn't bother to cover my body from his eyes. He had already seen and tasted everything on me.

I paused, waiting for that familiar thrill I got from his call, his touch, his very presence. I had loved this man. I had given up a lot to have him, but his lies and not following through on our plans had caused my love to fade.

"So if he loved you, if he chose you, if he couldn't get enough of you . . . then why the hell ain't he with you."

*I flinched as Aria's mocking words came back to me.
There was truth there. A truth that pained me deeply. The
man I loved didn't love me enough. I'd made the right decision. I had moved on. We were over.*

*I stroked him with my eyes, not missing his troubled
expression or the thin red scratch down the side of his
face.* "Can I assume Aria ran back like the little hood rat
she is to tell Jaime about us?" *I asked, calmly smoothing
my bangs back down into place even though I felt my nervousness rise.*

*He nodded as he continued to stare at me with the most
intensely dark eyes.*

*Turning on the padded bench to face him, I tilted my
head up.* "If you're this disturbed—or whatever it is you
are—about Jaime, then why did you tie my life up for all
this time with promises you had no intention of keeping?
Why did you lie to me, Eric?"

His jaw clenched. "She is my wife," *he stressed.*

*I smiled softly. Sadly. Perhaps even bitterly. His words
tore my heart and my soul to shreds.* "And I was the
friend and then the love of your life. Remember?"

"I do love you, Jessa, and you know it."

I shook my head, looking away from him. "Not
enough because you never really were here in this relationship with me. I was falling in love with a storyline, with
lies, with a man who knew he had no intention of leaving
his wife."

"I don't want to lose you, Jessa."

"And I wanted to be loved and cherished, not placated,
Eric."

*He raised his hands and pressed them against my bare
shoulders. I shivered at his touch.*

*From that one moment our awareness of each other
changed; Eric's touch or look warmed me. Our chemistry—that unseen connection between two people—had
always been intense. Emotional. Electrifying. Undeniable.*

At first our lovemaking was awkward as if he were a virgin, but I had taught him well and in time the physical caught up with our chemistry. And yes, there was added thrill because we were sneaking. Hiding. Catching quick fucks here and there. Sharing a look as we both sat among our friends with our privates still damp from each other's juices.

Even now that my heart was broken under the weight of his lies and my trust in him destroyed, my clit throbbed with new life as my nipples hardened in tight chocolate buds. As his hands eased down to stroke my breasts I felt my head drifting backward and a gasp of pleasure escaping through my open lips. No, Jessa.

I jumped up to my feet, brushing his hands away. "It's over, Eric," I told him sharply.

"No, it's not." Eric reached out and grabbed my upper arms. "I'm not losing you, too."

My brows furrowed at his words and the tight feel of his hands on me. "Let me go, Eric."

He jerked my body close to his and wrapped his arms around me tightly as he pressed kisses to my face, neck, and shoulders. "Don't leave me," he whispered in a voice that disturbed me. "I need you, Jessa."

I could barely breathe because he was holding me so tightly. I fought him to be freed as I felt my panic rising.

"Please give me my pussy. Please," he begged.

I kicked at his shins and tried to knee him in the nuts as he whirled me and then pushed me down onto the bed stuck under his weight. "Eric," I shouted in shock.

"I had to fuck Jaime, but I want to fuck you, Jessa. Fuck me. I need some pussy. I need your pussy," he moaned in my ear before he ground his hard dick against my stomach.

I felt repulsed that he was aroused by his forcefulness with me. I felt helpless and out of control. At a disadvantage. Afraid. Eric had never been this way with me. Never.

"I can't lose you, too. I can't." He shifted his hand down between us and I heard his zipper just seconds before I felt the smooth tip of his dick stroke my pussy lips. *"I can't."*

"GET. THE. FUCK. OFF. ME!" I bit down hard on his cheek. He hollered out and rolled off of me. I was free. Thinking fast I raced across the room and grabbed my car keys. There was a can of pepper spray on it. Ironically, Eric had purchased it for me after my husband died. I never imagined I would have to use it on him like a stranger in the street.

"Get out, Eric. I mean it. Get out. Right now or I will fuck you up real good with this shit. I mean it." I held my hand out with my index finger poised and ready over the dispenser.

He rose to his feet, his hand pressed to his cheek. *"I'm sorry, Jessa. I'm so sorry. Please forgive me,"* he said, the crazed look gone from his eyes as he stepped in my direction.

What the hell?

"Just get out, Eric. Please get out," I begged, the fight leaving me as tears of frustration, anger, and hurt rose.

Long after he finally took his leave, I double-locked my front door and wept like a baby.

Chapter 7

"Nah. I'm good."

Jaime pulled her cell phone from her face in total shock. She couldn't believe Pleasure had turned down her offer to redesign a room in his apartment for him. *Son of a bitch. That Negro shot me down.*

"Listen, I know the only thing you're concerned with is my pussy and purse, but I'm trying to get back into interior design and I need a portfolio of before and after photos." Jaime wiped the sweat from her brow with her hand. "I need your help, Pleasure."

He fell silent.

Jaime walked out the front door to sit down on her couch. "All I need is a week and a five-hundred-dollar budget to do one room. Trust me, I'm as good at design as you are at dick laying."

"To be honest, Jaime, I've never had any of y'all at my apartment," he said. "I consider that separate from my, uh, business."

Jaime propped her elbows on her knees. "So you never had a girlfriend, a date, a booty call over to your apartment?" she asked in disbelief, her eyes shifting to take in her next-door neighbor, Lucas Neal, climbing out of his Ford Expedition with a chubby girl of eight or nine years of age.

"I didn't say my girl doesn't come over," he stressed, like Jaime was slow to understand.

"Oh. Okay." Jaime smiled and waved at her portly neighbor even though she felt embarrassed to be classed in with the rest of Pleasure's "dick divas." She had never been to his apartment and had no clue where he lived. His dick she could spot in a lineup, but she knew nada about him. Not even his real name.

She wasn't shit but a female john and he was her trick. Jaime frowned at the truth of their "relationship."

"What's your real name, Pleasure?" she asked.

"You finally ask me that?" Pleasure chuckled deeply. "It's Mikel."

"So you have a girlfriend?" she asked, hating the sting of jealousy she felt.

"Does it matter?"

Yes. "Does she know you dealing dick?" Jaime asked smugly.

"Does your husband know you my best client?" he volleyed back.

Jaime sat up straighter. "Fuck you, Pleasure."

"Your dime. My time. Tell me when and where. You know how we get down."

Jaime's mind flashed back to just last night when he'd rubbed her naked body with oil and then pressed her to the wall while he fucked her from behind. Each hard thrust of his dick had pressed her body against the wall. Intense. Bizarre. Sexy as fuck.

"Fuck you and that rat trap you probably living in," she snapped, sick of his cocky bravado as she slapped her phone closed.

She sat her cell phone on the brick step beside her, hating that her pussy was warm and moist at the memory of the way he'd fucked her like she was the only pussy in his life.

"Bullshit," she swore.

Your thing with Pleasure is what it is, she thought. *Stop trying to make it more. Stop trying to pretend like it's more.*

Jaime closed her eyes and tilted her head back to allow the summer rays to warm her face. Sitting on a stoop outside her rented town house was a long way from lounging in their spacious backyard that resembled an outdoor living room with its stone fireplace, pavers, and high-end patio furniture.

Everything was different. She was no snob really, but everything about her life was a long way from her upbringing and from the life Eric had given them in Richmond Hills.

Truth be told, there were parts of her life she wanted back. The expensive weaves, spa days, shopping at only the finest stores, her home, her leisure.

Eric was a bastard in the days following their divorce, but he always had been a good provider. Always.

If I want that life I have to do it for myself. "My marriage is over, my parents have damn near disowned me, and I pay the man in my life for sex and attention," she muttered about the truth of her life.

Just me, myself, and I.

Bzzzzzz.

Jaime looked down at her cell phone. A picture text came in. She opened it. It was from Pleasure. She paused and licked her lips instantly thinking it was a dick shot and liking the idea. A lot. *That nigga got me sprung.*

Jaime opened the text and her eyes widened at the picture of a stylish upscale living room. Large windows. Sleek leather furniture. Tiled floor. Fur rug. Flat screen on the wall. Fireplace with lit glass beneath it.

Her eyes dropped down to the words below the picture:

BUSINESS IS BOOMING. RAT TRAP
MY ASS. LOL.

"What the hell?" Jaime snapped, thinking if that one room was really his and was any indication of the rest of his crib that dick-slinging motherfucking stripper was living better than *she*.

She'd pictured him struggling and enjoying any time he spent at her shit to keep from being at home. "Dayum," she said. "Oh hell no, I have got to get back on point. I have to."

Jaime climbed to her feet, sliding her cell phone into the back pocket of her jeans before she brushed any debris from her behind. Her eyes were locked on Lucas's front door as she jogged down the few steps and crossed the lawn into his yard.

The front door opened before she'd stepped one foot onto his step. That surprised her and she paused. "Uh, hi, Lucas," Jaime said with much hesitation as she looked up at his round, bearded face.

Lucas smiled, his eyes bright and friendly as he stepped out onto the stoop. He looked surprised as well. "I was just headed back out. Well, *we* were headed back out, but you're a nice surprise."

Jaime felt relief that he wasn't sitting his ass in the window looking at her, but the look of interest in his eyes made her pause. "We?" she asked, shifting her eyes to the girl stepping past him onto the porch.

"This is my daughter, Kellie," he said, placing his hand warmly on his daughter's shoulder.

Jaime gave her a smile before looking back at Lucas. "I just wanted to let you know that I'm an interior designer and I'm starting my own business—"

"Who's getting towed?" Lucas said, looking past Jaime as he stepped down a step.

Jaime turned and her face filled with first surprise and then confusion at the tow truck parking on the street in front of her Volvo. A tall and slender pock-faced man climbed down from the passenger seat with a clipboard in hand, and headed up the walk to her front door. Her heart pounded like crazy. Her stomach was nothing but anxiety. She made her way across to her own front yard, almost tripping over herself with her quick steps. "Excuse me. Helloooo. Excuse me," she called out to him. He looked over at her. "Hi. Yeah, can I . . . can I help you?"

"Ms. Hall?" the tall man asked, referring to a notepad on his clipboard.

"Yes," she said, shifting past him to look over as a big burly, red-haired driver climbed down out of his truck and began hooking it up to her vehicle. Jaime looked around at her neighbors taking in the spectacle. *What the hell?*

"This car is registered to Eric Hall and he has authorized us to repossess the vehicle," he said, with a Southern twang that was way more Tennessee than New Jersey.

"What?" Jaime snapped, snatching the paperwork.

"Yes, ma'am," he assured her, pointing out the name of the finance company and the paperwork showing Eric as the sole name on the vehicle registration and insurance.

"But he's my *husband*."

"Ma'am, I'm sorry, but you'll have to speak to the vehicle owner about that," Pock-Face stressed, his *you'll* sounding more like *jewel*.

"Is everything okay, Jaime?" Lucas asked from behind her.

The old Jaime came out of hiding as she felt the curious eyes of her neighbors on her. In that moment, as she felt embarrassment warming her neck and cheeks, the cloak felt familiar.

She put on a smile as fake as cubic zirconias to diamonds as she turned to face him. "I'm having car trouble and was afraid to drive it so I'm getting it towed to my mechanic," she lied with well-practiced ease.

Lucas' eyes shifted past her as he nodded in understanding. "Smart move, you don't want to cause more damage."

"Right," she said, turning from him to watch as the men loaded up her Volvo. Soon they were pulling away loudly with her Volvo securely attached.

Inside she seethed. Her hatred of Eric was growing.

"Hey, Jaime, I was wondering: would you like to come over for dinner one night?" Lucas asked.

Jaime closed her eyes as irritation was added to the stack of emotions building inside of her. No need to take it out on him. "Sure, but right now I need to call my . . . uh . . . mechanic," she said, her teeth and gums hurting from smiling so hugely. So brightly. So falsely.

"I'll walk over later and we'll plan the night and every-thing," he offered, his face bright and filled with hope.

"Sure, okay, yeah," she said, distracted and unable to hide it.

It took everything in her to walk into her house calmly under his watchful gaze. As soon as her front door closed behind her, Jaime yanked her cell phone from her back pocket and dialed Eric's number. So many questions bombarded her that she felt dizzy. She leaned back against the door heavily.

"Hello, Mrs. Hall," Eric said, his voice slightly mock-ing.

"Eric, what the hell are you doing? How dare you— after everything I've done for you and the bullshit I've taken from you and the front I put on for you—how dare you repossess my fucking car!" she roared, her voice climbing steadily until her throat ached.

"I'm confused, wife," he said coldly. "You don't want me, which I assumed meant you don't want the things that I have and can still do for you. It's a package deal."

Jaime massaged her forehead with her fingertips as she found just enough strength to pace in her small foyer. "You are unbelievable."

"No. I am your husband. And if you want to move out

of that shithole you're in and back into our beautiful home, and not flit around town in a luxury vehicle without a penny to your name to pay the note . . . then come home. Simple. It's a package deal," he repeated.

"And this makes you feel like a man to blackmail or strong-arm someone into being with you, Eric," she asked in a low voice brimming with just a fraction of her anger.

"I'm fighting for my marriage and my vows. There's no shame in that."

Jaime felt choked with frustration and drowning in the lack of control. "Who told you where I lived?" she asked, having to get the answer to the question that was nudging her the most.

"Your mother only wants what's best for *us.*"

Jaime could only shake her head. "And I only want what's best for *me,*" she said. "And that's not you."

Eric sighed like he was bored. "You will be home. Choice is yours. Sooner? Or later?"

Click.

Jaime fought the urge to throw her cell phone against the wall as she clutched it so tightly that it hurt her palms. She paced. Back and forth. Thinking. Thinking. Thinking.

Insult on top of injury was an understatement for the crap Eric just pulled.

Without a penny to your name.

She paused for just a millisecond before she flipped her phone opened and dialed the toll free number for her bank. Her heart pounded and she was already denying it, as she entered her information.

"Your checking account balance is currently in a negative balance—"

Jaime stumbled backward as she felt the blood drain from her body. She felt chilled to the bone. It had to be Eric.

Without a penny to your name.

The thousands of dollars she had had that very morning was gone.

You will be home. Choice is yours. Sooner? Or later?

———— ∞∞∞ ————

Renee sat inside her dark two-car garage, parked in her car, enjoying the taste and feel of the Firefly Sweet Tea in her decanter. Truth? She didn't want to go in the house knowing she would be alone. Since she was supposed to fly to Denver this evening for work, the kids were both spending the night at friends.

After a long and lonely lunch in her office with way too many drinks, Renee had slept right through her three o' clock flight out of Newark / New York International Airport. Without Darren working that day to keep her on her toes, Renee hadn't awakened, and came from behind her locked office door well after nine. With a pounding headache and her breathe tasting—and probably smelling—like dog shit, she made a new flight for first thing in the morning. She would arrive just an hour before the charity event. *Yet another fuckup.*

Her cell phone softly played Etta James's "At Last." She reached and flipped the BlackBerry over. She was surprised to see Jackson's number displayed.

They had already argued earlier because Renee hadn't forced the children to spend the weekend with him. Hell, she was a grown-ass, educated woman still trying to process the bullshit of her husband fucking and getting another woman pregnant; how the hell did he expect the children to grasp it so quickly? They loved their father, but they had yet to forgive him.

Renee answered the call. "I don't feel like arguing with you, Jackson. The kids are already at their friends' so it's a done deal," she sighed, letting her head fall back against the soft leather of the headrest.

"Can I come over?" Jackson asked.

Renee's eyes were heavy from the effects of the liquor, but they popped open at that. "Excuse me?" she asked, her grip tightening on the cool metal of the silver decanter.

"Can I come over, Renee?" he asked again.

Renee sat up. "For what, Jackson?"

"Listen, I want to make love to my wife," he said, as if it was the most common thing in the world. As if he hadn't crashed her world into a billion tiny pieces.

For one moment—one small moment—Renee allowed herself to remember the days when the very thought of Jackson had made her wet. They used to share everything. She was the epitome of a lady in the street and a freak in the bedroom. Nothing was off limits. All doors were opened and thoroughly explored.

And sometimes when the liquor wasn't her lover for the night she missed and craved Jackson until her clit literally ached.

She shook her head, not letting the liquor, her memories, or her horniness nudge her into something she would regret. "Sorry, no baby mama drop-in sex here, Jackson. You made a choice, remember, you like white meat now?"

She thought her turn of words was clever and giggled. It turned to a hiccup.

"You know you want this dick, Renee," he said calmly. Too calmly.

Renee sat up and looked behind her, expecting to find him sitting in his truck behind her. "No, I don't," she said, only half lying and sounding like it as she turned around feeling slightly disappointed.

"So my affair means I'm dirty now?" Jackson asked.

Renee fingered her flask at the sound of anger in his tone. "What?" she asked, frowning as she stroke the metal side like a pet.

Jackson laughed bitterly. "Look here, Mrs. Perfect," he said, the coldness of his voice not veiled at all. "If I found out that your assistant almost fucked you the night of your awards banquet—if I had known that then—should I have left you? Should I think of my wife as dirty? Huh?"

Total shock. It sobered her.

"That's a lie," she said defensively. "Don't you dare try and handle me like I'm the adulterer, Jackson. Don't put your shit off on me."

"So you're denying you and Darren got a hotel room?" he asked calmly. Again, too calmly.

Renee flashed back to a scene of Darren chewing on her clit like gum. She shivered in repulsion. It was clear that man-child assistant knew NOTHING about the joys to be found in a pussy. N.O.T.H.I.N.G. He probably was a whiz with a dick, but pussy wasn't his shtick.

"Since you think you know so damn much, why don't you tell it and not ask it," she snapped, unscrewing her decanter to take a healthy swig.

"Why don't I tell you this, Renee? I fucked up because our marriage was fucked up. I apologize for everything that I put you through and that you're going through, but everything . . . *everything* . . . I told you about that damn job was confirmed for me. I never wanted you to have that job, I was—I *am*—a damn good provider. It wasn't money you were looking for. It was dick. I knew you weren't any different. I knew it—"

Renee froze. *Say what now?* "Different from who? What the hell are you talking about?"

How in the hell had the tables gotten turned?

"Listen, Jackson, the damage to our marriage was done when you got *Anga* pregnant," she said sarcastically. "Don't put your shit on me because you don't know what you're talking about."

"I knew it. I knew it," he said.

"Knew what?" she snapped.

Click.

Renee couldn't do a damn thing but lower her BlackBerry

and stare at it. Jackson's anger about Darren had been more about her job than the actual man. She shook her head as if that would clear it and make what he'd said make sense.

But Renee didn't bother with it. She didn't feel like fussing and fighting. In that moment she really didn't give a fuck. Her thinking was too fuzzy and all she wanted to do was rest up for her early flight in the morning. "No more of you," she said to the decanter, pushing it down into the side pocket of her Coach briefcase before she climbed out of her vehicle. She yawned as she made her way around the front of the car and up the few steps into the kitchen.

As soon as she entered her house she dropped her purse and briefcase onto the large island. She was a bit unsteady on her feet, but didn't bother with the lights and regretted that decision before she even reached the bottom of the stairs.

"Shit," she swore, looking up at what seemed like a thousand dimly lit stairs. She waved her hand like "fuck it" and made her way over to the living room to flop down onto one of the plush sofas, glad for the quiet and the darkness.

And soon she was just as glad for the sleep.

"Hmmmmmmmmmm."

Renee frowned as she lay somewhere in that zone between sleep and wakefulness. She shifted onto her side with a wince, trying to decide to which side of the zone she wanted to be in. Awake or asleep.

"Hmmmmmmmmm."

What the hell? Renee's eyes opened, adjusting to the darkness of the living room. *Is that moaning?*

She rolled over onto her back and sat up straight. She gasped at the sudden sound of a harshly whispered voice and the steady squeak of some furniture.

"Fuck me harder, Daddy."

Renee whirled toward the sound of the voices. She gasped in shock and horror at the sight of her son's naked ass high in the air as he bent over the steps while Darren slid his hard inches in and out of him. "What the fuck is going on?" she roared.

They jumped apart, dicks flying like wailing arms. Naked brown bodies showing more than she wanted to see. Renee hated the image of her son's anus still spread and open from the invasion of Darren's dick.

Renee went from shocked to ballistic in less than three counts. She jumped over the sofa and flew dead at Darren where he stood, pushing him hard with both hands against his bare chest. "You bastard. I trusted you around my fucking kid, not offered him up to get your rocks off."

Darren stumbled back a few steps, holding up his large masculine hands with his dick glistening and greasy.

Renee's stomach lurched, knowing it was lubricant. "I'm calling the police, you pedophile," she told him.

Aaron stepped forward, trying to cover his nakedness with a shirt as he reached for arm. "Ma, wait—"

Renee whirled on him, snatched her arm away, and slapped him across the mouth in one fluid motion that couldn't have been choreographed better by Alvin Ailey. She raised her foot to snatch off her shoe and started whaling on him. Anywhere and everywhere she could get a lick in. Across his upraised arms. His thighs. His ass. His chest. He turned and tried to block the blows and Renee was dead on his ass.

"Ma! Stop!" he cried out.

Renee barely heard him. She barely knew what she was doing. There was a white noise like static building in her ears. Her tears flowed freely and she was losing focus on her target. A target that she loved. A target that was getting the brunt of all her frustration. Anger. Disappointment. Rage.

Darren grabbed her arms from behind, his flaccid dick grazing her behind as she struggled against his strength.

She dropped the shoe. He released her as Aaron turned and raced up the stairs.

"Your ass is fired," she told him coldly, punctuating her words with a finger to his chest. "Get your shit and get the fuck out!"

"I'm sorry, Renee, I never thought Aaron and I would like each other—"

Oh God, my son is gay. Renee closed her eyes at the image of their sex act.

"And I understand that having sex in your house was disrespectful. . . ."

Renee opened her eyes feeling like this motherfucker had a but coming. . . .

"But I am good at my job and I will not be pushed out of it because your son and I have feelings for each other," Darren said, still naked and holding his clothes in a bundle under his arm.

Renee frowned. "Your ass is fucking fired," she said, her mind on the bar against the far wall of her living room.

"My job and my relationship with Aaron—"

"Relationship?"

"I'm sorry, Renee. If you fire me for this I will sue you for sexual harassment," he said, his eyes boldly locking with hers.

Renee knew he was talking about the night of the awards banquet when they had tried like hell to fuck and failed miserably. *Guess Aaron finished the job for me,* she thought sarcastically as she stormed to the front door. "Get. Out."

Naked as he pleased, Darren strolled to the door. "I really am sorry you found out about us like this," he said.

Renee stood behind him and shoved hard with both her hands to his back, pushing him out of her house. She raised her foot and nudged him hard square in the crack of his ass for good measure. He stumbled forward, recovered, and then quickly scurried to his car now parked in her drive.

With the house dark and her car in the garage, her son and his lover never knew she was home when they got there. That was clear.

Feeling her head spinning like crazy, Renee stepped back and slammed the front door closed.

WHAM!

Aaron was gay.

Maybe in a different time and place she could have handled the news. She could've talked to him. Tried to adjust to the idea. Be the good mother she knew she was.

But now?

Now it was just the straw that broke the camel's back.

She arched her back and released a wail from her gut as if she were trying to free a million demons from her soul. It echoed against the wall as though she stood inside the Grand Canyon.

Still, it was nothing to the rage still building and burning deep within her.

"Why am I here, Dr. Matheson?"

Aria would always be known for being straight and to the point. She hardly ever had time for bullshit. Regardless of whom it was. Including their marriage counselor.

"To save your marriage."

Dr. Matheson was pulling no punches either. Aria froze as she looked at him where he sat in his normal spot across from her. She had been crossing and uncrossing her legs in the dark skinny jeans she wore with sky-high alligator stilettos that added four inches to her height. But now she was as frozen in time as a statue.

"Then why isn't Kingston here as well?" she asked, trying to ignore the deafening pounding of her heart.

Dr. Matheson opened his leather portfolio and removed the pen she recognized as a Caran d'Ache, a Swiss maker of luxury pens. As a writer she enjoyed the feel of pen to paper and had invested in several fine pens over the years. Kingston had surprised her with one of their 18-carat pens when she'd sold her first story as a freelancer.

Odd thought in that moment. Very odd. But Aria would love to focus on anything but the heavy words the doc dropped on her like boulders.

To save your marriage.

What the fuck was going on?

"Kingston will be here, but I suggested first talking with you." He scribbled something on his pad with his five-hundred-dollar pen.

"So you've talked to *my* husband," she said, her ire and attitude spiking like crazy. It was all starting to feel like a mystery he expected her to solve with all the double talk and vague answers.

Aria wasn't in the fucking mood. Period. Point blank.

"Yes, he called me and I suggested meeting with you first."

Aria crossed her legs again and settled back in her chair, stiffening her spine. "You seem to be running the show in our marriage. Kudos to you."

Dr. Matheson leveled his eyes on her. Steady. Unwavering. Understanding. Concerned.

It was the concern that made her feel even more afraid at the sudden turn of events.

She and Kingston had awakened this morning, made love in the shower, and gotten dressed for the work day with eyes of love. He'd left for an early-morning surgery and she'd dressed to head into the city for lunch with the editor of *Sessions* magazine, who'd freelanced her to do the Nona King interview. They were going to dine and then she would personally turn in the completed interview.

That morning she had been focused on how proud she was of that interview. She was her own worst critic when it came to her writing . . . especially the interviews. It was more than just the right words, intonations, and plotting. It was all about the right conversation. Everything was invested in the direction of the questions. Her ability to get the answers no one else had. Nona King had given a million interviews during her career, but Aria wanted this one to be a class above the rest.

And she honestly felt like it was.

With Nona's revelation of childhood abuse during her follow-up phone interview, Aria knew it was major. She felt that familiar excitement whenever a project was complete and there was nothing she could do to make the interview or her insights better.

To make a living doing what she loved was way more than this little ghetto girl had ever dreamed of. She definitely felt blessed. A good career. A good marriage. Good family. Good friends. A damn good life.

The lunch went well. But then she got this call from Dr. Matheson and here she was questioning everything she thought was okay.

She eyed him in return, thinking of all the reconnecting she and Kingston had done in the days after finding out that Eric was Jessa's lover. And not just sex. Communication. Intimacy. Love and affection.

No more counseling sessions.

No more arguing.

No more cold and angry silence that screamed of building resentment.

But here she was.

To save your marriage.

Something had changed.

"He knows the truth, doesn't he?" she asked, uncrossing her legs and sitting forward to press her elbows into her thighs. "Jessa Bell told him, didn't she?"

Dr. Matheson nodded as his eyes studied her carefully.

Aria's stomach clenched like it had been pierced by a sharp blade. She wiped her face with her hands.

To save your marriage.

"When Kingston comes I will get into both of your feelings and try to work through what is undeniably a huge breach in the trust of your relationship." Dr. Matheson closed his portfolio.

Aria leaned back and closed her eyes, trying to fight back the tears that filled them. Failure. They flooded her lids and raced down her cheeks. *Kingston knows.*

"So the temporary restraining order she has against me wasn't enough, she had to destroy my marriage," Aria said bitterly, thinking of the countless calls she'd made that Kingston hadn't answered. Wouldn't answer. "I'm gonna beat her ass."

"And what would that change?" he asked calmly, as he scribbled furiously.

Aria shifted her hostile eyes to his face.

"You're losing focus, Aria. This isn't about Jessa Bell. Is it?"

Aria shifted her eyes to the beautiful landscape through the windows behind him. The summer skies might as well be overshadowed by dark, tumultuous clouds. "No, no, I know it isn't. I lied to him. I betrayed him. I fucked up. I fucked up," she finished softly, her eyes filling with more tears as pain tightened her chest.

Dr. Matheson leaned forward and pressed a box of tissues into her hands.

This one show of compassion weakened her even more until her shoulders slumped and then shook with tears. She didn't feel like she deserved it.

"Why did you keep these secrets from Kingston, Aria?"

"There are things about me that I want to forget.

Things that I regret. Why would I want to tell him?" she asked in anguish, clutching the box of tissues so tightly that the cardboard sides buckled.

"Things like what?"

Aria eyed him like he was crazy. "I just said I want to forget."

"But you haven't forgotten, have you. You'll never forget."

No. Never.

"How old were you?"

"I'm lucky to be alive," she admitted in a shaky tone.

Dr. Matheson leaned forward in his chair and pierced her with his eyes. "You deserve to be alive. Do you know that?"

The truth hit home like a ton of bricks. She didn't believe she deserved anything. Nothing. Not even her life.

And definitely not to bear a life.

"Kingston hates me, doesn't he?" she asked, voicing her worst fears.

"I can't speak for him," he said.

A long cry from simply, "No, he doesn't."

"Is he coming?" she asked, her fears evident in her voice.

"I honestly can't say. He is supposed to be here in thirty minutes." Dr. Matheson held up his hands.

"I love my husband," she said, voicing her heart.

"Even more than working on your marriage, Aria, you have to deal with your unresolved issues, your guilt about your past. The first step is talking about it. Tell me about it."

Aria closed her eyes and let her head fall back as she opened a door to a past she wished she could erase.

But she couldn't.

"Before the age of sixteen I had slept with more than a hundred men and had more than one abortion," she admitted in a whisper swollen with shame. "I know things that could make a whore blush. I *was* a whore. Instead of getting paid up front, I stole from the men. I robbed them in their sleep."

"Why?"

"For the money. For the thrill, I guess. I don't know." Aria shook her head, trying to free it of a vivid image of nearly being gagged by the dick of this old man in the back of his car.

"My cousin seemed so cool to me and it was exciting being out and about, sneaking, making money, partying."

"How old was this cousin?" he asked, making more notes.

"Eighteen or nineteen."

Dr. Matheson looked up. "And do you understand that you were a child being influenced by someone not more than a child herself?"

Aria shrugged, giving in to the urge to kick off her shoes and pull her feet beneath her in the chair. Fuck it. He wanted to get to the real scoop. Then she had to be as real as she could. The realest bitch ever. "I smoked weed. Drank. I even tried to pop pills once, but that . . . that . . . that took me out of my game too much. It was too risky to be that high," she admitted, pushing back a memory that could very well send her crazy . . . if she let it. That memory she would never share. Never.

"But weed is still a drug and a lot of the decisions you made were under the influence?"

Aria pressed her chin to her knuckles, allowing her eyes to go distant as she allowed the memories to come rushing at her like an oncoming train going full speed. "Yes. I mean I was a ho. This was beyond being fast and hot in the ass. This was straight criminal activity and promiscuity."

"Do you think there are other young girls who could learn from your story?" he asked.

She cut her eyes over at him. "Only if I tell it . . . and I won't," she said with certainty.

He fell silent for a second and Aria knew he was switching gears. "Tell me about the abortions?"

Aria felt nauseous. She shook her head, feeling like she was no more than a child.

He waited. No words. No real actions. Just waited.

"No," she stated emphatically. Translation? Move the fuck on, doc.

He scribbled away.

That angered her. "My life is more than whatever you're writing in that pad. My marriage might be over and all you're worrying about is keeping shit on the record?" she snapped, needing an outlet, a bull's-eye, for her anger.

"Do you want to know what I just wrote?" he asked calmly.

"Yes."

"I made a note to speak with you about a referral to another counselor to deal with your guilt about your past."

Aria released a heavy breath. "Where is Kingston?"

"The choice is his whether to show up or not."

Aria checked her watch. "I don't have anything else to say until my husband arrives."

"And if he doesn't?" Dr. Matheson asked.

Aria just pressed her lips closed and watched the clock. She meant what she'd said. The only thing that mattered was her marriage. She had nothing else to say until Kingston arrived.

The appointed time for his arrival came and went.

Kingston never showed.

Chapter 8

Betrayal. Once again Jessa Bell's venom left them momentarily paralyzed. Jaime didn't know if she would ever recover. How could she when financially she was ass out? No ends. No dinero. Nothing.

"I hate that bitch," Jaime drawled, as she sat in the back seat of the yellow taxicab.

It was the longest ride ever. It was about more than the miles or the sixty minutes to get there. Emotionally it felt like she crawled across glass on her knees to get where she had to go.

And she had to.

She had no choice.

As the taxi pulled to a gentle stop, Jaime licked the gloss from her lips and looked out the smudged window at the sprawling brick house.

"Thirty-five forty-six, ma'am," the fair-skinned driver said, looking at her with odd bluish green eyes through his rearview mirror.

"Yes, of course," she said, picking her clutch up from the cracked seat to look inside her wallet. President Grant was sitting there lonely as hell on her last fifty-dollar bill. All the money she had to her name.

She pulled it out of the wallet, folded it, and placed it in the metal slot in the bulletproof glass. Patiently she waited for her change. She needed it. The days of heavy tip-giving were gone. Long gone.

Smoothing her shirt over her hips, Jaime climbed out of the back of the cab and made her way up the long walk. They knew she was coming—she had to be announced at the gate—still she was nervous about their reaction to her upcoming request.

The ornate front door opened before she was halfway up the walk. Suddenly it felt like a walk of shame as her parents stood there watching her every step. Even though she knew her pale pink suit and pearls were presentable, Jaime knew their eyes scrutinized her. Judged her. Maybe even found their daughter—their only child—lacking.

"Hello, Mother. Hi, Daddy," she said softly, barely above a whisper, stepping up onto the step just below them, allowing them to look down on her—just like her mother wanted.

Virginia Osten-Pine nodded her perfectly coiffed head, her lips pursed as if she had just sucked on a dozen lemons or swallowed a shot of vinegar. She turned and entered the house.

Jaime knew she was headed for the formal living room, the place where they entertained guests.

"Come in, Jamison," her father said sternly, using her given name.

Her mother had an ally and Jaime knew it was two against one. *Lord help me,* she prayed silently.

Jaime walked into the living room. Sure enough, her mother sat perfectly poised on the edge of her French Provincial settee. Jaime took the seat opposite her. Her father, ever the referee, sat in the chair adjacent to them both.

"Well, Jamison, you called and asked to speak with us," her father began, resting his hands on the round swell of his belly, a sign of the good life he led. "But first, I must stress to you how disappointed your mother and I are in the way you've handled your marriage and yourself."

Jaime nodded, avoiding her mother's gaze. "I understand that you both feel that way, but there's a lot that you don't know." She chose her words carefully. Very much so. "My marriage is over and Eric was not all what he portrayed himself to be. He verbally and sexually abused me in the months after my affair—"

Her father stuttered as he fought hard to sit up straight. "What did you say?"

Her mother gasped and literally clutched her pearls.

Jaime ignored her. She swallowed the shame she felt and continued on. It was time for the truth. "And he has been having an affair of his own with Jessa."

"What?!" Virginia screeched like a banshee.

Her father jumped to his feet. "I will snap his neck."

"No, I will divorce him and move on with my life . . . with your help," she finished softly, finally turning to glance at her mother's face. She took some pleasure in shocking the café au lait complexion to a pale and sickly looking beige.

"I never wanted to embarrass you or the family. And I didn't want to be an imposition . . . but Eric has repossessed the car and took what little money I had from my bank account, leaving me penniless."

Jaime's eyes shifted to her father's hand balling up in a tight fist as if he had Eric's neck in his grasp.

"What are your . . . plans, Jaime?" her mother asked, her facade back in place and emotions hidden.

Jaime faced her mother. "I would like to keep my town house and continue rebuilding my interior design career."

She took a deep breath she hoped her mother didn't see. "I do need to borrow some money until my divorce is settled," she stated softly, too softly.

Her father rose from his chair and walked out of the living room.

"You want our money but not our advice?" her mother asked.

Jaime's spine turned to steel. "Actually I would love your support, your trust, and your love. That won't cost you anything."

Virginia's face showed disapproval.

She didn't raise her daughter to speak back. *Or to speak up,* Jaime thought.

"And the naked man in your living room? Where does he play into all of this?"

He is none of your fucking business.

Jaime's father walked back into the living room carrying a check and a set of car keys. He handed her both. "Jaime, never feel as if you have to keep things from us. We're your parents and we love you."

Jaime's relief far outweighed her shame in even having to ask. She folded the check, not looking at the amount. Whatever it was beat the hell out of what she came there with. The keys were to a Honda Accord—a car they kept just for any errands the staff had to run. She felt blessed to have it as she rose to her feet and wrapped her arms around her father. "Thank you, Daddy. I'll pay you back."

He squeezed her back and Jaime never thought a man's embrace could feel so comforting. Tears welled up, but she blinked them away.

"Franklin, a word please." Virginia walked over to the massive unlit fireplace against the far wall.

Here comes the bullshit, Jaime thought as her father released her and joined his wife. Their heads bent together.

Her mother spoke. Her father nodded enthusiastically.

Her life was planned in just that quick moment. Jaime just knew it.

"We have just two stipulations for the help we're giving you," her father said as he crossed the polished hardwood floors.

Jaime said nothing.

"Nothing would help your career more than all of the affiliations you pulled away from. The church, your sorority, and your charities could be a great way to network for clients."

Those words came straight from her mother's mouth into her father's ear and back out of his mouth.

"That makes a lot of sense and I missed everyone," she lied, playing the game. Her mother was the best at it but she had taught her well. "Anything else?"

"Regardless of both of the mistakes you and Eric made in your marriage, as a woman your reputation is everything. The, uh . . . young man . . . that, uh . . . was at your house."

Jaime squirmed where she stood, thinking of the look on her mother's face at the sight of Pleasure's naked body.

"Until your divorce is final he is not welcome in your life." Franklin slid his hands into the pocket of his pants as he gave her a hard look filled with his disapproval.

No Pleasure?

Her pussy throbbed in disappointment at the thought of turning loose that dick. *Sheeeee-it.* "I understand," she said.

"Do you *agree?*" Virginia asked, stepping forward to stand beside her husband.

Jaime locked eyes with her mother. The implication was clear. Play by our rules or get the fuck out of the game. "Yes, I agree," she said, feeling that familiar weight of obligation and falsehood causing her shoulders to droop.

"Excellent," her mother said in pure satisfaction, a smile as big as a skyscraper spreading across her face.

———— ◦∞∞◦ ————

As soon as Jaime could free herself from her parents' home and all of their questions and reminders of obligations, she did. Once she climbed behind the wheel of the

2008 Honda Accord and cruised past the metal gates of the subdivision where they lived, she felt some of the pressure ease.

Some but not all.

As she cruised up the brick-paved street lined with shade trees, Jaime reached for her cell phone. Sitting at a red light she dialed Pleasure's cell phone.

Until your divorce is final he is not welcome in your life.

Jaime made a face. "Picture that shit," she said, pressing the phone to her ear as it rang. The sun was finally going down, but it was already a quarter to nine and she knew where he was.

Her "dance" with Pleasure had begun more than five years ago while she was a senior in college. He'd performed at a bachelorette party she attended and he had her attention the minute he walked through the door with his dick swinging in this black sling-looking contraption. He was six foot nine inches of caramel-dipped muscles that screamed hot sex. It was her first real exposure to anything sexual due to the sheltered life she'd led under her mother's watch. After his up close and personal performance, Jaime had kept the business card he handed out. Within the month she pulled out that card and found the club where he worked.

And once a month her trip from suburbia to the Newark strip club became a ritual that she absolutely craved. Even after her marriage to Eric, she gave in to that one moment of defiance from the life she knew and enjoyed a secret life that gave her some sanity from the bullshit falsehood of her life. He came to recognize her and she knew that he knew he had her good and fucked up.

But the years of sexual frustration he had awakened in her exploded into a nasty, freaky fuckfest in one of the back rooms of the strip clubs last year. She'd never intended to cheat on Eric, but that sizzle Pleasure created deep within her was undeniable. She gave in just that once and she hadn't called on his services again until six months later when the message from Jessa Bell made her take a cold hard look at her marriage and find it unbearable. She left Eric and called Pleasure.

It had been on ever since.

She wasn't stopping now.

Jaime tried Pleasure's cell phone on and off during her drive on the Garden State Parkway toward Newark. No answer. She dropped it onto the seat before she grabbed the wheel and turned the Honda into the parking lot surrounding the brick building with neon flashing lights. The steady thump of the bass vibrated against the walls.

Her eyes skimmed the parking lot. Her clit thumped like a heartbeat at the sight of Pleasure's shiny black motorcycle.

Dressed in her prim and proper suit and her heels, Jaime was taken back to the time she'd snuck out to come here and see the man she was fixated on. *Maybe a session in the back room won't be so bad,* she thought, needing a dick fix.

Jaime used the last of her cash to pay her way into the club. Some rap song played, Jaime didn't know the name or artist and didn't care. She just liked how the loud bass seemed to pluck her clit and vibrate against her nipples. She paused to let her eyes adjust to the darkness as she made her way closer to the stage.

Jaime hadn't been inside the club since Pleasure had made home deliveries. The smell of the dancers' heavy colognes and body oils mingled with the smell of liquor and the scents of the women—between their thighs and otherwise—something about the atmosphere still repulsed her and turned her on all at once.

She took a seat by the front of the stage, her eyes locked on the dark-skinned bald stripper, who was flipping a three-hundred-pound girl like she was a featherweight. With the catcalls of the women and the music, the noise in the club was deafening.

Jaime watched the next few performers with only mild interest. "Excuse me," she said to the muscular waiter dressed in nothing but a black thong embossed with his name in white script: Man-Man.

"Yes," he said, bending down.

She had to swallow and blink her eyes from the over-whelming scent of whatever "supposed to be" sexy cologne he wore. "Pleasure—"

"Mr. Popularity is up next," Man-Man said, smiling like a hyena.

Jaime turned away, dismissing him. She looked around in the darkness as she clutched her car keys and the last few singles she had to her name. *Who else came just for a taste of Pleasure?* she wondered, jealousy creeping up on her.

And she knew it was irrational and foolish to be jealous of a man who was not her man, who stripped and sold his dick for living. But . . .

Out of sight, out of mind.

She hadn't been in the club again after that one night she'd fucked him in the back room.

The lights dimmed and the music shifted easily into the slow and sultry strains of the next song. Jaime sat up straighter. She recognized the song. It was "Invented Sex." Pleasure was always playing it on his iPod. The lights flashed like lightning during a rainstorm just before the curtains opened and Pleasure stepped onto the stage in a bright red bodysuit that was little more than shreds that exposed his muscular frame.

No one could deny the excitement that flared up among the crowd.

Jamie's pussy was singing "hello" as she eyed him snaking his body down to the floor before doing a back flip that made all the ladies go ca-ray-zy.

Through his entire set, Jaime waited anxiously for him to come to her, signal to her that he was ready for her. With every dollar bill shoved into his thong, her stomach clenched.

When he finally slow ground his hips toward her, Jaime forgot everybody and everything. She inhaled deeply of the scent of him as Pleasure straddled her chair and began to pop his strong hips to make his long dick flicker up and down against her chin in his thong.

Jaime leaned forward, causing the length of his dick to slide against the side of her face as she looked up into his eyes.

"Get it, girl," someone screamed above the music.

Pleasure danced his way around her and Jaime shivered as he began to slow grind his dick against the back of her neck. She moaned in pleasure and released a breath filled with the heat rising in her.

"You need some Pleasure, don't you?"

Her eyes opened at the feel of his breath suddenly against her cheek. She nodded desperately. She wanted to forget it all. Eric. Jessa. Her parents. She wanted him to fuck it all away. "Now or later?" he asked, the low intimacy of his voice a deep contrast to the noise surrounding them. It made what he said and how he said it all the more sexy to her. All the more alluring.

Pleasure had her fucked up for real.

"Now," she begged, her voice shaky as her panties clung to her intimacy and her heart beat like she had been surged with pure adrenaline.

Pleasure was her addiction and she didn't want to get clean.

He came around her again and Jaime eyed him as he did a handstand that caused every muscle in his arms, shoulders, and back to flex. Her pussy lips applauded him.

Pleasure bent over backward, putting his strong muscled thighs on each of her shoulders and his dick in her face. She knew for a fact that it was the ideal position to suck him to a creamy ending.

When he stayed like that she realized he was waiting for her to slide his fee inside his thong and wasn't just giving her a preview of his ruler-length dick.

She bit her bottom lip and clutched her purse tighter. Her father's check was no good to her in that moment. She needed cash and she didn't have it.

He eased to his feet and then bent down close to her. "Now or later?" he asked again near her ear.

Even as she shivered she knew: no dollars, no dick. "I'll pay you later," she breathed up to him.

"And I'll pleasure you later," he said, before he turned and danced away.

Jaime felt a deep disappointment, jealousy, and simmering anger as she watched a woman who looked as old as her mother slap Pleasure's smooth brown ass before she reached in front of him to push a wad of money inside his thong before she stroked his dick.

Jaime's eyes squinted as she watched him during the rest of his set. He never looked her way again. Not even once his set was over and he led the older woman to one of the back rooms.

She jumped to her feet and made her way out of the club. Man-Man the waiter stepped in her path with a huge grin on his face. Jaime wasn't a violent person, but she felt like slapping the hell out of him.

"Grandma Moses outbid you, huh?" he asked.

Jaime flushed with embarrassment, pushing him hard to free her path out the door. She didn't stop running until she was inside the car. She hated that images of Pleasure fucking the hell out of the older woman taunted her like a child being picked on in school. Was his dick even hard enough? Was he aroused by her? Did his dick have no preferences?

"Shit, shit, shit," she said, hammering her fists against the steering wheel.

She stopped and eyed the door of the club. She wanted to fly right back in there, storm that back room, and . . . and . . .

And what?

Jaime released a heavy breath and shook her head. "And get the fuck over it," she muttered, hating that she did exactly what she needed to do and left.

As she drove home she sang along to Chrisette Michele's "I'm Okay" on the satellite radio . . . but she was far from okay.

She was broke.

She was afraid.

She was alone.

She was lonely.

She was tired.

Her husband was fucking her friend. Her lover was fucking other women. She was just fucking alone.

She ate up the miles to get back to her little town house, ever aware that she was rushing to an empty-ass house. She considered calling Renee and Aria for a ladies' night out but decided against it. Renee was busy keeping an eye out for her teenage kids and Aria was busy being the only one still in her marriage.

"No, I made this lonely-ass bed and now I'm going to lie up in it."

She turned the Honda onto her small driveway, sitting and looking at the stylish contemporary home that easily fit inside the home she'd left behind in Richmond Hills.

"Life is all about choices," she said to herself, knowing that if she had the cash on hand she would have made the choice to slide that money into Pleasure's thong in a heartbeat.

She'd only had two lovers. Eric had been warm enough

and perfunctory. It had felt like nothing more than a wifely duty. And the days after he'd discovered her one-night stand the sex had been a tool of punishment.

Everything with Pleasure had been different. Everything.

He'd done more than sex her. He'd taught her, coached her, and made her enjoy sex. Made her want to have sex. Made her good at sex.

She hummed the chorus to Pleasure's favorite performance song, "Invented Sex," thinking it was a fitting statement to his prowess. She pressed her back against the seat and arched her hips forward as she massaged her inner thigh with a deep moan.

Long after Jaime had stopped her ritual trips to Pleasure and Eric began to torture her with sex, it was moments alone in her bedroom with nothing but a dildo and memories of that one steamy session on the dirty floor of that back room that had given her the only pleasure in her life. Once Pleasure had become her paramour she had discarded the fake dick, but she'd never regretted it as much as she did right then.

She bit her bottom lip as she inched her prim and proper skirt higher and slightly jerked the moist seat of her panties to the side to strum her swollen and aching clit slightly. She gasped hotly at the feel of her own touch as she remembered Pleasure's performance on stage. The slow and easy gyration of his hips or the hard thrust of his buttocks. The flicker of his tongue. The tightening of his rigid abdomen. The hard cylindrical length of his dick.

Knowing just how he took all his skill into the bedroom made her nipples harden in a rush. She eased her legs open wider as she massaged circles against her slickly wet clit with her forefingers.

"Pleasure," she moaned, feeling a quickening in her heart and thrill race up the center of her pussy that was just the beginning of that familiar ride.

She deepened the pressure, gyrating her hips in a slow wind that mirrored Pleasure's motion when he was fucking her.

She imagined the feel of his dick against her tongue.

She yearned for his touch on her nipples, a mix of softness and steady pressure that was intoxicating.

She badly wanted to feel his hand massaging oil on her soft buttocks before lubricating the length of him to help guide his inches deeply between her buttocks.

Jaime cried out a bit, her face a mix of pleasure and pain. She wanted him. She knew she shouldn't. Pleasure was no good for her, but she couldn't leave him alone. Not now. Not yet.

She gently guided her fingers inside her pussy, pretending, wishing, needing them to be Pleasure's dick instead.

"Pleasure," she moaned.

"Fuck me?" she begged with a tortured cry.

Jaime turned her head as she found a slow and steady rhythm easing her fingers in and out, up and down, around and around her core. A light sweat coated her brow and upper lip. Her heart hammered. Her pulse raced.

"I need this," she moaned, tears welling up in her eyes.

She blinked them away, catching just a blurred outline outside her driver's side window. Her heart stopped as she leaned away from the window and looked up at her neighbor, Lucas Neal, standing there transfixed with his dick hard and pressing against the zipper of his khakis like a fist trying to break free.

She pulled her fingers from her pussy and lowered the power window.

"I saw you sitting in the car and wanted to check on you—"

"Get in the back," Jaime told him, raising the window.

Maybe it was the upcoming divorce. Her parents' overprotectiveness. Her money troubles. Pleasure's rejection.

The sight of Lucas's hardness. Ego. Or just plain loneliness and horniness. Whatever. She was seizing the moment.

Lucas paused for just a second, his round face disbelieving before he hurried around the front of the car to climb inside. As soon as he closed the door, she threw the car in reverse and backed out into the street.

What am I doing? she wondered to herself.

Getting fucked for free, she answered.

He hesitated. "Jaime—"

Continuing her ride of impulsivity, Jaime whipped the Accord into the empty parking lot of a small strip mall. Parking in the dark area on the side of a shoe store, she turned and eyed him.

"Do you have a condom?" she asked, reaching out to massage his dick in the dim interior. *Not bad,* she thought. Far from Pleasure but better than Eric.

"In . . . in . . . my . . . my . . . wallet," he stammered nervously.

Truth?

After Eric's dominance and Pleasure's total control, it felt good to be the boss. It kicked everything up a notch for her.

"Put it on," she said, avoiding looking in his eyes. His face was not Pleasure's and she wasn't interested in it anyway.

Lucas hurriedly unzipped his dick before he raised up slightly to dig his wallet from his back pocket. He worked the condom packet free like his life depended on it.

Jaime worked off her panties, kicking them away with her heels, as she lowered her bucket seat to lay flat against the rear seat. She turned and climbed across the seat to settle across his lap. The scent of her pussy was clean but heavy with her arousal. His khakis were down around his knees and his hard dick stood up between their bellies like a chaperone.

She eyed his round belly and pale thighs briefly, her focus on the curving length of his dick. Again, no Pleasure but not bad.

"Jaime, are you sure 'bout this?" Lucas asked nervously.

She grabbed his dick and eased her pussy down onto it.

At the feel of her, his head dropped back against the headrest and he bit his bottom lip with a deep, guttural moan. "Shit," he swore.

Jaime felt the difference between him and Pleasure, but Lucas's dick was making a strong stand.

She brought his hands up to her ass beneath her skirt as she began to ride him in a way that brought her clit against the hard base of his dick.

"Shit," he swore again.

Jaime snatched off his glasses and then grabbed the back of his round head to guide his open and panting mouth to her titty.

"Oh shit. Oh shit. Oh shit," he hollered, his body going stiff.

Jaime stopped riding him. "No."

"I'm sorry," he said heavily, sweat soaking his hair and shirt as he panted like he'd just run a marathon.

She felt his dick go limp inside her.

Jaime lifted her hands and pulled the roots of her hair in frustration.

"I'm sorry but it was—"

"Don't worry about it," she said, meaning to cut him off, climbing off his lap to slump onto the driver's seat.

Feeling brash and hella spiteful, Jaime pressed her knees open wide. "Just for the record this is the last time you'll see this pussy," she told him, before she raised her seat back.

"I never been freaked before—"

Jaime whirled around to eye him. "Freaked?"

Lucas nodded as he picked up his glasses from the floor and slid them onto his round, boyish face. "Damn right. Freaked," he stressed. "Shit, a brotha was overexcited by your show in your driveway."

"I'm not a freak."

Lucas looked disbelieving. "Whatever."

Jaime reached up to turn on the interior light of the car. "You wanted this from the moment you came to my door to introduce yourself," she told him, watching him as he left the condom on his dick and pulled his boxers and pants back up around his round waist.

Lucas stopped working his zipper up to eye her through his glasses. "I wanted to take you out to dinner and get to know you better. I wanted to build on the attraction I had for you. My plan damn sure wasn't to screw you in a parking lot, but I took what *you* offered."

Jaime looked away from his anger, turning off the light and speeding away from their parking spot with a squeal of her tires.

He said nothing else to her.

That was fine with Jaime. It was more than fine.

As soon as she pulled into her driveway, he hopped out of the car and stalked away. She lowered her head into her hands. *What the hell am I doing?* She asked herself, ignoring the feel of the moist seat of her panties now stuck to her ankle.

She looked up at the knock on the window. It felt like déjà vu to have Lucas standing there looking down at her. She lowered the window.

"I apologize if you think I took advantage of you," he said, before turning and quickly walking across his lawn and into his house.

That only made her feel worse.

She reached down and grabbed her panties to shove

into her purse before she climbed out of the car. She ignored the stickiness between her thighs as she made her way to her front door. "I gots to get my shit together," she said.

As soon as she walked inside the door and locked it her cell phone vibrated. Pleasure?

She reached inside her purse and pulled it out, flipping it open without a cursory check of the caller ID. "Yeah," she said.

"Busy day, Mrs. Hall?"

Jaime froze at the sound of Eric's voice. She frowned. "What concern is it of yours?" she asked coldly.

"You're pissed about the car and the money you stole from me?" he asked.

The money you stole from me, she repeated in her head. It confirmed what she already figured. No one knew about that but Jessa. *I really owe that bitch a major ass whipping.*

"Should a married woman be at strip clubs and riding around with their single male neighbors?" he asked.

Jaime frowned, feeling the color drain from her face. She rushed to her front door and opened it wide. "Are you following me?" she asked, looking up and down the street.

"You're building quite a case for me for this divorce you keep harping on about," he said in total satisfaction.

Jaime stepped back and closed the door soundly before she put on all the locks. She felt violated.

"Let's put all this behind us. Come home, Jaime," he said. "Come home or I'll make you regret it. I promise you."

Click.

As he ended the call, Jaime felt chilled to the bone.

Chapter 9

Aria sat huddled in a chair by the front window of her mother's three-bedroom apartment in Newark. With dull eyes she watched nothing and everything about the street where she'd grown up too fast. The porches were filled with people trying to enjoy the cover of night and the little coolness it brought from the summer heat. A few kids still played under the streetlights in the street between parked cars. People arrived and left their homes in vehicles and cabs. The perimeter of Westside Park was empty, but Aria knew buff brothers were balling on the hardtops down by Eighteenth Avenue.

Thankfully, unlike the days she was growing up, the sounds of gunfire and the squeal of tires on stolen cars were much fewer. Less crime. Better-looking homes. Cleaner streets. More police presence. Not perfect, but definitely a better reflection of the good people who lived within the perimeters of the city. Kids had more of a chance of just being kids.

Aria was home and whenever the white-picket fence lifestyle of Richmond Hills got to be too much or she just needed a reality check she headed to her mother. Blunt, brash, honest, loving.

Where else could she turn after her husband walked away from their marriage?

Kingston had never shown for the appointment at Dr. Matheson. He never answered her calls. He didn't go in to his practice.

She didn't know whether to sit back and wait for him to make an appearance or call the police to report him missing. *Kingston is wrong. What if he's lying in a hospital hurt? How am I supposed to know?*

But she knew nothing kept Kingston from her but his own hurt and pain. That was the sole reason.

"Aria, it's going on ten," her mother said, walking into the dimly lit living room to come and stand by her. "When are you getting on that road home?"

Aria just shrugged and shifted in the chair to relieve the prickling pressure across her buttocks from sitting too long. She'd been in that chair since she first got to her mother's hours ago.

Aria sat, watched, thought, and alternated between calling Kingston and fighting not to call Jessa—something that could get her ass thrown in jail. "Punk bitch," she muttered.

"What's going on, Aria?" Heather Goines asked, reaching out to turn on the slender lamp on the table beside her daughter.

"How many times have I offered to move you, Mama?" Aria asked softly, instead of answering her mother's concerned question.

Heather pulled a chair from the small dining room off the living room. "Way too many times for you not to figure out I ain't going nowhere."

"Why not?"

"Newark is home."

Aria smiled. Her mother never minced words. "Good and bad, huh?"

Heather chuckled. "Girl, don't be naive. Mama tried to put plenty of common sense in that head before you went off to college for them book smarts."

Aria could only shake her head. Her mother was the self-proclaimed guru / Oprah / Confucius of the ghetto and there was more to come.

"Listen, every city has good and bad. Some of it is just covered up better, but once you get past them iron gates and big sprawling front doors you'll find a lot of the same shit that goes down around here. Bullshit is still bullshit even with icing on it."

"But the icing makes it easier to deal with," Aria countered.

Heather waved her hand dismissively. "Well, cleaning up the bullshit instead of living with it would be the easiest thing to do."

Hmph. Mama just summed up the same thing Dr. Matheson told me earlier. Dr. Matheson had some serious competition on his hands.

More than working on your marriage, Aria, you have to deal with your unresolved issues, your guilt about your past. The first step is talking about it. Tell me about it.

She had shared a lot with Dr. Matheson today. A lot but not all. Aria turned her face to look back out the window, locking her eyes on a lone figure walking down the street, his head down, chin nearly buried to his chest. She briefly wondered what his story was. What was his own pile of bullshit to deal with?

"There's a lot about me that you don't know," Aria began.

"I might know more than you think," her mother said.

Aria shook her head. "Never. Not about this, " she admitted softly. . . .

Aria took each step leading up to their second-floor apartment carefully. She definitely wasn't able to run up the stairs like she'd done earlier.

"You a'ight, cuz?" Jontae asked from behind her.

Aria paused on the landing and reached out for the banister. She nodded. "Just cramping up," she said, wincing as an intense spasm radiated across her lower back.

"It's gon' be like that all day," Jontae said around a wad of gum she was popping like fireworks on the fourth of July.

"I know, I remember from the last time," Aria said, taking a deep breath before she continued up the stairs to the front door of the apartment. It opened before she could use her key and she looked up at her mother standing there, wiping flour from her hands with a dish towel. Aria forced herself to stand up straighter and smile. "Hey Ma."

"Hey girls. What you two been up to today?" Heather asked, walking down the hall to the kitchen.

"We went downtown, Auntie, to look around in all the stores," Jontae offered up from behind her.

Liar, Aria thought as she fought not to wince while she made her way to her bedroom at the rear of the apartment.

"Aria, are you okay?" her mom asked from the kitchen just as she passed.

"I think something I ate messed up my stomach," she said, avoiding her mother's eyes. Liar, liar, pants on fire.

"You probably need to shit it out," Heather said, sliding battered chicken wings into the bubbling deep fryer.

That made Aria smile even through her discomfort. Her mother was off the chain. "I'm okay. I'm just gonna lie down, Ma," she said over her shoulder.

"I'll be in to check on you," Heather called back.

"I know." As soon as Aria stepped into her bedroom she kicked off her bright purple Reeboks and lay down on her side on her twin-sized bed covered with her Strawberry Shortcake comforter.

Jontae closed the door before she dropped down on the

other twin bed and reached over to turn on the radio. "On and On" by Erykah Badu filled the room.

Aria rolled her eyes heavenward as Jontae began to sing along completely off-key. Before she could reach the next chorus, Aria's bedroom door opened. She was facing the wall and turned to look over her shoulder as her mother stepped in.

"Jontae, since Aria isn't feeling well, why don't you head on back to your dad's."

That was a nicely worded order and not at all a request. Jontae was sneaky with her shit and never showed outward defiance. Playing nice and sweet got her way more freedom. "Okay, Auntie. Bye, Aria. Hope you feel better."

Behind Heather's back she motioned to Aria that she would call later and then she left. Aria loved her cousin and summer companion, but she was glad to see her ass go.

"You sure you okay, baby girl?" Heather asked, coming over to touch Aria's forehead.

Aria closed her eyes and enjoyed the smooth and warm feel of her mother's touch. Tears welled up in her eyes behind her lids. She fought like hell not to let them fall.

She fought like hell not to speak the truth. Mama, I just killed my baby.

She fought and won both times.

"I'm good, Mama," she said, feeling really tired and just wanting to hug her pillows to her stomach and wait for the cramping and bleeding to stop like the nurses at the clinic said it would.

Heather turned on the window air-conditioning unit and closed the blinds to block some of the sun's summer rays.

"If you don't feel better I'm going to give you a laxative," she said, pulling the pillow from the empty twin bed to settle gently under Aria's head.

Aria chanced a look up and she felt surrounded by the

love in her mother's eyes. That look eased the throbbing aches of the cramps.

"Mama don't want nothing wrong with her baby," Heather said, smoothing Aria's head before she softly patted her cheek.

Mama don't want me lying here recovering from a second abortion at just sixteen. *Aria couldn't stop the tear that raced down her cheek.*

Her mother's face filled with concern.

Tell her, tell her the truth. Let her help you through this, *she told herself, all the while knowing she wouldn't. She couldn't. Not ever.*

Aria reached up and wiped the tear away. "Something must be in my eye," *she lied.*

Heather sat up straight and crossed her arms over her chest as she eyed her daughter. "Somebody bothering you? Somebody hurt you? What you and Jontae been up to?"

Aria forced herself to smile. Her mother was in detective mode and that would end real fucked up for her. "Just not feeling good, Ma. That's all."

Her mother walked to the door. "I had you. I raised you. I know you, Aria. Mama here when you want to talk. You hear me?" *she asked over her shoulder.*

"I hear you, Ma."

Long after her mother stepped out of the room, closing the door softly behind her, Aria lay there with her eyes locked on the wall silently crying. . . .

Aria remained quiet and kept her gaze locked on the male figure getting smaller and smaller in the distance.

Her mother sighed and it was filled with a lot of things Aria recognized—regret, disappointment, anger—but still the love a mother has for her child, especially her only child. "Do you regret having the abortions?" she asked softly.

Aria turned in the dimly lit room to eye her mother in surprise.

"What, Aria, you think I'm gonna grab a brush and beat your ass like Diahann Carroll in *Claudine?*" she asked, leveling her eyes on her daughter's face. "Don't get me wrong, I woulda did it back then, but now? Now you're a grown woman living under her roof with her own husband."

"I'm sorry, Mama," she said.

Heather Goines smiled sadly. "So am I because you could've come to me. I don't care what the situation I always got your back, Aria. It hurts that you didn't know that."

"I should have," Aria admitted, looking down at her hand as she twisted her three-carat wedding band around her finger beneath her three-carat solitaire. "Just like I shoulda known not to keep secrets from Kingston."

"More secrets?"

If only you knew, she thought, thinking of all the things about those summers her mother still didn't know. If Heather "keep your panties up" Goines knew just how much sex and scheming her little girl had done. . . .

"More secrets, Aria?" her mother asked again.

"I fucked up, Ma. I fucked up bad. He might be gone for good." Aria's heart ached as she breathed life into her true feelings and her tears raced.

"What happened?"

"I need to talk to Kingston first," she said. "But I will tell you about it because in a way it affects you, too."

Heather Goines reached over and grasped her daughter's hand. "If it's God will then all things can and will be done, Aria. You remember that. Okay?"

And in that moment, nearly shielded by darkness with

just enough light to shimmer in their eyes, Aria knew that her mother had guessed about her infertility. And she also knew in that moment that the matter was set aside until Aria was ready to fully discuss it with her.

"Now, your old mama gon' give you some advice. Some tough love," Heather Goines said, rising to her feet and pushing the dining room chair back under the table.

Aria closed her eyes and smiled. *Picture Heather Goines not getting her nickel in,* she thought.

"To me—and it's just my opinion—you should be home waiting on your husband. If he walks through the door then you fight to let him know that you love him and if he never returns then you begin to rebuild your life without him."

Black and white. That was her Mama.

She looked over as her mother turned on the ceiling fan, basking the room with light from above. She continued on to the front door and opened it. "Go home, Aria," she said firmly with a soft smile.

"But Mama—"

Heather shook her head. "Go home. You can't keep running and hiding and lying about your problems. Where has it gotten you so far?"

Aria rose to her feet and grabbed her car keys. "I thought *I* was the college grad," she teased, reaching to playfully pinch her mother's cheek.

"Common sense can't be topped."

Aria hugged her mother close. "If I call for you—"

"I'm there. Me and Uncle One-Eye will tear that highway up," Heather finished, playfully swatting her daughter's buttock.

"Not Uncle One-Eye," Aria drawled, thinking of how well his nickname suited him.

Heather just laughed. "Go on. Get."

Aria walked out into the hall, turning to look back at

her mother. She saw the sadness her mother felt and turned away, just grateful that her mother chose not to ream her out for her deceptions in the past.

But she wasn't crazy. Aria knew she hadn't heard the last of it.

"Picture *that* shit."

Aria entered her passcode and waited patiently for the heavy iron gates of Richmond Hills to open for her. She waved to whichever security guard sat in the booth as she whizzed past, taking the long curving roads before she reached the first home in the subdivision. She eyed Renee's brick Colonial and her foot edged over to the brake. It seemed like every light in the house was lit, making the sizable structure beam against the backdrop of night.

The last time they'd spoken, it had sounded like Renee was crying or drunk. Renee had rushed off the phone and until her own drama had hit her like a Mack truck, Aria had meant to check on Renee. Be a better friend than she had the last month or so.

Tomorrow, she thought.

Tonight her thoughts were all fucked up with the mess waiting for her around her own door.

Go home, Aria.

Her mother's voice echoed in her head and she shifted her eyes to the home she shared with Kingston. She eased her foot off the brake and lowered it onto the accelerator.

Her stomach was tight with anxiety as she pulled into the drive, but her heart hammered like crazy to find the lights on in the living room. Kingston! *He must have parked in the garage*, she thought, feeling like her heart was about to explode in her chest.

Emotions overwhelmed her as she lowered her head to

the steering wheel and licked the last remnants of her gloss from her lips. What awaited her on the other side of that door? What story was about to unfold?

Aria was afraid.

Taking a deep steadying breath, she left her SUV and made her way up the stairs. Her thoughts were racing.

What do I say? How do I explain? How do I make it right? Why did I give Jessa the power? Why didn't I tell him myself?

Shit. Shit. Shit. Shit. Shit, Aria. SHIT!

Aria slid her key into the lock not even sure it would still work. *Click.* She felt relief as she pushed the door open and stepped inside the foyer. "King—"

The sound of laughter from the living room made her freeze. Aria frowned deeply as she held her keys so tightly as to almost pierce her flesh. She made her way to the living room with long strides like she was marching to war. *If a bitch is in my house, it's gonna* be *a war.*

At the front arched entry to the living room, she pulled up short. The anger dissipated from her face as Kingston and his parents turned their heads to look at her. She smiled stiffly as her eyes shifted to Kingston. Were they ALL here to kick her out? "Hello, hello, hello," she said, slightly cautious.

Kingston stood up and walked across the mahogany hardwood floor. Her eyes took in everything about him. His strong and handsome features, only softened by his long lashes. The way every movement of his muscled frame was like that of a panther in the loose-fitting jeans and pale blue shirt he wore.

Her eyes tried to search his as he came to slide his hand onto her back and kiss her cheek. Aria stiffened, unable to hide her surprise at his show of affection. "I forgot my parents were coming for dinner. I guess you did, too," he said, his voice seemingly warm. "I told them you had an interview to do and wouldn't get back until late."

Is this a Jaime-and-Eric-type, Emmy award–winning performance? Are we fronting now or is everything okay?

Aria smiled and slid her hands around Kingston's waist, aware of his parents' eyes on them. "You should have called and reminded me. I would have come straight home."

"Didn't want to bother you," he said.

Aria side-eyed him, not sure how to take it all in as he gently freed himself and reclaimed his seat by his father, Tony.

"You're always so busy. When are you going to slow down enough for you two to give us grandchildren?" his mother, Olivine, said as Aria moved forward to kiss her cheek and hug her close.

Aria froze. She shifted her gaze to Kingston and did not miss the tightening of his square jaw. "Are y'all staying the night?" she asked, moving over to hug her now-standing father-in-law. His parents now lived in upstate New York and usually avoided the forty-five minute ride home until the mornings.

"Yes, Eric filled us up with Chinese food and you know I hate to drive on a full stomach," Tony Livewell said, patting his slightly rounded belly. His tall and stocky frame was a testament to his fitness in his youth.

"So, Aria, back to my earlier question," Olivine said, crossing her ankles in the casual and flowing silk pantsuit she wore with large and bold colorful jewelry that Aria knew came straight from a high-end boutique. "Babies. When will I be able to rock some grandbabies?"

Aria turned and gave a long and hard look at Kingston. Even though he stared back willfully she saw the pain flash in his eyes.

Aria loved her mother-in-law to death. She was a sweet and affectionate woman who knew how to cleverly get her way without even seeming like it. Kingston was a classic mama's boy and Aria had literally poured the pussy on him to break some of the more ridiculous ties like him stopping by his mother's house for dinner almost every night.

Olivine Livewell was an overprotective mother whose main goal was to be an overprotective grandmother. She used to e-mail Aria articles on ways to increase fertility, working mothers, and anything else she thought would make Aria start popping out kids like her last name was Duggar or some shit.

Even though she didn't know it she was making shit real awkward for Aria. "Soon, Olivine. As a matter of fact I'll give you a buzz when I'm ovulating so you can be in on it from the beginning."

The corners of Olivine's red painted mouth dropped to the floor.

"Aria!" Kingston chopped out sharply.

She licked her lips, looked somewhere for a quick second, before she forced a smile and faced her mother-in-law. "I'm sorry, Olivine. I'm just a little grouchy today."

Olivine nodded, her asymmetrical bob swinging back and forth slightly. "I didn't mean anything by it. I was just asking."

"I'm going up to get your room together," Aria said, rising to her feet. The pretending was too much. Just too damn much.

"Kingston, what is going on?" his father asked as soon as Aria stepped out of the rear entrance of the living room.

She paused. It was hard to ignore their whispers floating from the room.

"Is she mad at *me?*" Olivine asked in obvious disbelief.

"No, Mother," Kingston answered, his voice distant.

"*Yes*, Mother," Aria mimed sarcastically, knowing she was being childish. Olivine was a cool mother-in-law. She had just caught Aria at the wrong damn time with her baby-making shit. *If I could, Olivine, I would. Damn.*

"Well, what's going on?" Olivine asked, still whispering.

Aria frowned as she pressed her back to the wall and leaned in closer to the arched entryway. She knew that her husband was slouched in his chair with his head leaned back on the chair, eyes closed, mouth a straight line.

"Ma, Aria and I are going through something right now—"

"Something like what?"

Aria stepped back into the room. Sure enough he was slouched in his chair just like she had guessed. "Kingston, I need help upstairs," she said, tired of the limbo she was floating in.

She wasn't going to stand there and ear hustle on the status of her marriage. She deserved to hear it first. Face to face. Was she fighting for her marriage or preparing to move on without him—something she couldn't imagine doing.

I fucked up, she thought, flushed with embarrassment.

"Aria, I really am sorry," Olivine said, rising to her feet.

"It's okay," she said. "Kingston?"

He rose to his feet and made his way past his father's seated figure to join her in the hall. Kingston turned and closed the double doors blocking that side of the living room from the hall with the rear stairs to the upper level.

Aria touched his arm, but he roughly brushed away her touch, shoving his hands into his pockets as he stalked back and forth. "Kingston, I am so sorry—"

He held up his hand, his frown so deep that his handsome face was decidedly devilish. He continued to pace, his shoulders tensed and squared up.

Aria held her hands out to him. "Kingston, please—"

He whirled on her. "I'm so fucking pissed at you right now, Aria, don't you get that?" he ground out in a low voice.

She stepped back from the angry tears in his eyes as he pierced her with a hard stare. She nodded, her words stuck inside her because she had never seen her husband so angry.

He took deep breaths.

She knew he was trying to calm down.

"I didn't want to do this with my parents here."

"Do what?" she asked softly. "Do what, Kingston?"

He smiled, but there was not one drop of humor there. "Don't play games, Aria, we're both smarter than that."

"Can I talk?" she asked him, her voice filled with so many emotions as a tear raced down her cheek.

Kingston's eyes locked on that tear before he turned away from her, crossing his arms over his chest as he dropped his head. "I can't do this right now, Aria."

"And I can't lose you, Kingston," she told him fiercely, filled with more fear than she'd ever known she had. "I'm sorry I can't have kids, but I love you—"

Kingston whirled on her, his face incredulous. "You think that's what I'm mad about, Aria? Seriously, Aria, that's what you think?" he asked, his deep voice filled with anguish.

Aria shook her head, bringing her hands up to cover her face. She felt helpless. Hopeless. Lost. Her world was spinning and she felt off center like she could crash at any moment.

"Let me explain something to you," Kingston said, stepping forward to jerk her hands from her face before he released her.

He can't even touch me. Aria felt weak and pressed her back to the wall.

"This is all about trust, Aria. Plain and simple. You don't trust me. You didn't trust me not to fuck your friend. You didn't trust me not to leave you. You never trusted me not to cheat. And *now?* Now I find out that you didn't even trust me to tell me that you couldn't have kids, Aria." Kingston threw his hands up in the air.

"My past. I didn't want you to be ashamed of me—"

Kingston stepped close to her, bending his head so that his fiery eyes locked with hers. "Did I ever do or say anything to make you think I was better than you? That I didn't love you for you?" he asked in hard tones. He patted his solid chest. "Tell me what the fuck I did to make you handle me like this, Aria. Huh? Huh? I didn't love you enough. Huh? I didn't respect you enough? Huh? What? I didn't put you first?"

She shook her head.

Kingston laughed bitterly. "You're damn right. I'm not perfect, but I was a damn good husband to you. But maybe I was too good? Huh? What's your problem? You don't know when somebody loves you?"

I was a damn good husband.

Aria reached out to wrap her hands around his waist. "Kingston, let me make this up to you," she begged, her tears wetting his strong neck as she pressed her face against his warm skin.

"Get the hell off me, Aria," he ordered, standing as still as a statue. "I'm sick of your shit. I'm serious. I'm sick of it. I. Am. Sick. Of. It. Around here smelling my drawers and rummaging though my pockets, treating me like a criminal or something in my own damn house when you are the one who can't be trusted. Man, fuck this shit."

She hugged him closer. "Kingston—"

The muscles in his arms flexed as he freed himself of her embrace. He pushed her back roughly.

Aria stumbled, but it was the thought of losing him that made her knees give out. "Kingston, please," she begged, all of the Newark bravado gone from her as tears and snot ran down her face and her heart continued to shatter.

He eyed her with his own tears as he licked his lips and clenched his fists. "You know how much I wanted a baby. A family. You knew this and you didn't say nothing. I'm a damn good man. A damn good husband. I didn't deserve this shit, Aria," he said fiercely, his voice low and filled with anger and pain.

The double doors suddenly opened and Aria saw him swipe at his tears with the sides of his strong hands. His mother looked back and forth at them both.

"Listen, kids, what is going on with you two?" she asked in obvious concern.

"It's nothing, Ma," Kingston said.

Aria pulled her knees to her chest and buried her face against her thighs as her tears racked her body.

I was a damn good husband.

"We're leaving so that the two of you can finish your conversation in privacy," Kingston's father said sternly.

Aria felt a presence standing over her. She looked up as her father-in-law offered her his hands. She took them and he pulled her to her feet with a gentle tug. He patted her back reassuringly before he led a sputtering Olivine out of the hall.

Kingston slumped down onto the bottom step, his arms bent on his knees and his head hung low between them. Aria walked over to him, but he stood and brushed past her to follow his parents' path. She hugged the banister close, needing some type of solid support as her world slipped out from under her.

"I'm driving my parents home."

Aria whirled around, feeling the swelling and grittiness

in her eyes from her tears as she faced him standing there not looking directly at her.

"I'm going to stay there."

Aria cried harder, slumping down to the staircase. "Kingston, please. I'm sorry. Please—"

"I'm sorry, too, Aria, because I honestly don't see myself coming back."

When she looked up he was gone and her world as she knew it had gone with him.

Chapter 10

Renee needed her friends. She needed them around her. She needed them to listen to her, advise her, just be there for her. Life was a raggedy, baldheaded, bummy bitch for her and it was too much. Just too fucking much stressing her.

Her marriage. Her career. Her son. Her sobriety.

Her fucking sanity.

She bit at the side of her nail as she eyed the bottle of tequila sitting on the center of the island. It was calling her so badly. Charming her. Winning her over.

Turning from the temptation, she took a deep sip of her cup of black coffee as she looked out the kitchen windows up the street to Aria and Kingston's home. She picked up her cordless and dialed Aria's cell phone number.

It rang three times and went to voice mail. "Maybe she's not up yet," Renee said aloud to herself, looking over her shoulder at the bottle. "Aria, call me when you get this."

It was time to get her shit together and everything about that bottle wasn't going to help a damn thing.

Seeing your son in the act with his lover had a way of making things clear. Liquor had had her lost to the fact that he was sexually active . . . with a man.

My son is gay? Experimenting? Bisexual?

Definitely not a virgin. That she'd seen firsthand.

Renee massaged the small bridge of her nose with her free hand, wishing she could shake the image out of her head and wishing even more that the shit had never gone down. From the corner of her eye she saw the sun glare through the window over the sink and make the clear bottle glisten.

Renee dialed Jaime. It went straight to voice mail. "Jaime, this is Renee, call me."

She set the cordless phone on the granite counter and turned to press her ass back against it, crossing her ankles in the wide-legged linen pants she wore with brown crocodile heels and a crisp white shirt. She licked her lips as her eyes caressed the bottle. It might as well have a DRINK ME tag hanging from it as if she were Alice in Wonderland. That's how badly she wanted it.

Renee stepped forward and grabbed the bottle by the neck. She pulled the cork stopper and turned the bottle upside down, sending the tequila down the drain. She let the bottle rest inside the drain and turned away, wrapping her arms around herself as she fought not to let the liquor empty down her throat instead.

But she wanted it. Craved it. Needed it.

Renee turned back to the sink and grabbed the bottle. It was empty. "Damn!" she shouted out in frustration, turning to fling the bottle against the wall. It dropped to the travertine tiled floor and shattered.

With wild eyes she spotted the drops of liquid inside the sink. Get it. She dragged her index finger through the droplets and raised it to her mouth to suckle. Her eyes closed at even the faintest taste of tequila against her tongue.

"Ma, did something crash?"

Her eyes popped open at the sound of her son's voice from behind her. She shook her head as she moved over to began picking up the shattered pieces of glass from the floor. "Just go get ready, Aaron," she said, her voice as weary as she felt. "Your grandma's picking you up in a little bit."

Come on, Renee, you're better than that. Smarter than that. Get your house in order. Get your shit together.

Renee was squatting and let her head hang low between her knees. She wanted a drink. "Damn," she swore, promising herself to break the ties liquor had on her.

"Ma, I can't stay home?"

Renee looked up in surprise. She thought he'd gone upstairs like she'd told him. She said nothing. She had nothing to say to him.

"Do you hate me because I had sex in your house or because I'm gay?" he asked.

Renee looked up at her son. The sound of pain in his voice hurt her like she had walked barefoot across the shards of glass. "I don't hate you, Aaron," she said, a wave of embarrassment filling her as she looked away from him and focused on picking up the glass.

"Do you hate that I'm gay?" he asked, insistent.

"I can't do this right now, Aaron," she said sharply. "Please."

He walked out of the room.

"I love you, Aaron," she said, resigned and knowing that as angry and disappointed as she was that he needed to hear that.

His tall and slender figure paused briefly, not looking back at her, before he left the kitchen and headed up the stairs.

As she rose and dumped the broken glass she was holding into the trash can, she wondered if he was still in communication with Darren. She gritted her teeth and clenched her hands at the thought of Darren.

She didn't give a flying fuck that Darren was only three years older than Aaron. His relationship with her son was—in the words of Aria—"a done dada."

Renee picked up the phone and called Jackson. She

walked around the island and out of the kitchen. The smell of the tequila still clung to the air and taunted her. "Jackson?"

"Yes?"

She ignored the coolness of his tone. "Listen, I need to talk to you today."

He paused. "You and your lover not working today?"

My lover. Negro, you are so far off, she thought. "I'm going in this morning, but I can be at your office by noon. I really don't give a flying fuck what Darren is doing, Jackson."

He paused again.

"Jackson?"

"I hear you," he said.

Renee closed her eyes and did a ten count. "Listen, I know you're pissed at me or all working women or what the fuck ever, Jackson, but we're parents and we need to discuss a . . . a . . . situation with Aaron."

"A situation like what?" Jackson asked, his tone softening just a bit.

Renee walked into the room that had once served as their joint office. She made her way to her desk and slid onto the leather executive chair. "I'd rather talk in person," she said, turning on her all-in-one desktop.

He fell silent again. "Even though I hated that you were working, I still never thought you would cheat on me, Renee."

Her fingers froze above the keyboard. Her brows furrowed. Trying to kick her newfound love of liquor and having the urge to drink nipping at her constantly like a dog on a rubber bone, Renee didn't have the time, patience, or will to play Dr. Phil. "Jackson, listen," she began, licking her lips and swallowing hard. "Cheating has nothing to do with time or place or opportunity. If it's in you to cheat it is in you. I don't care if it's a strip club or a church. Period."

"No, because my parents were fine until my mother went to work, Renee," he stressed. He released a heavy breath. "You know what? Just forget it."

Renee's face filled with surprise. "Jackson—"

"Just forget it, Renee. I'll see you later."

Click.

Renee was left with nothing but a dial tone in her ear. *Jackson's mama dipped out on his daddy. Say what say who now?*

She set the cordless on her desk and pressed her chin into her palm. *But Charesse doesn't work.*

The fact that her mother-in-law was always at home was the reason Renee was sending Aaron there, to be under her watchful eye.

Renee always assumed Jackson's beliefs about women working were because his mother was a stay-at-home mother. Obviously she was missing a big chunk of info on his parents' history and how it affected her husband.

Knowledge is power and maybe things between them could have been resolved if she knew she was working against his history. But now. Now it was just time to move on. She quickly finished typing her document and printed off two copies before sliding them into a folder.

As she pushed back in the chair her eyes dropped down to the lower drawer of her desk. She leaned back in the chair and crossed her legs as her eyes stayed locked on it. It was one of her stash spots. She licked her lips and blinked her eyes rapidly in nervous anxiety. *Is a bottle in there or not?*

She tapped the toe of her shoe against the drawer. A drink would rest her nerves and take away the jitters she felt. *Just one drink.*

Tap. Tap. Tap.

Just a sip would get me straight.

Tap. Tap. Tap.

Renee dropped her head before she forced herself to

wheel the chair back. One drink would lead to another . . . and another . . . and another. Then total blackout.

"No," she said forcefully, rising and striding out of the office with more strength and confidence than she'd felt in weeks.

She was just walking out the front door with her brief-case when a silver minivan turned into the drive. Renee smiled and waved at her mother-in-law, before she walked back up from the porch to push open the front door. "Aaron, your grandmother's here. Let's go. She's waiting," she yelled, before stepping back outside to walk up to the minivan.

"Thanks again for picking him up, Charesse. I appreci-ate it." Renee looked down at her mother-in-law, every bit of fifty-five and the epitome of a grandmother. She still couldn't swallow Jackson's insinuation.

"No problem at all. Anything I can do to help," Charesse said.

Renee flushed with embarrassment. Anytime she spoke to her in-laws they never discussed her and Jackson's sepa-ration. Until that moment, she didn't even know if they knew. Until that exact moment. It was hard to miss the compassion.

So had Jackson told his parents about his bastard? Did they decorate a room in their house into a nursery like they did for Kieran and Aaron? Did they call Jackson's bitch and check on her like they did me?

"I gotta go, Charesse, but thanks again," Renee said, turning to quickly walk to her car and climb in.

Behind the wheel she blinked away her tears and fought for composure, all the while the urge to drink whispering in her ear.

She looked over her shoulder to reverse the car down the drive, careful not to strike her mother-in-law. On the entire ride in to her office, she tried not to think about Jackson's lover's pregnancy and who all said what, where, when, and why about it. Between the usual stop-and-go morning traffic and fighting the urge to stop her car on the Garden State Parkway to check the car for an errant liquor bottle, Renee was almost successful.

As soon as she strolled into her office on the fourth floor of the fifth-story glass-and-steel building, Renee's hands slightly trembled.

She dropped down into her seat and covered her face with her hands. "The best way out is always through. The best way out is always through," she repeated the Robert Frost quote.

Feeling more steady she picked up the phone and dialed the extension for the receptionist. "Hi, Yolanda. Is Darren here today?" she asked, hoping otherwise. *Maybe his ass is too ashamed to show his face.*

"Yes, he just walked in."

Renee's stomach felt like it dropped to her heels. *This motherfucker is really trying me?* "Ask him to come into my office, please."

"Yes, Mrs. Clinton."

Renee hung up the phone and leaned back in her chair. Waiting.

Knock knock.

"Come in, Darren," she called out, crossing her hands to keep them from trembling.

The door opened and Renee smirked at the boldness of his walk and the way he held his head high. "So first you try to fuck me, then you fuck my son, and now you're trying to fuck me over."

Darren paused, his ass just inches above the chair, before he relaxed and sat down. "Renee, I really like Aaron," he said, looking as sharp as ever in a gray and white pinstriped suit.

Renee shifted her ass in her chair. "So much so that now you're blackmailing me to keep your job?" she asked.

Darren's dark and handsome face became incredulous.

"You're firing me when I have covered for you and helped you keep your job."

Renee sat up a bit straighter and nodded. "So I should thank you and forget that you're a twenty-year-old man fucking my seventeen-year-old son in my house. Nigga, please," she snapped, reaching for her phone and quickly punching numbers.

It was Darren's turn to sit up straighter. "I messed up about disrespecting your house, but—"

"Hi, this is Renee Clinton. I need security to escort my assistant from the building," she said, her eyes locked on Darren. "He is no longer an employee here."

Darren jumped to his feet as Renee hung up the phone and reached for her briefcase and the folder she'd placed inside. "Look, I like you, Renee, and I learned a lot working with you, but if you think I will sit back and let you ruin my career—"

Renee held up her hand. "Say what you want to whomever you want. I don't give a shit." She pushed the folder across the desk toward him.

He frowned as he opened it and read the contents. "You're resigning."

"Effective immediately," she told him. "Looks like neither one of us will be working at CancerCure."

If it was at all possible for Darren's deeply dark complexion to blanch . . . it did.

"Security will escort you to human resources. You have a choice to make when you get there. Resign and get the hell on with your college career and a new internship. Try to badmouth me or see my son again and I will call the police and have your ass arrested for statutory rape."

Knock knock.

"Come in."

Darren's face closed up and he rose to his feet as two burly security guards all in black entered her office. "I didn't deserve this and I won't forget it."

Renee nodded as sweat covered her upper lip. "Good, maybe you'll learn something from it," she said, rising to begin gathering personal items into her briefcase. "Never bite the hand that feeds you . . . or stick your dick where it don't belong."

The security guards snickered as Darren walked out of the office between them. He looked over his broad shoulder and gave Renee a hard stare that stayed with her long after the door closed behind them.

By the time noon swung around, Renee wondered if she was going to make it through the day. She was just beat the fuck down mentally, and not having a drink to numb the awareness was really fucking with her.

It didn't help that her supervisor at CancerCure easily accepted her resignation. Renee knew she had made mistakes in the last few weeks that outweighed her successes of the past, but in her opinion she hadn't reached a point of no return.

"To hell with it," she muttered, pulling her car into the parking lot of the massive office building where Jackson worked.

Sitting behind the wheel of her car, she picked up her cell phone. She had two missed calls, one from Jaime and the other from Aria. She decided to call them back after her talk with Jackson.

Renee pulled her keys from the ignition and left her car, sliding her oversized dark shades over her eyes. The summer sun was beating down on her as she hurried across the massive parking lot and inside the building.

"Good afternoon, Mrs. Clinton."

Renee removed her shades and smiled at Saad, sitting behind the security console in the lobby of the building.

"How are you, Saad?" she asked the slender African with a pure smile that made Renee wish she could be that happy.

"I'm excellent. You?"

"As well," she lied as she signed in. "Have a good one."

Renee gave him another smile before she moved around the security desk to the large elevators. Just before the doors opened she glanced over her shoulder and saw Saad turn in his chair to look at her.

She bit her lip as she paused before the elevator. The doors closed in front of her. *He knows. They all know about Jackson and his whore. They knew before I did.*

Renee hitched her head higher, constantly fighting the urge to immerse herself in a liquor bottle. Constantly fighting to deal with her life sober. *I'm not the one who should be ashamed.*

But she was.

She turned and pulled her BlackBerry from the holster on her hip. "Jackson? I'm downstairs in the lobby. I'd rather not run into your pregnant whore," she told him in clipped tones as she slid on her shades and walked out of the building with a brief wave to Saad.

"I'll be right down."

My husband has a baby on the way with another woman.

Pain clutched at her heart as a tear as solitary as she felt raced from beneath her shades and down her cheek. *When is this shit gonna stop hurting so bad? God, please. Please.*

She forced herself not to pace until the doors slid open and Jackson walked through. Renee had to look away from him, hating that her heart still pounded at the sight of his tall and broad frame, square handsome face, and even the slightest glint of silver hairs at his temple.

She loved this man. Still.

He lightly rested his hand on her lower back. She shivered and her nipples tingled.

She wanted this man. Still.

"I thought we could go to lunch and talk," he said, his voice just as comforting and strong as always. "Is that okay?"

Renee nodded and stepped forward to free her body of his touch. "I'll follow you," she said, glad that her shades shielded her eyes.

"Renee, we can ride together."

She shook her head and raised her keys up in answer.

"Okay. Where are you parked?" Jackson asked.

She pointed to her car as she headed in that direction. She already knew his BMW was parked in his reserved parking spot for executives at the front of the building.

In her car, she followed his car, frowning when he got onto the Parkway and headed in the opposite direction. Renee reached for her BlackBerry, dialing him. "Jackson, where are you going?" she asked, turning on her left-turn signal as she switched lanes behind him.

"Home."

Click.

"Home?" she asked in confusion. "He moved?"

In time she knew he was headed to their home in Richmond Hills. *Her* home. It wasn't *their* home anymore.

For the rest of the ride, Renee repeated the Robert Frost quote. "The best way out is always through."

Her getting free from the alcohol, her marriage, and her struggles with her children was "to go through" this season. Fight through it. Survive it. Even learn from it.

"The best way out is through."

Still, she would have given her all to rewind the hands of time and have her little family unit make better decisions so that her "happily ever after" wasn't blown to hell.

Jackson was the love of her life, but he was no longer the man in her life.

She watched his BMW slow down as he pulled up to the security gate. The gate opened and he entered Richmond

Hills. Renee waved to Lucky, the potbellied, red-faced security guard, as she closely followed Jackson inside.

It felt like the old days of them coming home at the same time and then meeting at the door to make love against the wall like the day they'd spent apart had been too much to bear.

From behind the wheel of her car she watched him unfold his tall frame, wave to their next-door neighbor, Mr. Thimble, and jog up the steps to unlock the front door and deactivate the alarm.

It would be so easy to tell him to come home. So easy. Until the repercussions of his affair left her with plenty of baggage to carry. Baggage she didn't have the strength to deal with.

Renee left her vehicle and followed him inside. As soon as she stepped into the foyer, Jackson reached for her body and pulled her close to him. His mouth nuzzled her neck as his hands cupped her buttocks with well-practiced ease.

Renee felt faint. That familiar chemistry was there between them. She shivered and gasped, completely losing her breath as he placed kisses up and down her throat.

"Renee, please, I miss you. Please," he begged, his voice deep. Tortured. Haunting.

Her nipples throbbed. Her clit ached. Her pulse raced. Her heart found renewed strength. In that moment everything was okay.

She hated it.

She couldn't fight it.

Sex had never been their problem. Never.

"Feel how hard my dick is." He pressed her hips forward and circled his hips, grinding the thick and heavy length of him against her belly.

"I missed you so much, Renee," he whispered against her mouth.

She tilted her head back, allowing his mouth to press to her chin hotly. Drops landed on her cheeks and her eyes fluttered open to find Jackson silently crying. She raised her head and kissed the track of his tears.

"I'm so sorry," he whispered into that intimate space between their open mouths.

Renee pressed her mouth to his, silencing him, erasing his words, getting lost in the physical. As his tongue circled hers with a heated familiarity that made her ache, Renee clasped her arms around his neck.

Just this once, she promised herself as Jackson jerked her body up into his arms and carried her up the stairs like she weighed nothing.

Like their problems weighed nothing.

Renee shivered as he pressed her body onto the bed and then rose to tear the front of her shirt in one solid rip before he unbuttoned her pants and worked them down her hips along with the sheer white thongs she wore. Jackson dropped to his knees and used his strong hands to press her knees open wide.

The first stroke of his tongue tortured her as she cried out and pressed her hands to the back of his soft hair. "Jackson," she sighed, closing her eyes.

He moaned as he sucked her throbbing clit into his mouth. Spasms radiated from her core to the center of her belly as she bit her bottom lip.

From that moment on time seemed endless as Jackson used the skill of his tongue to bring her to a climax that made the soles of her feet warm as he licked up every drop of cum.

She thought of all they had built together and even more about what they were losing. The tears flowed as she was caught up in the rapture and flooded with grief.

Jackson moved from her.

She felt the loss of him as she lay in the center of the unmade bed, her body wracked with tears that she couldn't stop to save her life. "Why, Jackson, why?" she asked, speaking the torture she felt in her soul.

The bed dipped under his weight. When he gathered her into his arms, her skin was warmed by his. "I love you, Renee. Forgive me, please, baby, I want to come home. Baby, please, can I come home?"

She cried harder.

Jackson pushed her back down on the bed, wiping her tears with his fingertips as he settled his body on top of hers. She felt the smoothness of his dick slide across her inner thigh.

An image of his dick easing across a pale white thigh flashed. Renee shook her head but the images played in her head like a movie. Jackson's dick wet with juices, surrounded by pink flesh and short blond hairs.

This is my husband. My husband. Mine.

Jackson cupped one of her breasts, teasing the chocolate nipple with first his fingertip and then his tongue.

Renee arched her back, wordlessly urging him to kiss them, suck them, adore them. He complied.

Everything between them in the center of that bed was raw, untamed, emotional, simple yet complex. It was everything and the only thing . . . in that moment.

As Jackson spread her legs with one strong motion of his knee, Renee gave in to the moment. *Just this once.*

Jackson leveled his body above hers and arched his hips. With one solid thrust his dick entered her, filling her, spreading her. Completing her.

"Damn, I missed this," he moaned into her ear. "Move them hips. Give me that pussy."

Renee hated the pleasure she felt with each stroke of his dick. She hated herself.

I'm weak.

She opened her eyes and Jackson's face was directly above hers. He dipped his head down and kissed her lips. "I love you, Renee. You know I love you."

She shook her head and closed her eyes. Renee couldn't look at him. She just couldn't. Her tears came harder.

And Jackson stroked her harder, using his hips to circle deep against her walls as he kissed away her tears.

"Renee," he moaned. "Renee . . ."

She gasped and then bit down on his shoulder with each spasm of her walls against his dick. "Aah," she sighed, holding his sweat-dampened body close before she eased her hands down to grip his ass, urging him deeper inside of her.

He cried out, his body stiffening for just a moment before he moaned against her neck and stroked his dick like a piston. "Renee. Renee," Jackson cried out, the veins in his neck stretched and his face contorted as his nut filled her.

With one final moan and a soft kiss to her lips, Jackson rolled over onto his back, pulling her body with him.

"Damn, that was good."

Renee lay there, sex sore and wondering where all her strength and good sense had gone. As the afternoon sun glared through the sheer curtains of the French doors and onto their nude bodies, Renee listened to the beating of Jackson's heart as he fell asleep.

Sex had been her stress reliever in the past, but giving in to her desires for Jackson just felt like another weight on her shoulders. Another noose around her neck. Another damn complication. Another reason to get fucked up.

She rolled out of bed and padded barefoot and naked to the adjoining bathroom. She stood before the vanity and stared at her reflection. She closed her eyes, sick of the sight of herself. "What the hell was I thinking?" she whispered up to the ceiling.

Renee sat down on the cedar bench in front of her dressing table, not caring that her pussy pressed against the wood. "Fuck," she said harshly, wiping her face with her hands.

When she opened her eyes they fell on her makeup bag. An imaginary light went off above her head and she jumped to her feet to snatch it open. Buried among the designer makeup was a mouthwash bottle filled with tequila. She'd hidden it there weeks ago.

She needed it now.

Her hands shook as she unscrewed the cap and took a healthy swig of the liquor, some of it overflowing and running down the sides of her mouth. It burned going down, but she enjoyed the familiar warmth in her belly. She enjoyed the taste of it against her tongue. She craved the numbness it would bring for a little while at least.

Slumping back down onto the cedar bench, she nursed the liquor and wiped her tears.

"Tomorrow . . . I promise. Tomorrow," she whispered into the rigid opening of the twenty-ounce bottle before she swallowed another healthy dose.

The minutes ticked by and Renee sat there losing track of time and fighting her demons. Renee felt disappointment when the bottle was empty. She wasn't done yet. She wanted—needed—more.

All of it was still there fucking with her. All of it.

When she finally rose and left the bathroom she stumbled just a bit. Jackson was still sprawled naked across the bed, his mouth open as he snored in his sleep. Renee turned away from the scene of her betrayal of her self and her sensibilities.

"Cheating bastard," she muttered, her voice slurring as the liquor took effect.

Renee started to take her foot and kick him in the balls. The thought of that made her chuckle as she reached for her robe at the foot of her bed, sliding it over her nakedness. The room spun slightly and she reached for the edge of the dresser to steady herself. "Damn," she whispered, blinking her eyes rapidly as she left the room and made her way down the stairs to the kitchen.

Brrrrrrng.

She jumped, startled by the sudden and loud ringing of the telephone. Taking a deep steadying breath, she picked up the cordless sitting on the counter. "Yes," she snapped, irritated.

"Mrs. Clinton, you have a guest here at the front gate," Lucky, the security guard, said.

Renee frowned. "Who is it?"

"Inga Brantley."

Renee's eyes popped open wide. Her heart hammered in her chest. She sobered the fuck up.

"She says she's looking for Mr. Clinton," Lucky added.

Renee laughed even though there wasn't shit funny.

"Mrs. Clinton?"

Renee hung up the line. "I know this bitch ain't trying to come to my home looking for my husband. Hell to the motherfucking no."

She snatched up her extra set of keys and stormed out of the front door to pass Jackson's car and hop into the driver's seat of her own. She knew she left skid marks reversing out the drive and zooming toward the front gate area like she was a NASCAR driver.

"I will beat her ass," Renee promised herself. "And then I'm going back to beat Jackson's ass for bringing this bullshit into my life."

Renee was moving full speed and didn't slow down as she neared the gate. She spotted Inga near the booth, her arms flailing as she obviously was trying to force Lucky to let her into the gated community.

Renee watched as the bitch climbed into her car and reversed it to try and drive through the exit gate—which usually stayed open.

Everything from then on moved in slow motion for Renee. All rhyme and reason? Lost.

Hatred burned her soul and fueled her rage. The audacity, she thought. The nerve.

"No. No. No. No. No!" she roared, gripping the steering wheel and slamming her foot down on the accelerator.

Somewhere in the distance she heard voices hollering and a car horn blaring, but her eyes were locked on her target.

As Inga's car veered right and hit the side of the security booth, Renee shook her head for clarity. She slammed on her brakes and jerked her steering wheel to the right. "No. Oh no. What am I doing?" she whispered, just seconds before the sound of metal crashing echoed in the air.

Jessa Bell

I can't help the smile that spreads across my face as I take a sip of wine. Do I regret spilling the secrets of my ex-friends as if I were an opened Pandora's box? No, not at all.

It was me they worried about when truly their own secrets should have been their biggest fears. Hmph. What's done in the dark always . . .

Although it was Jaime's husband that I claimed, I took the greatest joy in exposing Aria. Did she really think she was going to get away with marring my face? Did she really believe that? If so, the bitch is stupid. More than any of them she knows me. And she had to know I wasn't going to let that ride.

I could entertain myself for the night with what I visualized and hoped had happened. When I called Kingston he said nothing, but during his silence I knew he ate up every single, solitary word. I'd bet my last dollar that her bed was as empty as mine tonight. I pouted like I gave a fuck as I took another sip of my wine.

Oh, and poor Jackson was so angry to hear about Renee's little tryst. Who cares if I left out that Darren was gay? I shrugged. Not my problem and neither was the little bastard Jackson had on the way. Wasn't even looking to run into that information.

And Eric. He was the most shocked of them all. Jaime stealing his money? A secret account? He didn't believe me, but I bet he swallowed up the truth from that detective he hired. I still cannot believe he had her car repossessed. Oooh, to be a bird on the limb of the tree over that scene.

Not that I didn't have problems of my own.

In the morning, the delivery truck would arrive to pack me up and move my things back to Richmond Hills. I couldn't wait. Enough pretending. The life I thought I was going to have with Eric was over and this house was a part of that dream.

Taking another sip of wine, I walked across the hard-wood floors to pull back the silk curtains. I gasped and dropped the wineglass. It shattered to the floor as I looked at Eric through the glass. He was standing there, cloaked by the bushes and shadows of night, watching me. My heart pounded. Even though the glass separated us, I stepped back from him in my Louboutins.

"You changed the locks," *he said loudly through the glass, his voice accusing, his eyes blazing.*

I eyed him as I pulled my BlackBerry phone from the snug back pocket of my skinny jeans. His anger was palpable. I dialed his cell number and he answered, his eyes still locked on me.

"Eric, listen, what do you want from me? I gave up a lot to have you and you didn't even though you said you would and so I'm tired of the lies. Tired of being alone. Tired of the bullshit. But you want me to open my mouth wide and let you keep shoveling it in?"

Eric shoved his hands into the pocket of his slacks. "You're not leaving me," *he said.*

My heart dipped in my chest.

"You can't have it all. I gave you the choice. Me or Jaime. Right?" *I pointed to the house.* "Do you live here? Did you move in? Huh? Do you have divorce papers for *me to see? No. Where's my engagement ring? When's our wedding date? Huh?"*

Eric dipped his head down and looked at me hard. *"So you fuck up my marriage and now you just want to move on?"*

That hurt. I fucked up his marriage? "Look, leave me the fuck alone, Eric. *I don't know what kind of games you playing or what kicks you get out of fucking two women, but you need to find some other fool for your fake-ass ménage. Okay?"*

I dropped the curtain and flipped my phone closed.

Seconds later, he began banging on the door.

I tried to ignore him. I tried. But the knocking continued.

It was all so damn juvenile.

Flipping the phone back open, I dialed his cell number again. The knocking stopped.

"Listen, Eric, stop acting so damn crazy," I snapped. *"It's over. You're freaking me out. And if you do not get the hell away from my door I will call the police."*

"I love you, Jessa. Don't leave me. Please. Don't leave me."

This man that I loved was now a stranger to me. This erratic, angry, and emotional being was nothing like the cool, calm, and collected man who was first my friend and then my lover. His behavior confused me.

My heart ached to hear him sounding so pitiful, but I couldn't cave. I couldn't bend. It was over and he had to understand that. I'd played the role of mistress for too long. I've never been happy with second place. Never.

"Jessa," he moaned.

I moved back to the window to pull back the curtain. Eric stood there, his head bent back with his eyes closed, his phone pressed to his ear and his free hand massaging the length of his dick with a fast and furious pace.

"*Eric,*" *I snapped into the phone, knocking on the window.*

He shifted his head to look directly at me, a weird smile spreading across his handsome face as he continued to jack off with a moan deep in the back of his throat. "I miss your pussy, Jessa," he said, flicking his tongue at me like a snake.

My eyes dropped down to his dick.

"*That's right. Watch me,*" *he said, his voice raspy.*

"*Stop it, Eric,*" *I said, looking up and down the street to see if anyone saw him. My eyes widened at car lights moving up the street. "A car is coming."*

"*No one can see me but you,*" *he said, before biting his bottom lip and pulling on his dick harder.*

Had he done this perverted shit before? Standing outside my home, watching me . . . and masturbating? Eric Livewell? An intelligent man who owned his own architectural firm, attended church regularly, and was a respected philanthropist, was getting off in my front yard?

Thoroughly disgusted, I dropped the sheer curtain and reached up to pull the silk curtains closed. "You're sick," I said into the phone.

"*I'm coming,*" *he moaned. "Uhhhmmmmmm."*

What in the hell?

I ended the call and flung my BlackBerry across the floor. I couldn't wait to move back to Richmond Hills. Eric was all about his image and he would never pull these kind of antics in their gated community. Never. I knew that for sure.

I paced the room, my heels echoing throughout the house. The minutes ticked by. No knocking. My cell phone didn't ring.

Shaking my head, I moved back to the window and pulled back the curtains. Relief and disgust filled me. Eric was gone, but his cum was splattered against my windows.

Chapter 11

Aria sat up straight in bed, gasping for air as she escaped from the nightmare. She pulled her knees up and hugged them to her chest as she forced herself to settle down. The sight and sound of Renee's car crashing into that fence had scared the shit out of her that day and still shook her up in her dreams.

She had been driving up to the gate to leave the subdivision when she'd spotted Renee's car barreling at another car and then turning off suddenly and slamming into the towering stone walls flanking the entrance. Aria had slammed on her brakes and barely put her Range Rover into park, to rush over and pull Renee from the car. Everything after that was a blur of ambulances, tow trucks, spectators, and being questioned by the police.

Renee was arrested for a DUI and Jackson had rushed his future baby's mama to the hospital to be examined.

Aria wiped her face with her hands before she climbed out of the pulled-out sofa bed in her office. Sleeping in their bed without Kingston didn't feel right. Living here without him wasn't right.

She glanced at the clock. It was just after midnight and the entire house was quiet. She climbed out of the bed and walked to her desk, easing down into the chair and turning on her computer.

Her muse was gone.

For the past week the words wouldn't come. Her creative energy was shot. *Too much going the fuck on.*

The return of Jessa. Renee's arrest. Her separation from Kingston.

"Humph, I'm lucky *I'm* not hitting the bottle," she muttered and then regretted it.

Renee's drinking wasn't shit to joke about. At all.

She shook her head to free it of the image of Renee's forehead cut and bleeding from going headfirst into the windshield during the collision. Thankfully she was fine physically, but the thought of Renee in jail? She wouldn't even have a bail hearing until Monday.

It completely weakened Aria.

Aria smoothed her hands over her scarf-covered head as she looked out the office door to her empty house. In the past Kingston would miss her warmth and search for her in the house, usually finding her in her office.

She reached for her cordless phone, holding it for endless minutes before she finally turned it over and dialed Kingston's cell number.

For every ring her heart beat a thousand times more.

When it eventually sent her to his voice mail, Aria felt bitter disappointment. She closed her eyes. "Kingston, I . . . I have so much I want to say to you. So much. But you won't answer my calls. You won't reach out to me."

Aria leaned back in her chair, pressing a hand to her stomach to settle the butterflies. "I miss you so much. I love you so much. I'm sorry, baby. If I could let you feel what I'm feeling you would know how sorry I am. Please don't hate me."

She wiped away a tear. "I just wanted to be good enough for you," she admitted truthfully, hanging her head down.

Aria ended the call, sitting the phone back on its base.

What more could she say? How much more could she beg?

She reached out and touched the picture album holding their wedding pictures. She smiled thinking of their first dance at their reception to Donny Hathaway's "A Song for You."

A memory she couldn't forget . . .

———— ∝≫≪∝ ————

"Introducing Mr. and Mrs. Kingston Livewell."

The double doors leading into the ballroom opened. Aria and Kingston walked in holding hands to the thunderous applause of the family and friends among the elegant and romantic decor. Towering floral centerpieces, silk tablecloths, crystals hanging from the ceiling, and a soft lavender lighting with their names rotating around the dimly lit room. Everything was just as they'd planned. A perfect accoutrement to his hand-tailored tuxedo and her strapless trumpet dress with touches of Swarovski crystal at the waist and hem.

"Ready, Mrs. Livewell?" Kingston asked, looking down at her as he pulled her body close to his in the center of the dance floor.

Aria leaned back in his embrace and lightly stroked his cheek, her eyes filled with joy and love. "I've been ready for this since the first day I met you," she whispered up to him.

The smile that spread across his handsome face made her melt as she snuggled her face close to his. The opening moments of "A Song for You" began with the piano solo and Kingston lead their bodies in a back and forth sway. The sounds of the keys was haunting and touching all at once.

"I've been so many places in my life and time," he sang softly into her ear.

Aria nearly swooned as chills covered her body.

"Kingston," she sighed in surprise and pleasure before she pressed a kiss to his cheek.

"But we're alone now and I'm singing this song for you," he sang softly.

And that's how it felt. Like the room of two hundred guests and staff faded and it was just them. A man and his wife, completely lost in each other and the moment.

They held each other tighter as they slowly twirled around the floor together. Everything was there in that moment. Their love. Their passion. Their commitment.

Aria had never loved him more. Never.

It was the best two minutes of her life.

As the song came to an end, Aria held him close, pressing her hands to his lower back. Kingston pressed a row of intimate kisses from just behind her ear and down her neck and back again. "Thank you for being my wife. I will spend every day of our lives together loving you, taking care of you, and being there for you. I swear."

Aria leaned back in his strong embrace without a fear that she wasn't safe. "And I promise you the same, Kingston. I swear."

Brrrnnnggg.

The sound of the phone ringing pulled Aria from her memory. She snatched up the cordless and felt weak at the sight of Kingston's cell number on the phone.

"Hello."

"I don't hate you, Aria."

She pressed the phone closer to her ear.

"But I don't know if I can forgive you."

She shifted troubled eyes to their wedding photo.

"You hurt me. You really fucked me up, Aria. Because there is nothing in this world I wouldn't do for you."

"Even if you knew everything, I mean *everything* about me?" she asked.

"Yes, because your past has nothing to do with the woman I *thought* I married, Aria."

"I miss you, Kingston."

"I miss you, too, but right now I can't even look at you, Aria. This shit hurts. What else are you keeping from me? You don't think that shit runs through my mind?"

"I wanted so badly to be able to give you a baby. I guess I was hoping God would give us an immaculate conception," she admitted softly, shifting her hands over to the other half of the bifold frame to touch the photo of the teddy bear. The photo of their baby was supposed to replace it one day.

"Come on, Columbia University, you're smarter than this shit. We could have gone through fertility treatments or just adopted, Aria. But when you're so busy sneaking and lying and fighting this truth alone like I'm less of a man and can't help you through this? Damn."

Aria wiped her face with her hand.

"I need time, Aria. I need to work this shit through in my head and in my heart."

Aria said nothing. Neither did he.

"And I'm singing this song for you. . . ."

Aria's eyes widened and she pressed the phone closer to her ear.

"I'll call you soon, okay. Bye, Aria."

Click.

Long after the call ended, Aria held on to the fact that Kingston had been listening to their wedding song. Maybe the memories of all the good they'd shared would outweigh the bad and bring him home to her.

Maybe.

The hope she felt made it possible for Aria to climb back into bed, clutching one of Kingston's shirts to her body, and sleep. This time her dreams were filled with visions of her and Kingston and their daughter with his eyes and her face. The dream was so damn good that she was angry when the ringing phone awakened her.

Crawling from the sofa she blindly reached for the cordless phone from the edge of her desk. "Kingston," she said, her voice still thick and heavy with sleep.

"No, this your mama. Call down to the raggedy gate and tell this white boy to let your mama in before he catch one across the cheek."

"Yes, ma'am."

Click.

Aria smiled as she called and gave Lucky the okay. No matter how many times her mother visited she was not feeling the whole gate thing. She called it a reverse prison.

Stretching her tall curvaceous frame quickly, Aria rushed out of the room and down the stairs to yank the door open. Love filled her as her mother bustled past her, playfully swatting her buttocks as she did. Uncle One-Eye followed close behind. Aria knew his rusty dilapidated hooptie was proudly parked in her drive, but she didn't care. Her family was here. She needed them. They knew it. Simple.

"Gal, go put some clothes on," Uncle One-Eye said, his one good eye purposefully diverted from her long legs in the shorts and tank top she'd worn to bed.

By the time she'd showered and come back downstairs dressed in a comfortable print maxi dress, the scent of food was thick in the air. Aria's stomach grumbled. She couldn't remember the last time she'd eaten something.

Aria paused at the foot of the stairs thinking that with all its size and decor, her house was not a home. Not without Kingston.

She made her way into the kitchen and her mother turned

from the stove with a plate piled high with grits, crispy fried slab bacon, corned beef hash, and scrambled eggs. Her favorites. "Sit. Eat."

Uncle One-Eye was already stirring his over easy eggs into his grits. Her people lived in Newark but they brought the country of Hawkinsville, Georgia with them.

"I'm not hungry, Ma," she said, her appetite lost as she looked out the window at Renee's empty home. "I'm worried about my friend."

Heather wiped her hands with a dish towel. "I bet. But she'll be okay."

As soon as Aria had gotten back from the police station checking on Renee she had called her mother and Jaime, trying to find solace after the collapse of Renee's world. And trying not to feel guilty because her friend had turned to alcohol to deal. "I pulled away from our friendship and I didn't have a clue she was drinking like that."

"Yes, but this isn't about you, Aria," Heather said simply.

"Huh?" Aria picked up her fork and stirred the square of margarine into her grits. She side-eyed Uncle One-Eye with his face buried in the plate, but he raised his head to lock his one good eye with her mama's.

Aria frowned.

"Well, baby girl, you can be a little critical of folks, you know," Heather said gently.

What the hell?

"*And* . . . you tend to relate everything back to you. Sometimes it's good, most times it's not."

"I thought you came to comfort me through all this ish I'm going through," Aria grumbled. "I'm already in therapy. I don't need the ghetto Oprah analyzing me."

"What's that saying Mama used to tell us about truth?" Heather asked One-Eye as he chewed away on the hard rind of a slice of bacon.

" 'Truth is the light, don't live in darkness,' " he said, smacking between each word.

Oh, shut up, Uncle One-Eye, Aria thought—thinking it but not daring to say it out loud.

"Amen," Heather said, before scooping a spoonful of grits and egg into her mouth.

"Oh, Lord, so now we in church?" Aria snapped sarcastically.

Her mother and uncle laughed.

"Steppin' on dem toes, Heather. You steppin' on dem toes," Uncle One-Eye warned.

"Time for some mommy-daughter time. Take your plate in the den and watch TV," Heather said.

"Re-up my plate first." He handed the plate to his sister.

Heather quickly gave him a second helping and then guided him by the elbow off his stool and out of the kitchen.

Aria just shook her head at them.

"Now let's get to the really real, baby," Heather said, sliding onto the stool she'd just helped her brother out of.

Aria turned on her own stool to face her mother and the truth.

"You got angry with Renee for her affair. What that had to do with you? You're not Jackson? It wasn't your pussy or your business. Right? Right."

Aria drummed her fingertips against the marble top of the island.

Her mother shifted her eyes to Aria's hand. Hard.

Aria flattened her hand against the marble.

"You've always ridden Kingston so hard when you knew you had secrets of your own."

Aria felt like she was gut punched.

"You were so busy judging him and living life waiting for the other shoe to drop your life wasn't even as good as it could've been." Heather reached over and squeezed her daughter's hands. "Sometimes life is half full."

"It's hard to believe that when I can't have children, Mama," Aria admitted in a husky whisper.

Heather nodded. "I figured that's what it was. You love kids too much not to have one. No career, no goal, or nothing would've stopped my baby from having a baby."

Aria looked upward and blinked her long lashes for what seemed a million times.

"I remember you playing with your dolls and you would mix baby powder and water together and feed them. Bless your heart."

Aria nodded, clearly picturing the doll and the little red and white outfit. "And I'd sew clothes by hand. And take them with me everywhere. And name them. And rock them. And love them," she admitted, with a teary smile.

"And *mother* them," Heather added.

"Oh, Mama, I wanted to be a mother so bad," she admitted out loud for the first time ever. Before, she'd been too busy regretting that she couldn't be a mother to claim what she wanted.

Heather leaned forward to wipe away a tear. "All these beautiful black babies in foster care and waiting to be adopted? You can be a mother anytime you get ready, Aria."

We could have gone through fertility treatments or just adopted, Aria.

Kingston's words haunted her.

"Madonna and Sandra Bullock and Angelina doing what black folks don't want to do," Heather spouted, waving her hand. "All of you wealthy educated black folks letting white people out-do you. Y'all better get up off it."

Aria laughed a little as she looked down at the floor.

"And I'll say this. Doing it with Kingston is beautiful.

Real Cosbylike. But I raised you to be strong enough and smart enough to do it alone." She reached for her plate. No nonsense = Heather Goines.

Aria tilted her head to cast her eyes on her mother. "You did damn good without help."

Heather winked as she bit into a slice of bacon. "You're a testament to the *damn* good job I did."

"Are y'all done?" Uncle One-Eye asked, walking back into the kitchen with his empty plate and glass in his hand.

"I guess so since you don't have the patience God gave a gnat." Heather took the plate and walked to the sink to slide it into the sudsy dishwater she'd made.

Aria tried to finish her food but her appetite was gone and her thoughts filled. Adoption. The journalist in her wanted to know more and she felt that familiar nudge from her muse.

"Well, tell me where there's a bathroom in this big ole house," Uncle One-Eye said, already unbuckling his belt. "Grits run right through me."

Aria dropped her fork and made a face of horror. "Why don't you carry that upstairs. First door on the left," she said, pushing away her plate.

He laughed as he walked back out of the kitchen.

"And remember," Heather hollered behind him over her shoulder. "Drop one, flush one!"

Aria couldn't do shit but laugh.

———— ∞ ————

"Forgiveness, Aria. What does it mean for you, Aria?"

Aria looked across at Dr. Kellee as she wrote notes. Dr. Matheson had set up a consult for her with the therapist and even scheduled a Saturday appointment. "Forgiveness?" she asked, wanting to make the therapist look up at her.

She did, leveling hazel green eyes on her that contrasted

sharply with her deep chocolate complexion. It made Aria feel like the older woman was looking directly into her soul.

"Yes. What does it mean to you?"

"It's an ability to pardon someone for something they did wrong . . . for a mistake," Aria answered, settling into the chair and crossing her legs in the fuchsia ruffled dress she wore.

Dr. Kellee jotted something down again.

Aria released a heavy breath.

"What's irritating you, Aria?" Dr. Kellee asked, just the slightest tinge of her Jamaican accent around the edges of her voice.

"I hate the note-taking during therapy sessions, just throwing that out there," she said.

Dr. Kellee nodded as she closed her journal. "Okay, so let's *refocus* on our purpose here today. What does forgiveness mean to you?" she asked again.

Aria's bronzed face became incredulous. "See, I answered that, but you were so busy jotting down notes that you didn't even hear me."

Dr. Kellee laughed softly as she crossed her healthy legs in the navy pantsuit she wore. "I heard you give me the dictionary definition, Aria. My question is what does it mean to *you?*"

"Oh." Aria looked out the window. "It means letting God. It means moving on and moving past. It means accepting an apology and accepting that people do things that they think is best or in hindsight know is wrong."

Dr. Kellee nodded. "And can you think of anyone whom you need to forgive?"

"I will never forgive Jessa if Dr. Matheson filled you in on that drama," Aria said in a hard voice.

"We can discuss the topic of Jessa Bell another time. Let's refocus."

Aria nodded and scratched her scalp before she shook

her head. "No, I cannot think of anyone that I should forgive.

Dr. Kellee leaned forward. "I'm going to say that in time you will need to forgive your abusers."

Aria looked confused. "I wasn't abused?"

"You were a fifteen-year-old child having sex with grown men who didn't care that you were a child. Who didn't care that you were misguided. Who didn't care that it was a crime to have sex with a minor. Aria. Aria, you were abused."

She shook her head. "No, I'm the one who needs to ask those men for their forgiveness. I stole from them. I seduced them. I wasn't a victim, Dr. Kellee. I was far from a victim," she finished softly.

"You were a child, Aria," she stressed again. "A babe in the woods."

"*I'm* the one who needs to be forgiven."

"Okay, then forgiveness like anything else can go both ways, but I feel it's very important for you to take another look with mature eyes and sensibilities at your past, Aria."

Aria frowned as she continued to shake her head. "No. No, Dr. Kellee, I don't agree at all."

"So if you heard about a man of thirty sleeping with a child of fifteen would you call the police, Aria?" she asked, those eyes seeing through her.

"Of course I would," Aria stressed.

Dr. Kellee widened her eyes as she stared at Aria and nodded as if to say, "Exactly, Aria. Exactly."

Aria released a heavy breath and leaned back in her chair to hold her head in her hand with her elbow pressed into the arm of the chair.

"It's time to take a new look at your past, Aria, because the guilt, shame, and pain you carry with you has built this boundary around you that affects everything you see, you hear, how you react, how you feel. Everything. *Everything.*"

"But I'm not the type to hold other people responsible

for what I did," Aria balked, feeling her irritation rise. "I'm a grown-ass woman—"

"Who is stuck in her past. Who is still the sixteen-year-old crying after her second abortion. Who is still in so much pain," she finished with emphasis and compassion.

Aria had never felt so confused in her life. She'd thought therapy clarified things? *Bullshit.*

Dr. Kellee rose and walked over to a full-length mirror in the corner of her stylish and comfortable office. "Come on over, Aria," she prompted with a wave of her hand.

Between Dr. Matheson, Dr. Kellee, and her mother's ghetto psych 101, Aria felt all "therapied" the hell out. Truly. Still she rose and walked over to the mirror.

Dr. Kellee pressed a marker into her hand and then stepped to the side of Aria. "How many men do you think you have slept with?"

Aria shifted her eyes away from her reflection. "I don't know," she admitted, shaking her head.

"Ten? Twenty? Fifty?"

Aria closed her eyes as shame coursed over her body in waves. "More."

"I want you to draw a line for each man, Aria. Each one you can remember."

Still raw with emotions, Aria raised her hand and began drawing lines of four and then drawing a line across them representing five. And she did it again. And again. And again. Until nearly the entire full length mirror was covered. She had to squat to finish her task. Each line lowered what was left of her self-esteem inch by inch. *Whore. Ho. Slut. Trick. You ain't shit, Aria. Just a big fucking front.*

"What was the scheme your cousin and you did? What did you call it?" Dr. Kellee asked.

"Fuck and pluck."

Dr. Kellee nodded. "Was it right that you robbed those men?"

Aria shook her head, barely seeing her reflection past the thick black lines covering the mirror.

"Of course not. Of course not. Let's officially acknowledge that. But was it right for these men to have sex with a minor? To abuse you. To use you just as much as you thought you were using them."

Aria's eyes dulled at the thought of all the men. Faces she remembered. The many more she'd forgotten. "No," she answered.

Dr. Kellee pressed a board eraser into Aria's hand. "Erase the men. Erase them. Erase them, Aria."

If only it was that easy, she thought, accepting the eraser and cleaning the mirror with circular motions.

"Who do you see?" Dr. Kellee asked.

Aria started to be flip and answer, "Me," but she didn't. "I see an educated, attractive woman."

"Look deeper," Dr. Kellee nudged softly but firmly.

Aria studied her reflection. Her asymmetrical hair that she was growing out, her pretty summer dress and pale gold heels. Her bronzed brown complexion. Her sheer makeup. Her wedding ring.

"Beyond the physical, Aria."

Aria looked into her own eyes in the reflection. They mirrored her soul. Her emotions. Her being. Her fears. Her everything.

Emotions swelled up.

"I am . . . am afraid that I will never outrun my past," she admitted.

"Good. Keep going," Dr. Kellee urged, stepping back from the mirror and Aria's moment in time.

Aria opened and closed her hands at her sides. "I am scared that I am still *that* person."

"Yes."

"I am afraid to fail."

"Yes, Aria. Speak what you feel," Dr Kellee urged from somewhere in the distance, her voice an urgent whisper.

"I don't feel I deserve to be loved." Her lip quivered and she bit it deeply as her shoulders slumped under the truth of her words.

"Why, Aria? Why?"

"I hate myself," she admitted with an emotional gasp as she covered her mouth with her quivering hands. Her knees weakened and she stumbled back.

Dr. Kellee stepped forward and caught her, pushing her upright. "Stand up, Aria," she urged. "Stand up."

Aria did, wrapping her arms around herself, her emotions running on high. She felt drained.

"They took from you, from your foundation. Just as much as you took from them." Dr. Kellee stepped forward and embraced Aria tightly, massaging her back like a true nurturer.

"We will work on rebuilding that foundation, Aria. You and I. Okay?"

Aria nodded, glad for the comfort, the compassion, and the support. Even glad for the truth. A little piece of her felt just a tiny bit freer.

"We will work through it all so that you can forgive the most important person of all in this, Aria," she said, rocking her back and forth like she was soothing a baby.

She looked up over Dr. Kellee's rounded shoulder, knowing the answer before she even said it.

"You, Aria. You have to forgive and love yourself."

Chapter 12

The ties binding Jaime felt more restrictive than all of the years with Eric. She felt strangled by her mother's whims and weighed down by her father's restrictions. She felt like a child.

The last week had been filled with soirees, charity functions, and the like. Jaime was tired of smiling and nodding. Tired of endless chatter. Tired of being her mother's puppet.

But what choice did she have?

Money makes the world go around and her parents held the purse strings. It was them or Eric. Either way she wasn't in charge of her own life.

She raked her manicured fingers through the layers of her hair and then straightened the row of cultured pearls she wore around her neck. The jewelry perfectly suited the pink short-sleeve cardigan she wore over a crisp white Ann Taylor sheath dress. Soft perfume. Neutral makeup. Kitten heels.

The perfect socialite costume.

"Hmph." Jaime bit off a bit of her pale pink lip gloss as she studied herself.

This woman in the mirror was Jamison "Goody-Two-Shoes" Pine who became Jaime "Mrs. Stepford Wife" Livewell. Neither one fit her.

Turning away from the reflection, Jaime grabbed her Coach straw purse and keys, leaving her bedroom. It was time to go and get some Jesus, and Virginia Osten-Pine didn't like to be late. It was the first time Jaime would walk into a church since she'd left Eric.

And with everything going on among their circle of friends, Jaime could honestly say she needed to talk long and hard to God.

Her kitten heels clicked against the floor as she made her way out the front door. She paused and looked up and down the quiet street. She hated that she felt like she was being watched. Her life tracked. Her movements monitored. Eric was controlling her life from a distance by fear of her own actions.

She hated it.

As Jaime made her way to the Honda Accord, she spotted Lucas walking along the side of his house into his backyard. He turned, spotted her, and instantly turned away. No wave. No friendly smile. Nothing.

It had been that way since that night in her car. The night she'd let hurt pride and horniness push her into a one-night stand with her neighbor. They hadn't exchanged words or even a direct look since that night.

I wanted to take you out to dinner and get to know you better. I wanted to build on the attraction I had for you. My plan damn sure wasn't to screw you in a parking lot, but I took what you *offered."*

"Lucas," she called out, following an impulse, walking across her lawn to reach his.

He stopped and looked at her over his shoulder. She gave him a hesitant smile and a wave.

His round, boyishly handsome face showed his surprise for a quick second before he threw his hand up quickly and then continued on his way.

She started to go behind him but stopped herself, instead turning to walk to the car. She eyed the cars parked or passing by on the street. She hadn't seen Eric in days but he'd called. He'd taunted her. He'd tried to lure her to come back with threats and bullying tactics.

No romance. No words of apology. No wooing.

Just get your slave behind back to the plantation. That's how it felt.

Jaime had even considered it for a hot second, but good sense prevailed and she was moving on. "I can't go back," she said, climbing into the car and then reversing down the drive. "I'm not going back."

If Eric was having her followed then she was leading her shadows straight to the doors of church. She even listened to gospel music to help her get her mind focused.

To not think too heavily on Eric. Or Jessa. Or Lucas. Or . . . or . . . Renee.

She was even glad to pull the Honda into the fenced parking of the Church of Distinction. As soon as she'd grabbed her embossed, leather-bound Bible and stepped out of the car she saw her mother walking away from a crowd to approach her in a peach silk suit with matching shoes, purse, and wide-brimmed hat. Pulling from endless years of fronting, Jaime plastered her pageant smile on her face. "Morning, Mother," she said, hating that she wondered if her outfit would get a thumbs-up.

It didn't.

"Jaime, you really should have on hosiery."

"Of course," Jaime answered, feeling twelve years old and ready to scream and throw something like a two-year-old might.

"And the car could use a good washing, Jamison."

"I'll have it detailed first thing tomorrow," she replied, her voice monotone.

"I hope you will heed everything we said about your friendship with Renee," her mother said, as they crossed the parking lot.

Jaime's anger sparked and she literally had to bite her

bottom lip to stop herself from telling her own mother— on church grounds—to shut the hell up.

"Remember, Jaime, people think birds of feather flock together. Do you understand that a woman's reputation is everything?"

She eyed her mother and damn near rubbed her hands raw.

See, this shit right here is not working, Jaime thought, the whole time she gave her mother a smile more fake than gold-plated jewelry sold at one of those dollar stores.

"Hi, Baby Girl," her father said, snapping his cell phone closed before giving her a close hug and then holding her close to his side with one solid arm around her shoulders.

"Eric denied the settlement offer," he said to her as they walked toward the front of the large brick church that was just as much a high-society gathering as a place of worship.

"What settlement offer?" she asked, wishing she had her shades to block the sun from her eyes.

"The attorney made a reasonable offer to your husband—"

Jaime paused in her steps. "But I haven't spoken to an attorney," she protested, looking at her father's profile.

"Oh, there's no need," he scoffed, waving his free hand dismissively. "You let me and Cole Jennings take care of it."

What the fuck? Jaime reached up and squeezed the bridge of her nose and forced herself to count to ten— three times.

Do something, Jaime. Say something.

"Daddy, can I use your cell phone?" she asked. "I left mine home and I need to check on something really quickly."

I'll just add lying on church grounds to my other sins.

He handed her the phone and Jaime walked away from

him, scrolled to recent calls, and dialed back the last number on the list.

"Yes, Mr. Pine."

Jaime paused at the deep voice. A brotha. "Actually, this is his daughter, Jamison. Are you Cole Jennings . . . my attorney," she asked, glancing over her shoulder to be sure her father was preoccupied.

"Yes, I am. I wasn't expecting to speak to you today."

Jaime smirked. "You probably weren't expecting to speak to me at all," she quipped.

He chuckled.

"Listen, I need you to e-mail me a settlement arrangement and let me approve them or make suggestions . . . because no one knows what I want or deserve like me."

"Okay, anything else?"

Jaime felt stronger, mentally and physically. *Life is what you make it, Jaime, so fuck it; make it about you.*

"Yes, from now on my father is out of my business and out of the loop," she told him, feeling like she could tear off her going-to-church cardigan and burn it.

"Should I send you my bill then?"

Jaime arched a brow. "No," she stressed. "Now, my degree isn't pre-law *but*—true or not true—your expenses can be covered as part of the settlement arrangement?"

He sighed. Jaime's frown deepened.

"Your father and I have a lot of business ties outside of your divorce matter. Let me speak to him first and then—"

"Oh hell no," Jaime snapped.

"Oh my word."

She whirled around as an older woman made a face and hurried past her. "Sorry," she said even though she turned her back on the woman.

"Mrs. Livewell, let's make an appointment for you and your father to come in to my office tomorrow morning?" he offered.

Jaime rolled her eyes. "I'll call you back," she said, watching her father motioning to her that it was time to go inside.

She snapped the phone closed and made her way to them. "Bathroom break. I'll see you inside," she said, turning to walk up the driveway and into the side entrance to the church.

Once she married Eric she attended his church, but she was baptized and reared in the Church of Distinction. The minister of the last three years was new to her but the church was not. She was grateful for the air-conditioning as she made her way down the stairs to the basement and turned the corner leading to the ladies' room.

The sounds of the organ music filled the church as Jaime used the facilities and then washed her hands. She studied her reflection in the mirror.

Not to fluff her hair or arrange her clothing or even to check her makeup.

"Who are you?" she asked her reflection softly, tapping her hand against the vanity as she crossed one slender ankle over the other.

Her parents' daughter. Eric's wife. Pleasure's trick. Jessa's fool. Lucas's one-night stand. And now her parents' charity case.

Every step of the time line of her life was about somebody else. She'd thought her "relationship" with Pleasure was empowering her when in truth she'd let his dick whip her into submission. She paid but *he* controlled.

Jaime left the restroom and climbed the stairs to the main church. She joined the line of people entering the church, seeing her mother turned around in the pew and looking for her. She was just sitting down next to her mother when her cell phone vibrated.

Jaime looked down inside her pocketbook as she opened an incoming text. The sight of a glistening wet and hard as steel dick made her jump in her seat.

Several people looked around at her. She ignored them, looking back down in her purse at the words below the pic.

Cum and get it?

Pleasure.

Sunday was usually their day and she would work him and his dick for every red cent she paid him.

Even as her pussy throbbed and she crossed her legs to press down on it, she snapped the phone closed, resolving to kick her addiction. She hadn't called him since he left her pussy high and dry in the strip club that night.

She paid, but he controlled.

Jaime knew that in all aspects of her life, she had to get like Janet and get some more control.

ASAP.

Richmond Hills's Architectural and Landscaping Committee didn't play around. Nothing about the stately entrance showed evidence that Renee had crashed into the front exit gate. Everything was back in place. The gate repaired. The once-missing landscape replaced. And she knew the bill had been promptly sent to Renee and if she'd failed to pay the bill, the fines would accrue, and the committee had every right to place a levy against her home.

As Jaime pulled up to the control box and entered her passcode, she made a mental note to talk to Aria about that.

"I'm sorry, Mrs. Hall, but your passcode no longer works," Lucky said through the window of the security booth.

I really hate Eric, she thought. "Of course. I'm sorry.

Just call Mrs. Livewell," she said in an authoritative tone, slightly embarrassed.

"Right away."

Soon the gates of Richmond Hills opened and Jaime cruised through, ignoring Lucky's wave. She still had plenty bougie in her.

As she drove to Aria and Kingston's home she avoided looking at her old house or Jessa Bell's up the street. Now her husband and friend could really get it on. They did as much under everyone's noses.

Aria walked out onto the porch as Jaime parked in the drive behind her SUV. "Oh Lord, Pollyanna's back," she teased.

Jaime smiled. "You can stick these pearls where the sun don't shine on you."

Aria made a playful face. "Looks like you pulled the stick out of your dark spot," she said. "The old Jaime would've got offended and made a prune face."

She shrugged. "Just trying to get my ish together, as you would say."

"Aren't we all," Aria said sadly.

"Kingston is still at his parents'?" Jaime asked.

Aria nodded and leaned her back against the column. "Yup. He is so mad at me."

"Because the news didn't come from you," Jaime said, turning her eyes up the street to lock on Jessa's home. "It was your business to tell. Not hers."

"Trust and believe that restraining order is the ONLY thing keeping me from digging in that ass," Aria said.

Jaime thought back to the day Jessa had sent the message and the hell they all went through waiting and wanting to know which husband had strayed with their friend. Jaime never wanted to feel like that again. Lost in the sauce and mad confused. The waiting game was hell.

And then to find out it was she that had been betrayed.

"All of this is Jessa Bell's fault," Jaime said, the anger in her voice barely contained.

"Don't get me wrong. I hate the bitch. But we created our own secrets. Told our own lies. We gave her the power to destroy us."

Jaime looked up at Aria, incredulous. "Because she was our friend, Aria. We trusted a friend."

They both looked back down the street at Jessa's house. "I know Mark is spinning in his grave," Aria said.

"Yeah, I bet," Jaime agreed softly.

They fell silent for a moment. Jaime knew her thoughts were on the man who passed on way too soon but was a fun, friendly, and loyal presence during his time. A man who didn't deserve for his legacy to be marred by a whoring widow.

"Think Eric is in there?" Jaime asked.

"Do you care?" Aria countered.

She really didn't. "That man put me through hell and I helped him by sitting there taking it, pretending that we were fine. Hell, better than fine."

"We all did some pretending, sugar," Aria said in a Southern drawl that was completely random.

The two friends looked at each other and then laughed.

But Jaime's eyes were drawn back to Jessa's house. "It just doesn't feel right that she gets to live here and I'm in some second-rate town house," Jaime admitted, surprised by her own truthfulness. "What nerve does she have— after everything she put us all through—to move back."

"Man, Jessa Bell is straight crazy," Aria said, making a fist. "And I have all the psych meds she needs in this left and this right."

Jaime shook her head. "No, I'm serious. What the hell is she thinking?" she asked, even as she moved down the steps.

"Jaime. Hello, Jaime. Where are you going?" Aria called out behind her.

"To have the conversation Jessa and I should have had a long time ago," she said over her shoulder with her eyes locked on Jessa's door.

The appropriate thing to do was to continue to ignore her. Say nothing. Tilt her head up high and walk past her like she never existed.

Fuck that.

Jaime's steps paused as Jessa's front door opened before she even reached it. *Still playing games,* she thought, continuing up the walkway to stand before the door.

She looked over her shoulder at Aria standing in the middle of the street, looking like one wrong move and she would say to hell with the restraining order. Jaime closed the door as she stepped inside the foyer.

"I'm in the living room," Jessa called out.

Jaime headed that way, noticing that Jessa's home was back to being fully furnished. *The bitch and whoever she hired has been busy.*

Jessa was just lounging on the sofa in front of the windows. She was dressed in an all-white strapless jumpsuit, her ebony hair loosely twisted atop her head, a glass of wine in her hand.

Even in such casual attire, with her face free of makeup, the bitch was stunning.

"I was watching you while you both were watching my home," Jessa said, her slanted ebony eyes locked on Jaime. "Your friend looks ready to pounce . . . again."

"You used to be our friend but that . . . was that . . . an act?" Jaime asked, leaning against the wall, her head cocked to the side as she looked at this woman who deserved a beatdown to top all beatdowns.

"Listen, Jaime, I regret getting involved with Eric," she said. "Is that what you want to hear?"

Jaime laughed bitterly. "Bitch, please. An apology cannot erase the miles you put on my husband's dick."

Jessa pressed her elbows into the cushions of the chair

and then her chin in her hands. "You sound so possessive? If you're here to let me know that you two have reconciled I'm tickled pink for you."

Jaime crossed her arms over her chest as she strolled farther into the room. "Is *my* husband here? I wouldn't want to intrude."

"Listen, Jaime, Eric is not welcome here so please don't stalk my house looking for *your* husband," Jessa drawled, crossing her legs at the ankle.

Jaime arched a brow as she eyed her. Hard. "You're so fucking carefree about wrecking lives. So blasé about your bullshit. Nothing but a pretty package wrapped around a pile of bullshit and spite."

Jessa's eyes flashed. "Don't judge me. You don't know me."

"You're damn right, I don't. I never did. We never did and I doubt Mark did either," Jaime said coldly, coming to stand over Jessa's sitting figure.

"Low blow, Jaime," Jessa said in a voice barely above a whisper.

"Fucking my husband. Taunting your friends with your affair. Revealing secrets we told you as a friend. Those aren't low blows?" Jaime asked, ticking each offense off on her manicured fingers.

"What do you want from me? Why are you here?" Jessa asked, moving to rise to her feet in front of Jaime.

Jaime didn't back down. "To look your pathetic ass in the face and tell you that it is low class of you to move back into Richmond Hills after the stunts you pulled. Low class and ignorant."

Jessa's eyes became amused. "Not as upstanding as fucking a stripper, huh?"

Jaime swung.

WHAP.

Her hand landed solidly against Jessa's cheek, sending her flying back down onto the sofa. She moved to get up and Jaime used both her hands to shove her back down before she picked up the goblet of wine and tossed it in Jessa's face with a wickedly loud splash.

Jessa cried out dramatically, wiping the liquor from her face with trembling hands. "Get the hell out of my house!" she screeched.

Jaime stepped back to survey her handiwork. She didn't know she had it in her. Aria would've snatched her bald and dotted both her eyes, but Jaime thought she didn't do half bad considering she'd never gotten into a fight before.

"You're dead to us, Jessa," she said.

Jessa laughed. "I'm not dead to Eric, though. Please tell your husband to leave me the hell alone," she snapped.

Jaime shrugged. "Who cares, bitch," she said.

Jesse snatched her cell phone up from the chair. "Your husband. That's who."

You have thirty saved messages.

Jaime's eyes dropped to the BlackBerry in Jessa's hand. "They're all from your husband just this week."

Beep.

"Jessa . . . Jessa pick up. I need you. Don't do this to me. Don't leave me, baby."

Jaime stiffened at the sound of his voice. It was the same hushed and urgent tones he'd used when he ordered her to do his sexual bidding. It gave her the creeps.

Message after message after message from just that morning played, each becoming more disturbing than the last.

Beep.

"Jessa, I miss the feel of your mouth on my dick. Come get this dick. Don't make me jack off . . . unless you want to watch again."

Jaime's frown deepened as she played one message where he was crying. No words. Just tears. What the hell?

Beep.

"Uh . . . I just jacked this dick. Come and suck up my cum."

"Okay, that's enough," Jaime said.

Jessa shrugged as she exited her voice mail box. "I don't want the pervert. I'm sick of him stalking me. Handle it, please."

"*You* handle it," Jaime said, her voice hard. "You started it, now finish it."

With one last glare and then a shake of her head that was filled with pity, Jaime turned and walked back out of Jessa's life.

Aria met her in the street. "What did she say? Did she apologize? Did you slap her? You shoulda slapped her ass. Is there a knot on her head from me tossing that phone at her slick ass? Ooh, I want to beat that bitch ass soooooooooo bad! Oooh!"

Jaime actually laughed at the animation in Aria's voice. "She thinks Eric and I are back together."

Aria frowned. "She's dumb."

"I let her think that."

"You're dumb, too."

Jaime smiled, knowing Aria was just being Aria. "I wanted to know what was going on with them. That perverted bastard wants everything back to the way it was. Degrading me in private and fucking Jessa on the low. Ugh. Ew. She played these voice mails he left on her phone. Just. Done. Just. So. Done."

"Maybe he gets off like that."

They turned and walked up the middle of the empty street together. "I just want to be free and he's making it so hard while he's crying like a bitch and begging his mistress to take him back."

"Instead of taking it so hard, why don't you give it just as hard."

They came to stand on the sidewalk in front of Aria's house. Jaime eyed her.

"Life is all about the scales," Aria said, moving her hands up and down, palms up to the blue skies.

"Tip them in my favor, huh?" Jaime asked, biting the corner of her bottom lip.

Aria arched her brow. "And with nothing but the truth."

Jaime reached in her Vuitton bag for her cell phone and dialed Eric's number.

It rang once.

"Have you come to your senses?"

Jaime felt repulsed, thinking of the voice mails. "Yes, the night I left you," she snapped, turning away slightly as Aria gave her some privacy by walking up onto her porch.

"Listen, let's meet and talk about getting our marriage back on track."

Jaime took a deep breath, shaking her head as she paced. "No, Eric, what we need to get straight is our divorce."

"If you think I'm going to front your lifestyle while you're lying up with strippers your ass is crazy. It's simple, Jaime, get a job or get your ass back home. Matter of fact, have your ass home today. It's enough of this."

Jaime froze and licked her lips as her eyes squinted like a tiger locking on its prey: the house that used to be her home. "No, motherfucker, your ass is crazy and you're right this shit ends today. You are forcing my hand."

She thought about walking over to the house but a flash of their last meeting ending with bruises on her neck kept her locked where she was.

"Tomorrow you will receive another settlement offer from my attorney and you will sign it, Eric."

He laughed.

Jaime swallowed back her nerves. "If you don't then I will release the photos I took of my neck after you assaulted me when I confronted you about your mistress. I can imagine what your parents, your business associates, and your church family will have to say."

He said nothing. Image was everything to him. Everything.

"Now, picture me revealing that weird sex you liked to have, Mr. Whip It Good," she spat, her eyes blazing. Enough was enough.

Still, he said nothing.

"And then we'll top it all off with those creepy voice mails you left on your mistress's phone. The way she feels about you right now? I'll subpoena that bitch and dare her to catch a perjury charge for your ass."

Jaime felt stronger with each word. "Adultery and abuse of the woman who gave up a career to stay home and lick your boots. Bullshit. I gave up everything for you. Everything. I'm far from perfect, but I didn't deserve to be degraded, to be mistreated. Then for you to tell me that I'm ass out on the street with nothing. It's not happening, Eric."

She heard nothing but his slow and steady breathing into the phone. His silence angered her.

Jaime looked down at her feet and shook her head. "You can sign the settlement agreement or picture me taking you for half of everything, Eric. Your pension, stocks, real estate properties. Everything."

"Don't play this game, Jaime. You'll lose."

"Wrong," she said, looking up to eye the house again. "I've had these cards in my hands all along and didn't want to play them, but enough is enough. It's over, Eric. Our marriage is so over."

"Jaime—"

"Sign the fucking papers, Eric," she snapped coldly, before ending the call.

Aria came down the stairs and pulled Jaime into a tight sisterly embrace.

In that moment it felt damn good to have a friend.

Chapter 13

"I'm in jail. How did I get here?"

Renee knew the answer to that question literally. The police had hauled her to the city jail after she'd started to drive her car into Inga's in a drunken rage and then crashed it into the wall surrounding the entrance to Richmond Hills.

But how did my life get here? To this *point,* she wondered, looking around the small barren cell as she sat on the metal bench attached to the wall. It was little more than a metal slab with a thin mattress. She looked out between the bars but saw nothing beyond her prison.

She shifted her eyes over when her cell mate began to moan from her spot huddled in a ball on the opposite bunk. This was Renee's first jail experience, but she knew the overly thin girl was going through withdrawal from some drug she was hooked on.

Renee released a heavy breath and crossed her arms over her chest as she rested her head against the wall. One of the jailers had already told her she was in there for the weekend until her bail hearing sometime Monday.

She hated it. The smell of it. The dreary sight of it. All of it.

But she knew she deserved nothing less.

She flinched as the sound of the metal crashing against

the walls replayed in her head. The feel of her head crashing into the glass replayed. She would never forget it.

"I could have killed her," Renee whispered to herself. "Oh my God, I could have taken a life. Her and her baby's life."

She was utterly ashamed of herself. Her drinking. Her anger. Her life.

Everything had spiraled horribly out of control because she'd put all of her control and common sense aside for alcohol.

Even now her mouth watered at the thought of alcohol. Her addiction cried out for it.

Her cell mate rolled over and raised her head just enough to vomit. Renee turned her head from the sight of it and held her breath from the smell as she moved her feet to keep the liquidly vomit from running close to her bare feet.

Arrested for driving under the influence in nothing but a robe and in a cell with a junkie? Renee knew her life had truly hit bottom.

She rose to her feet, her body aching everywhere as she moved to the bars keeping them locked in their cells like animals in cages. "Jailer," she called out, her hand lightly gripping the bars.

"Pssst."

Renee looked over at the cell across from her. A big butch-looking bitch with shoulders just as broad as Jackson's made a V with her fingers and then licked between them. "Looking good in that robe," she said, her eyes burning holes.

Renee looked down and saw that her robe was slightly ajar and her cleavage showing. Frowning in disgust, Renee tightened her robe. "Jailer," she called again.

"Don't knock it 'til you try it, fish," her admirer said.

Renee fought her tears and her fears.

"Wish you was in my cell, fish, I'll bang that pussy real good."

"Who's calling me?" the jailer called down the long row separating the cells of the city prison.

"Me. Mrs. Clinton," Renee called down between the bars.

A short and plump woman with braids walked up in her uniform. "Yes," she asked, not at all sounding like she was in the mood to be bothered.

"Um, she's throwing up," Renee said, pointing to her cell mate shivering on the floor. "I think she needs medical attention."

"That ain't what she needs," her admirer called over.

Several female prisoners laughed from the cells.

The jailer looked past Renee to the woman on the floor. "I'll get someone in to clean it," she said, turning away.

"Um, excuse me, but can I have something to change into?" she asked in a whisper.

"When you get transferred to Clinton they'll give you a uniform," she said, but she cut her eyes over to the other cell, seeing the butch eyeing the imprint of Renee's body through the thin silk. "But I'll bring you a blanket."

"Thank you," Renee said, moving back deeper into her cell.

"You haven't made a call yet, have you?"

Renee shook her head as she reclaimed her seat on the bench. "I don't have anyone to call," she said.

The jailer shrugged and walked away.

Call who? Jackson? And be hurt and devastated if he was angry that she even thought about doing something that would kill his unborn child? She couldn't handle that.

Aria? And say what? *I'm still here in jail.*

Her kids? Renee shook her head, biting her bottom lip. She refused to have her children accepting collect calls from a jail. She refused to integrate that into their lives and their knowledge base.

Renee absolutely refused.

"Pssst. Fish. Open your legs and just let me eyeball that pussy."

Renee ignored her and silently said a Hallelujah and thank God they didn't share cells. She used to work out regularly and was pretty strong, but Renee wasn't sure she could take that big bitch.

What if I don't get out for weeks? Months? Years?

That thought weakened her to her core.

Jackson and his bullshit wasn't worth jail time. Who would be a mother to her children while she languished away in a prison?

What effect will my shit have on them? What have I done to my children? What will they face because of me?

Renee dropped her head into her hands. "Forgive me," she begged, her tears wetting her hands.

The nights in the jail were no better. The darkness seemed to hold secrets and encourage fears.

Renee tried her best to find comfort on the thin, plastic-covered mattress on the bench and some warmth under the coarse, plain-smelling blanket that scratched her skin more than it comforted her.

The laughter of the jailers filtered to their cells, mingling in the air with the moans and vomiting of her cell mate, the off-key singing of someone from a distant cell, and the grunts of the dyke across from her as she openly masturbated.

All of that coupled with her craving for a drink kept sleep from her.

Renee tried her very best to close her eyes as she used the side of her arms as a makeshift pillow.

"I'm so cold. It's so cold."

Renee raised her head to look over at the shadow of her

cell mate on the opposite bunk. Her voice was weak and shaky. It scared her.

Flinging back her cover, Renee sat up. "Are you okay?" she asked.

"I'm so cold. And it hurts. It hurts so bad."

Renee gathered up her blanket and moved to lay it across the woman's thin figure on the mat. The scent of shit and vomit and unwashed hair rose up. Renee gagged.

She rose to her feet and moved back to the bars. "Jailer," she called out, resting her head against the bars.

"Psst, fish."

"Shut the hell up," Renee snapped. "No, I do not want you to eat my pussy. No, I do not care how good my ass and titties look in this robe. No, I'm not gay, can't be turned gay, and wouldn't choose you if I was gay . . . so get the fuck over it!"

"That's what they all say."

Renee didn't know if she had just made a prison enemy or turned the dyke on even more.

A tall and thin jailer walked up to her cell. "Yes?"

"Can I get another blanket?" she asked.

She shook her head. "We're at full capacity so we're all out."

Renee didn't even put up a fight as she turned and walked back to sit on the bench.

"You can take your blanket back. I don't need both," came the muffled reply from beneath the blanket.

Renee shook her head. "I'll be fine."

The thin and weak laugh surprised her. "Nobody ever gave me shit in life so thank you."

"No problem."

The off-key serenade continued into the silence. "*If you don't know me by now . . .*"

"I really wish she would shut the fuck up," her cell mate said suddenly, her voice barely audible beneath the blankets.

Renee laughed.

"*You will never never never know me . . .*"

Renee laughed harder.

Her cell mate moved the covers off her face. "Shit, I stink. I'm choking my damn self under this cover," she joked.

Renee smiled, looking down at the thin and sallow face in the little bit of light from the hall. "How can you crack jokes at a time like this?" she asked.

"Time like what? Sheeit. This bougie shit is heaven compared to other city jails like Newark," she said. "Besides I'm home. I been in and out of jails since I was thirteen."

Renee opened her mouth but then closed it.

"Because it's better being in jail than bein' beat and raped by your own fucking father," she said, answering Renee's unspoken question.

Renee frowned in the darkness. "What'd you do to get locked up?"

"I shoplift a lot and obviously I either ain't good at it or I really do love these three hots and a cot because I get caught a lot." She laughed again. "But this time my old man and me was arguing in the parking lot at the mall and I missed and stabbed him when he hit me."

Missed and stabbed him? What the hell?

"Don't worry, I ain't violent or nothing," she said, shifting to sit her frail frame up on the mat.

No, you're not violent. You just miss and stab people. Yeah. Okay.

"He fought me like a dog in the street over which store to boost from," she said. "I done tricked to help get that nigga high and he was beating on me and . . . and it reminded me of my sperm donor and all the ass cuttings I took from *his* no-good ass. No not more. Not for me."

Renee realized she couldn't judge her. She snapped and

thought about driving headfirst into the car of her husband's pregnant mistress.

They both were addicts.

They both were in jail.

Who was she to judge?

"I bet a lot of women locked up behind some man's bullshit, just like me and you," Renee admitted, revealing that and nothing more. The last thing she needed was a jailhouse confession coming back to haunt her.

"Hmph. But I'll tell anybody not to let it get you to that point. You know?" she asked, bending over suddenly.

Renee turned her head, thinking she was about to vomit again.

Her cell mate swallowed hard. "I been getting high since I was sixteen. That's fifteen fucking years."

Renee's mouth fell open. The woman looked more like she was fifty-one than thirty-one.

"And you know what? Not one shot or sniff or lick of dope made me forget that shit my Daddy did to me. Trust me, I tried to fuck up on enough dope to forget my name was Basheera but it never worked. Never."

Renee thought of her own love of alcohol. She'd gone from a casual drinker to an alcoholic because she couldn't handle life. She didn't want to handle it. She'd come to a fork in the road and chosen the easy way out and it never worked. Never.

"Will y'all shut the fuck up over there?"

"Will you suck a dick and call it Rick?" Basheera called back even as she shivered and pulled the cover around her small frame.

Renee dropped her head in her hands and smiled before she fell silent, lost in her thoughts, her regrets, and her prayers.

Renee ran her hands through her hair, feeling the dry texture of her natural curls as she paced the short length of her cell. She breathed deeply, trying to beat off the desire to taste alcohol. She craved it and the deep sleep she would slip into because of it.

Renee sighed, turning to look over her shoulder at Basheera's empty bed. Sometime late last night they'd finally transferred her to a hospital for medication to deal with her withdrawal. Renee actually missed the communication from someone she probably would have never fraternized with on the outside.

"Good Lord, I'm even thinking like a lifelong criminal," she muttered, pulling her robe tighter around her frame as her admirer across the hall turned in her sleep.

What is going to happen to me? she wondered as she looked around the cell, hating that it had already become familiar to her in a way.

Renee glanced across the cell and then down at the shiny metal commode in the corner. With the lascivious lesbian always peering into her cell like a Macy's window display during the Christmas season, Renee had gotten quite good at holding her pee. She hurried to fling up her robe and squat over the commode, hating how the sound of her urine echoed inside the bowl. She rolled her eyes heavenward as she finished.

"I can give you a real golden shower."

Renee gladly flushed to mask the harassment from across the hall. *Fucking pervert,* Renee thought as she washed her hands. Not because of her sexual orientation but her relentless pursuit.

"Clinton. You have a visitor," a male jailer said at the door.

Renee looked up at the stained mirror, her curiosity clear in the depths of her eyes. Her eyes took in everything. The puffiness of her face from her tears. The darkness around her eyes from stress and lack of sleep. The wrinkled and disheveled state of her robe. The lopsided lean of her hair from sleeping on that side.

She looked absolutely nothing like Renee Clinton. Nothing at all.

"Let's go, Clinton," the jailer said, his voice hard.

She quickly rinsed her face and tightened the belt of her robe as she made her way to a small amount of freedom from her cell.

"One of the jailers called your husband and asked him to bring you a change of clothes," the jailer said as he signaled up the hall for the cell to be unlocked.

Ka-dang!

The door slid open slowly with an almost rusted-sounding grind.

Jackson. Renee paused momentarily before she stepped out of the cell for the first time in three days.

Physically? Barely washed.

Spiritually? Not cleansed.

Mentally? Totally undone.

She barely listened as the jailer explained the visiting procedure to her and how after a search of the garments they would bring the change of clothing to her cell.

As they waited for the heavy door at the end of the hall to open, Renee spotted Jackson sitting at a small table in a nice-sized room. He looked one the better than she did.

Did he comfort Inga as I lay in a jail cell?

And then she hated that even now jealousy ruled her.

Renee thought about the last time they'd been together.

And as good as it had felt to have Jackson's dick buried inside of her again, Renee had felt relief when he'd eased every delicious and traitorous inch out. *We weren't ready for sex. As much as I wanted it. Enjoyed it. Needed it. We weren't ready,* she admitted to herself.

Renee eyed him as she made her way to his table. Some of the hair on his head was silver. The squareness of his shoulder had rounded just a bit and his middle was softer, but Renee knew that she would have loved this man and stayed with this man until his hair was snow white and his body the epitome of old age. And she would have felt the same way as she did when she'd sworn to be his wife. Until death. Not until an affair.

Renee blinked away tears as he looked up at her as she sat down in the chair opposite him. She made sure to press her knees close together and tried to gather the ends of her robe, aware of the curious eyes of the other visitors and prisoners. She closed her eyes and released a breath filled with all her stress.

"Jackson," she began, opening her eyes to look at his profile as he sat at some spot beyond her.

He turned and looked at her. "I brought you a change of clothing," he said, his tone emotionless.

She nodded, forcing herself not to look away from his eyes. "They told me. Thank you . . . I . . . I . . . uh."

Jackson shook his head and balled his fist on top of the table. "We're better than this, Renee," he said, piercing her with eyes now filled with some anger and some sadness. "I fucked up . . . but you're better than this. What about the kids? What about you? What were you thinking?"

"In that moment?" she asked. "I wanted her dead."

Jackson dropped his head into his hand as he shook it.

"The alcohol, the jealousy, the hatred . . . all of it fueled one of the dumbest and the most dangerous things I've ever done," Renee admitted. "But I couldn't do it and I turned the car into the wall instead."

Jackson looked up. "You could have killed yourself."

Renee bit her bottom lip as she tilted her head back. "Everything . . . *everything* is all a fucking mess," she said in a harsh and emotion-filled whisper as one tear raced down her cheek.

"We will get through this," he insisted.

She swiped away her tears. "How? Through conjugal

visits?" she asked bitterly, her eyes brilliantly glassy with unshed tears.

"I have my attorneys already looking at the case and they'll be here for your bond hearing tomorrow and they're confident you will get a bond," he told her, his eyes filled with his desire to reach for her. To touch her. To comfort her.

Renee felt some comfort that Jackson was not ready to turn his back on her, but it wasn't enough to beat out the truth of the situation. "Jackson," she said, leaning in close. "I was going to kill your baby mama and she knows it. I am in jail," she stressed, almost choking on the words. "I'm an alcoholic. Friday was not the first day I've been drinking."

Her final words stunned him. He leaned back in his chair and wiped his mouth with his hands.

"Jackson," she said again, firmly. Insistent. "Jackson, it's over."

"What have I done to you?" he asked heavily.

For a moment, Renee wondered why she, on the side of the table for inmates, was consoling her husband, a visitor free to leave at any time.

"We loved each other . . . just not enough," she said with sad honesty. With a soft smile, she noticed the scattered gray hairs now filling the soft curls of his hair. "To be honest, Jackson, when I thought you fucked Jessa, I was prepared to forgive you. I was willing to fight for you."

He shifted his eyes up to hers.

Renee smiled sadly at the familiar wave of chemistry that floated over her body.

Jackson bit his bottom lip as he tilted his head back and looked up to the ceiling. "You never miss your water until your well runs dry," he said.

She shifted her eyes to look out of the window. Freedom. She missed it like crazy. How long before she felt it again?

They both fell silent. The minutes slipped by. Neither said or did anything. They were in limbo. They were at a crossroads.

"I have to go. Visitation is over," Jackson said, rising to his feet. He looked down at her. "I'll see you tomorrow when I pick you up to take you home."

Renee focused on his eyes, his jeans and T-shirt. Fifteen minutes was especially short in a jail. "I'll be okay, Jackson," she assured him, the words sounding hollow even to her own ears.

There's no turning back now, Renee thought the next morning as she sat in the holding cell awaiting her arraignment.

She took a deep breath and she rocked back and forth on the bench, trying hard to calm herself, to settle her nerves. "I made the right decision," she told herself. "I am a mother first and foremost. I am doing what is ultimately right for my children."

The door to the holding room opened and Renee looked up at the uniformed court officer motioning his finger for her to step out of the room.

Her stomach tightened into a tight knot and she even felt like her bowels might run. "Get it together, Renee," she told herself as she stepped out of the room at the end of the long hall.

She looked forward as she followed the officer through a large wooden door into the courtroom. As she was led to the defendant's table next to her attorney she saw Jackson, Aria, and Jaime sitting directly behind him. She gave them a soft smile, trying to reassure them that she was okay. She had survived the weekend in jail and was ready to survive more if necessary. It was completely out of her hands.

"I love you, Renee," Jackson mouthed.

Renee just looked away from him even as her heart tugged. She couldn't forget that outside of this courtroom the rest of the world moved on and her husband cheated and his mistress was pregnant.

"Justin Harringer representing the defendant, Your Honor," her attorney said, looking like he was worth every bit of the huge sum Jackson paid him.

The white-haired judge nodded as he looked through the open file. "Do you waive the reading?" the judge asked, eyeing him over the rim of his spectacles.

"Yes, Your Honor."

Renee stood motionless. That morning he had already explained that this was a formality, waiving the public reading of her charges.

Driving Under the Influence, Criminal Mischief, Misdemeanor Assault. Her charges. Possible jail time? Up to three years.

Shit.

But that was to come later once a trial date was set. For now she was taking Justin's advice and focusing on getting out of jail. *Quick, fast, and in a hurry,* Renee thought, as the judge asked the prosecution for the specifics of the case.

"Mrs. Clinton drove the vehicle under the influence of alcohol with the initial intent to run into the vehicle of Inga Brantley, the pregnant mistress of her husband—"

BAM. His words felt like a slap to the face and Renee had to force herself to show no emotion just the way her attorney instructed her.

"Mrs. Clinton lost control of the vehicle before the impact and instead crashed her vehicle into the main gate of the Richmond Hills subdivision where she lives."

Renee gasped. "I didn't lose control," she said, leaning forward to eye the female prosecutor.

The judge tapped his gavel.

Justin lightly touched her arm and leaned over to whisper in her ear. "You can't speak out in corner unless addressed by the judge."

"But—"

Justin's grip tightened just a bit. "But nothing, Renee. Now is not the time."

She pressed her lips closed. "I apologize, Your Honor," she said.

The prosecution continued with the details of that day.

"Recommendations for bail?" the judge asked, eyeing the prosecutor.

"The state requests a hundred thousand dollar bond."

Renee's knees went weak as her line of supporters behind her gasped.

The judge slammed his gavel again. "Defense," he said sternly, jotting down notes.

"After discussion with my client this morning I would suggest she be ROR. She has no criminal record, minor children that depend on her, and great ties to her community. She is not a flight risk."

Renee looked up to the judge.

"Attempting to run over her husband's mistress in a drunken rage?" the judge shook his head. "I am not inclined for an ROR, counselor."

Justin cleared his throat. "My client has volunteered to enter a thirty-day rehabilitation program with the ROR."

The judge briefly shifted his eyes to her. "Does the prosecution accept the conditional ROR?"

The prosecutor looked through her file briefly. "We stand by our suggestion for bond."

Lord, please. Please. Don't send me back to jail. Please don't let him send me back to jail, she prayed.

The judged quickly wrote something and flipped the file closed before handing it to his court clerk. "Mrs. Clinton is ROR with the condition that she enters an alcohol rehabilitation program within the next twenty-four hours."

Justin turned to her and was saying something, but

Renee had already turned to lean across the wooden divider for Jaime and Aria to wrap their arms around her. Tears of relief flooded her eyes as she looked over her friends' shoulders at her husband.

Her mind flashed back to the last few years of their lives. Nothing was how she'd thought it would be . . . and she doubted it ever would be.

Chapter 14

One Month Later

M*y wife,*
*I wish that I could turn back the hands of time to the
moment just before I decided to let anger and resentment lead to me the bed of another woman. I was a
fool. A weak-minded fool who let my past dictate
the way I viewed my marriage—our marriage. I
loved you and I feared every day that your career,
your life outside our home, would take you from me.
Every day I waited for you to come to me and say
our life was not enough. And that scared the shit out
of me. Losing you was my biggest fear, reliving the
pain my mother caused my father haunted me.
Instead of realizing that you had my back and you
were my backbone. Instead I began to resent you
like an enemy. I hate myself for it, because my fears
caused a lot of the destruction of our marriage. Our
lives.*

*You are not my mother. You are nothing like her. I
should have realized that years ago. I should have
done better by you, Renee. I should have loved and
trusted you.*

*And now we are facing you going to jail and my
having a child with another woman. Back when we*

were dating you used to say that we were a team and there was nothing we couldn't accomplish together. We can get through this. The trial, the baby, rebuilding our family. We can do this, Renee. I want to do this.

Please don't give up on us. We need each other now more than ever.

I miss you. I crave you. I love you.

Yours,
JC

Renee released a heavy breath as she allowed her fingers to trace Jackson's handwritten words. She had made the choice to have no visitors during her monthlong stay at the upscale rehabilitation center. But Jackson had written her nearly every day and Renee had to admit that the letters had been a bright spot in her day. And the topic of many sessions with the facility's therapist.

She folded the monogrammed stationery and pressed the letter down atop the others in the box before she put on the lid. She rose from the cushioned club chair by the window of her suite and looked around at the French country decor. Her suitcase was packed and sitting by the door.

She was sober. It felt good. She felt alive. Refreshed. Renewed.

Better than she had before she even began drinking.

"God is good," she said, digging into the box to pull out another letter.

Ma,
Dad told me that you didn't want us to visit and I guess I understand. I do hope that you get better, but I can't help but wonder how our family went to the left like that. I know you were mad at Dad for the

baby, but I hope finding out I was gay wasn't part of the reason you began drinking so badly. I wish you hadn't found out that way, but Ma I've known I was gay for years . . . and Darren was not my first boyfriend. . . .

Renee fanned herself with the letter as she released a heavy breath. This was far from the first time she'd read the letter, but each and every time her son's revelations stunned her. She felt like she didn't know her own child and she ached to know that he'd kept this secret, dealing with it all alone. She literally ached deep in her gut as she shook her head and refocused her eyes on the letter.

I know you might be saying why is he telling me this now, especially with everything you're going through, but I want you to deal with it in there instead of coming home and having it knock you on your ass again. Especially since I want you to accept that I love Darren and we are still seeing each other.

Another long breath. Renee had already placed her former assistant in her "don't fuck with me" category and now this? The anger she felt about that still set deeply with her. She didn't want someone she'd almost fucked fucking her son. Had Darren told him the truth about their relationship? Had he told Aaron that he'd eaten her pussy? Horribly so, but still, the mouth he kissed her son with had been places on her where the sun didn't shine.

Renee pulled back the sheer curtain to her window, enjoying the feel of the sun on her face. Mostly the letters were from Jackson with some from Aria and Jaime. Everyone had honored her request to write. Almost everyone. There were none from her daughter, Kieran. That hurt. That and the fact that Kieran had moved out of their home in Richmond Hills and in with Jackson's mother.

It seemed Kieran was angry and sick of both Renee and Jackson.

"Give her time," Jackson said in his letters.

Renee thought about the possibility of being thrown in jail. Time wasn't on her side and she still had many other issues on her plate. Her back-and-forth decision to reclaim Jackson and the love he swore he had for her. The anger of her children at her. Her upcoming trial.

But now she was better prepared to face it sober and clear headed. Her struggle for sobriety had just begun, but Renee had deepened her faith and strengthened her resolve to not fall back under the control of her vice.

"Ready, Mrs. Clinton?"

Renee turned to find Orie the rehab tech standing at her door. She cleared her throat as she nodded. "Yes, I'm ready," she said, pushing aside her fears of reentering the real world and all its stressors . . . and temptations.

Renee tucked her box of letters under her arm and grabbed the handle of her suitcase as she walked out of the room into the wide hall of the stylishly decorated facility. As she made her way out of the building all of the staff and most of the residents stepped forward to hug her and wish her well.

On the day of Renee's arraignment, as soon as she'd walked out of the courtroom they had all traveled in a chauffeur-driven Yukon to the rehabilitation facility. In the last thirty-one days she had really connected with a lot of the residents. Their stories had haunted her. Their resolve had impressed her. Their friendship had strengthened her.

Some she had exchanged contact information with.

With one final wave, Renee walked out of the frosted glass door to the outer area of the clinic. She smiled as Jaime and Aria rose to their feet. Her friends. "Oooh, it feels good to lay eyes on you heifers," she teased, stepping up as they formed a small circle hugging each other close.

"How are you?" Aria asked, her chocolate face filled with concern.

"Better," Renee said without hesitation.

"Good," Jaime said.

Renee looked past their shoulders and out the door. "Where's Jackson? Parking the car?" she asked, running her hand through her fuller and softer natural curls.

Aria and Jaime exchanged a look before they both looked at her. Each one took one of her hands.

Renee felt her shoulders droop. *Now what?*

"He asked us to pick you up because um . . . um . . ."

Renee squeezed Aria's hand as she saw her usually wordy friend struggle for the right words. "It's okay. I'm good. I'm a big girl. I can take it."

"Something about Inga going into premature labor and rushing to the hospital," she said, her eyes pained.

Renee nodded through her disappointment. "It's all right. Jackson has other priorities. He has this other person that he's responsible to. It is what it is," she finished.

Jaime and Aria looked unsure.

"Listen, I'm good because a month ago I would have been craving a drink and right now I'm hurt and I'm disappointed but I'm okay," she assured them.

As they gathered up her luggage and left the facility, anxious to fill her in on everything she'd missed in the last month, Renee's mind was on her husband at the bedside of another woman having his child.

In that moment, the letters and all of the emotions they evoked meant nothing because she and Jackson's love for each other could not—would not—change the fact that Jackson had a choice to make and she was not his pick. It was the first of many such choices.

It wasn't the marriage she wanted to have and she was ready to move on.

Finally.

Days later, Jaime smoothed her hands down the side of Pleasure's face as she looked down into his face. His hands grasped her buttocks tightly as she circled her hips, bringing his long and thick dick deep inside her core before easing him out, just to circle and take him deeply within her again.

She moaned in the back of her throat as she eased her body up enough for him to take one hard and thrusting nipple into his mouth.

"Aah," she gasped out sharply at the feel of his tongue circling, stroking, and then suckling her nipple.

"Why did it take you a month to call for this Pleasure?" he asked, his dreads spread out on the sheet beneath his head as he looked up at her hotly.

Jaime smiled with a little sultry bite of her bottom lip as she quickened the pace of her hips. She sat up, pressing her hands against the hard sweaty muscles of his chest. "Didn't want it until now," she told him huskily.

"Picture that shit," he said, all smug and shit.

Jaime shifted one of her hands up to cover his mouth. "Shut the fuck up," she told him. "I called you over here to fuck, not talk."

His eyes got a little bigger as she rode him harder with an arch of her eyebrow.

"I don't give a fuck what's on your mind or for all that gigolo bullshit you dish out. You got a big dick and I felt like fucking so here you are," she told him, loving how powerful she felt. *Fuck his mind games. I'm going for mine.*

Today was a new damn day.

She felt her nut rising and thrust her hips harder and faster, pressing the base of his hard dick against her clit. "You always did talk too much. Pleasure this. Pleasure that," she mimicked even as a shiver raced across her sweat-soaked body and an anticipation began to build deep within her pussy.

"Hmmmmmm," she moaned, flinging her head back as she kept her hand locked over his mouth.

Jaime bounced up and down on his dick, her breasts jiggling in all directions. She looked down at him fiercely as the first wave of her nut coated every inch of his dick. He brought his hands up to grab at her waist and she shoved them away.

"Ooh, your pussy hot," he moaned, now that his mouth was free.

Jaime massaged her own breasts as explosion after explosion after explosion fired off inside her core. She cried out hoarsely and sweat dripped from her body down onto him. Tears filled her eyes.

"Yessssssss," she sighed, feeling an amazing sense of calm in the midst of the electricity.

"Ooh. Make this dick come," Pleasure moaned.

Jaime didn't even give a fuck about him or his nut.

As soon as she shuddered with the last wave, she hopped right up off his dick and stood up from the floor.

"Hey," he called out, his condom-covered dick hard and glistening wet as it stood up like a soldier between his muscled thighs.

Jaime stumbled a bit on weak and wobbly legs as she brushed her new bangs from her face. "I'm done. You can get the fuck out," she told him over her shoulder as she left her empty bedroom with an unsteady gait.

"Jaime," he called out behind her. "Stop playing."

She stopped and turned around to eye him in the middle of the bed. Dick still swinging like a flagpole. "Thank you for the last two hours of incredible sex. I needed it. I got it. It's over. Bye-bye," she told him with a wave of her hand. "Lock the front door on your way out."

Fuck him.

She walked into the bathroom, locking the door behind

her. It was empty save for the one washcloth, towel, bar of soap, makeup bag, and change of clothes she had sitting on the commode.

"Can I at least get a shower?" Pleasure asked through the door.

"You sell dick for a living," she told him as she turned on the shower. "I'm sure this isn't your first or last time with a dirty dick."

She stepped into the shower, enjoying the feel of the spray hitting against her skin.

"What about my money, Jaime?"

She rolled her eyes heavenward. "Bill me," she hollered out before snapping the shower curtain closed.

Jaime was done with Pleasure. The night he'd chosen Granny over her because she couldn't scrape two nickels together she knew she had to find her pleasure elsewhere . . . but since she was in a good mood she'd allowed herself one last fuck. Crass but true. A little pleasure and revenge mixed all in one.

It felt damn good to go for hers and leave his dick blowing in the wind. Damn good. "Sooooo relaxing," she said with a little laugh.

Jaime finished her shower and dressed in the crisp white sundress she'd selected earlier. She freshened up her lightweight summer makeup and stepped back to review her reflection with a smile. "Looking good, girl," she said, feeling more like the old stylish and sophisticated Jaime, but better. Not just an image but the real deal. Real feelings. Real emotions.

True to herself.

It was about damn time.

Jaime left the bathroom and was pleased to find Pleasure had left the way she'd told him to. Hmph. *Deuces.*

Pleasure had nothing to offer her but a wet ass.

Her heels clicked against the wood as she walked

through the entire house one last time. She had discovered a lot about herself during the months she'd lived here. It was her first place all on her own. The place where she fully gave in and discovered that she had a healthy sexual appetite. The place where she had finally found the strength to walk away from a marriage that had failed a long time ago. The place where she'd learned more about herself than she had her entire life.

Jaime would miss it, but she had to move on. She had no choice. In life you had to play the cards you were dealt.

In the bedroom she bent down to scoop the sweaty sheet from the floor. She allowed herself a moment to inhale the scent of him and their sex. She purred a little in the back of her throat at the memory of all the explosive sex they'd shared. She would miss him—or rather *it*. His dick.

In truth she didn't know enough about him to miss him.

Balling the sheet up, Jaime walked out of the house and locked the door. She paused long enough to toss the sheet into the large garbage can on the side of the house. For a moment she considered keeping the sheet, but just like her lust for Pleasure she had no real use for it.

Jaime spared Lucas's house one last look. He had to have seen the moving trucks and known she was moving. Still, he'd barely spoken when he saw her. She tried to apologize, even sending him flowers and knocking on his door a couple of times, but everything was ignored. So now her attitude was fuck it.

She climbed into the Honda and smoothly reversed down the driveway, giving her town house, Lucas, and the neighborhood a final wave.

Jaime turned the air on full blast as she steered the car onto the Garden State Parkway. She enjoyed the quiet of the car. No music. Her cell phone on vibrate. Nothing but her thoughts and her plans as she drove.

In the last month she had lined up two decorating jobs. They were small, just a bedroom in one home and a den in another, but she was determined that everything she did from here on out was to build her interior design business and brand.

Jaime turned the Honda up to the wrought-iron entrance gate of Richmond Hills. She allowed herself to relish the moment. Her return. It felt damn good.

"Good morning, Lucky," she said to the portly security guard as she pulled up to his glass booth and entered her security code.

"Morning, Mrs. Hall," he said, his face already flushed.

"Um, Lucky, I'm not sure if you know, but Mr. Hall and I are divorcing and he is no longer permitted on the premises," she said.

Lucky made a sad face. "I'm sorry to hear that."

Jaime gave him a smile. "I'm not," she said before pulling through the now-open gates.

She laughed and blew her horn as she sped around the curve. It was hilarious to her how just a few months ago she would have plotted, planned, and schemed to keep her business from "the help," and now she really didn't give a flying fuck who knew that her marriage to Eric was over.

There was nothing but the formality of signing a document dissolving the lie.

"I'm ready to sign them papers," Jaime sang loud as hell, completing feeling Usher's ode to divorce.

She waved at *her* neighbors as she breezed past and eventually pulled into the driveway of *her* home. *Well, for now.*

Yesterday her attorney had delivered word that Eric had vacated the premises per their temporary settlement agreement. Their home, her showcase, was hers. As was her repossessed Volvo, a temporary monthly alimony payment, half of his 401K, a temporary income from his architectural business, and shared summer usage of their vacation home in Martha's Vineyard.

She already planned to invite Renee and Aria down for

a mini-retreat just for the ladies. They all could use a vacay to get over the aftermath of Jessa Bell the Jezebel.

Jaime parked the Honda next to her Volvo in the three-car garage. She started to call her girls over to enjoy this moment with her, but decided she wanted to step into her destiny alone. Independent. Self-assured.

Yes, she was wrong for the years she'd snuck away to watch Pleasure dance and even more wrong for cheating on her husband that night on the floor of that back room in the strip club. But discovering that her husband had been fucking Jessa—her friend—for years, long before her affair, she felt absolved and *more* than deserving of everything she got from him.

Jaime's step faltered as soon as she walked through the front door. Her mouth fell open, but she had no words. None.

"Oh my God," she whispered, raising her hand to her fast-beating heart.

Furniture shredded and destroyed. Glass broken into shards. The words SLUT, WHORE, and BITCH painted on the walls in shocking red paint. The smell of pee in the air and the sight of defecation smeared on the walls.

She felt fear like nothing else ever and backed out of the house, not quite sure Eric wasn't still lurking and waiting to take his rage out on her.

She doubted a hurricane could have caused such destruction. No, this scene before her was pure unadulterated rage.

Aria stuck her pencil behind her ear after making a note in the margin of the book she was reading.

Her research on the adoption process had led to a discovery of the vast amount of women—particularly African-American women—dealing with infertility. The more she read and researched and discovered, the more she wanted to know, research, and discover.

She felt a kinship with the women on blogs sharing their stories about struggling to do something that should be the most natural thing in the world: have a baby.

The more she read the more she wanted to break the ugly stigma attached to it.

"I felt like less of a woman. . . ."

Or

"I told people I didn't want children to keep from admitting that I couldn't. . . ."

Or

"Seeing or hearing stories of other women abusing or mistreating their own children when I couldn't be blessed to have a child ate me up. . . ."

Aria understood it all. All of it.

She was so ashamed of her own infertility that she'd lied to her husband and kept the truth from her own mother. She'd shared with no one the ache or the tears she shed at the thought of never bearing Kingston's child.

Aria sighed as she closed the book she was reading on herbal remedies to "heal the womb." She wasn't sure she believed it, but it was interesting reading nonetheless. If only sipping on false unicorn root once a day could reverse the injury she'd done to her womb.

She looked around at the people milling about the NetCafe, a cozy and comfortable coffeehouse that she loved to frequent to read or write when she needed a break from her house. She eyed her mini-laptop sitting on the round wooden table in front of her but didn't turn it on. It was intimidating to say the least.

Dr. Kellee was intrigued by her fascination with adoption and infertility. She felt Aria was using it as a shield or diversion from her personal struggles with herself and her marriage. And so she challenged Aria through an assignment that Aria's very next blog entry be about her own struggles with infertility. Because of it, Aria hadn't blogged in two weeks. Was she really ready to put her business out on front street like that? To have people side-eye her or pity her? She admired the women who shared their stories . . . but she didn't want to join them.

Hell to the no.

Dr. Kellee said she was ready.

Aria begged to differ.

She took a sip of her green tea before she stroked her fingers across the keyboard. *The truth is the light, Aria. So step out of the darkness.*

Dr. Kellee's words floated to her. Their sessions were raw and emotional, but Aria left there every week feeling more in control and in love with herself. Little by little. She was learning the power of forgiveness. Of herself. Of her past.

More and more Aria stood on solid emotional ground.

The power of forgiveness was necessary and amazing.

Aria looked down at her wedding band and engagement ring swinging from around her neck on a twenty-two-inch platinum chain. She fingered them with her right hand as she looked down at the bareness of her left hand.

Another of Dr. Kellee's assignments. She was not to put them back on until she felt completely free of her guilt and completely emotionally sound to be in a fulfilling, open, and honest relationship.

And until Aria felt Kingston felt the same.

That day had yet to arrive. But how could it? How could it?

She'd fucked up. True. But more and more, Aria's vision of their marriage was shifting. They'd both expected perfection and that didn't exist outside of fairy tales.

Plus, she was tired of waiting on his forgiveness. Tired of waiting for him to pull himself from his mother's bosom. Tired of him constantly throwing up her lie anytime they talked. Tired of waiting for him to bring his ass home. Just tired and sick of being tired.

Every week Dr. Kellee was moving her toward emotional health and with each bit of strengthening her will, she was losing patience with her husband, whom she loved and adored.

Sighing, Aria finished the last of her tea and gathered her laptop and book into her Coach satchel. As she strolled out of the busy coffeehouse, she slid on her aviator shades and pulled out her cell phone. She dialed Kingston's cell number, her heart pounding as she stood outside the coffee shop watching the busy traffic pass her by.

"Hey, Aria."

She closed her eyes. "Kingston, listen I love you. I . . . I adore you, but I have to take my life off of pause. I have to know where I'm headed. This limbo? This limbo is bullshit."

"Aria—"

She shook her head. "No, listen. I am sorry. I've said that a million times. I fucked up. I've said that a million more. But dammit. I can't . . . I won't do this. This is ridiculous, Kingston."

She fell silent and he offered no words. None. She felt weak. "You know, I realize now that I thought you were too good for me. That you were too perfect. But you're not."

"What does that mean?"

"You lack the power to forgive," she said softly, simply and honestly. "You have a flaw, Mr. Livewell."

"I never said I was perfect, Aria. I just ask not to be lied to and to be accused of fucking around when I wasn't."

"I am learning every day how to forgive myself for *everything* . . . and trust me, Kingston, this probably sounds really fucked up but I have a lot more on my plate that I did to myself than I ever did to you. A lot more."

"Aria—"

She balled her fist so tightly that her nails pressed into the flesh of her palm. "I need you to get off your Mama's tit, drink your milk from a cup, put on your big-boy drawers, and bring your black ass home before you don't have a home to come back to."

"And you feel you're in a position to deliver threats?" he asked, his voice low.

She couldn't distinguish the emotions in the depths. Anger? Annoyance?

Aria sighed. "I need you to learn how to forgive, Kingston. Life ain't black and white," she said, leaning her back against the metal lamppost as she ended the call. She pushed her shades up on top of her head as she wiped the sweat from around her eyes and nose.

She felt tired of the back and forth with Kingston. What more did he want from her? She didn't have shit else to give?

Aria pushed up off the lamppost and shifted her bag up higher on her shoulder as she walked past the tall man standing beside her. She couldn't wait to hear Dr. Kellee's thoughts on her ultimatum to Kingston. Too much? Too soon?

Aria sighed.

She felt a hand lightly touch her elbow and looked over her shoulder. She didn't recognize the older silver-haired gentleman. "Yes?" she asked.

He smiled. "I thought that was you," he said, smiling and showing off teeth so straight they had to be dentures.

He licked his lips. His eyes dropped down to her breasts in the V-neck tank she wore with fitted skinny jeans.

Aria felt repulsed. Her past was back again to fuck with her present. She remembered the last time one of her "tricks" ran into her when she was with Kingston. "Excuse me," she said, sliding her shades down onto her face as she turned and stepped out into the street.

"Hey," he called out behind her.

She barely heard over the long screech of tires against asphalt. Aria looked sideways. Her eyes widened just seconds before the oncoming black vehicle hit her.

She wasn't sure how much time had passed when she moaned and grunted softly in pain as she came to. Every part of her body throbbed or ached. She drifted somewhere in between the wake and sleep zone and she knew she was doped up on drugs.

The sound of a door opening and closing sounded and she tried to open her eyes, but they felt heavy like something weighed them down.

"How she doing?"

Mama.

"She's doing better. She's in stable condition. Thankfully she only has a broken leg and some contusions. It could have been much worse."

A nurse or doctor? She felt like she wanted to sit up, but a two-ton elephant weighed her down.

"Her face is so bruised and swollen."

Renee.

"I wish she would open her eyes."

Jaime.

"She's been out like a light since they brought her in."

Kingston!

Aria felt like she wanted to cry. Especially when she felt her hand being rubbed. She knew her husband's touch. She even recognized the familiar weight and coolness of her wedding bands on her finger. Had Kingston slipped them back on?

"Thankfully she didn't miscarry the pregnancy."

"Miscarry?" her mother, Kingston, and her friends all said in unison.

A baby? Oh my God. A baby!

"Yes, Aria is eight weeks pregnant."

The hold on her hand tightened.

"Oh my baby," her mother sighed happily, sounding like Claire Huxtable.

"We're going to be aunties!"

Through her haze, Aria felt the tears wetting her cheeks as she struggled to awaken. Suddenly she was enveloped by the scent of Kingston's spicy cologne just a moment before a kiss was pressed to her lips. Her tracks of tears. Her cheeks. Her forehead. Her ear lobe.

"Did you hear that, Aria? We're having a baby," he whispered near her ear. "You're going to be a mama."

Aria moaned slightly as she fought for total consciousness.

Her husband and her mother laughed.

Aria felt herself drifting back to sleep.

"I forgive you. I forgive you, Aria," he said, blessing her with more kisses.

She moaned and grunted slightly just before sleep consumed her.

Epilogue
"Goodbye, Jessa Bell"

*H*indsight is twenty-twenty.

I know now more than ever how true that is. But it is too late for regrets and what-ifs. The time to make different—better—decisions has passed.

It's ironic how the thought of stepping forward into my future without my man, my lover, my everything had been hurtful. Scary. Disappointing.

I cannot help but recognize that I drove the car that led my life down this road. I was the maker of my own destiny. The ruler of the domain of my life. Keeper of my pussy.

Now?

Now I know that welcoming him into my life and my bed was the biggest mistake I ever made . . . save for moving back to Richmond Hills at all.

It seemed the more he lost Jaime or lost out to something to Jaime, the more he clung to me and the more I resisted him, the angrier he became.

Vivid memories of messages or actions he took after our breakup shook me. Deeply disturbed me. That masturbation scene outside my windows was just the tip of the iceberg. His moods flipped between hating me and desperately needing me. Smothering me. Stalking me. Like an animal to prey.

"This is all your fault."

"You need me just like I need you."

"You destroyed me."

"You complete me."

"Both you bitches used me."

"Anything you want. It's yours. Just say the word."

"I hate you."

"I love you."

It was such utter madness.

There was no love in his actions. Just obsession. A crazed obsession that I didn't understand at all. A deluded obsession that I underestimated.

Tonight he bombarded his way into my home. He touched me with a brutality and cursed me with a cruelty.

"Bitch, you're the reason Jaime divorced me."

"You helped her take everything from me!"

"You destroyed me!"

Eric . . . this . . . person who paced and paced, his eyes darting about the room as he moved frenetically, was a stranger.

He is not my friend. He is not my lover. He is not the man I thought he was and I welcomed the illusion into my life and now I'm left to deal with the reality.

The finality.

I am looking into the eyes of crazy as I feel the life leaving my body from the tight clutch of his hands around my throat even as he presses his lips to mine with such rage. It is a kiss meant to punish. Meant to degrade.

My body is already trembling. The heat and life fading as the strength leaves my body.

"This is all your fault."

"You need me just like I need you."

"You destroyed me."

"You complete me."

"Both you bitches used me."

"Anything you want. It's yours. Just say the word."

"I hate you."

"I love you."

My eyes roll back into my head and finally he releases me. My body slumps to the floor. His cries mean nothing to me. His attempts to revive me are too late. I know that. If I could turn back time . . .

If I could go back to that moment just before he first slid his hand up my skirt.

Coulda, woulda, shoulda.

As I lay on the floor and take my last breath I hear a gunshot echo throughout the room.

I can only pray that he is joining me in hell.

Dear Readers of *Mistress No More,*

Well, it was a very long wait for this sequel and I thank you all for your patience and for caring about how it all unfolded. I hope all of your questions were answered and your wishes fulfilled. I feel drained of all of the emotions I poured into this book. At times I would end a sentence and have tears in my own eyes or laughter in my heart. I write from the soul and I'm grateful that a lot of you connect with that.

I cannot thank you all enough for the success of *Message from a Mistress*: the book clubs, the bloggers, the blog talk radio hosts, and every reader who supported this project. I thank you all from the bottom of my heart. For those who have been riding with me since 2000, I thank you and hope our journey continues. For those just introduced to me, I hope you're inspired to learn more and to read more.

Again, I thank you all.

Best,

N.

Connect With Niobia:

Web site:	www.NIOBIABRYANT.com
E-mail:	niobia_bryant@yahoo.com
Twitter:	/InfiniteInk
Myspace:	/niobiawrites
Facebook (Personal Page):	/InfiniteInk
Facebook (Announcement Page):	Niobia Bryant-Meesha Mink
Shelfari:	/Unlimited_Ink
Yahoo Group:	/Niobia_Bryant_News

When it comes to joining the ranks of Washington DC's glamorous elite, no social ladder is too high for these ambitious ladies to climb in Angela Winters's latest,

Back On Top

On sale in August 2011 from Dafina Books

Chapter 1

Sherise Robinson couldn't believe she had let herself run behind today of all days. Her first day back at work from maternity leave and she was going to show up late if she didn't speed things up. That was not the message she wanted to send.

As she rushed around the master bedroom of her elegant Georgetown town house on Washington DC's northwest side, Sherise felt panic start to set in. A lot was riding on how today went, no matter how much her husband, Justin, tried to tell her otherwise. The power-hungry, manipulative bitch, as her coworkers secretly referred to her, was coming back, and if she showed any signs of softening, weakening, she was dead. The barracuda was now a mama and she could just imagine what they were all thinking: *She's vulnerable.*

She was going to show them they were wrong and as she stopped to look in the full-length mirror that covered her walk-in closet door, her confidence was lifted. Finally she had found her missing Missoni stacked pumps and her outfit was complete. She looked sharp and sexy, and at twenty-seven, Sherise felt certain she showed no signs of having just given birth six months ago. That was thanks to very expensive underwear that tucked everything in, but also to the fact that she had made sure not to gain more than the twenty-five pounds her doctor told her was the minimum amount of healthy weight gain during her pregnancy. While there was still a stubborn pound or two hanging around, everything was tightening up nicely.

From head to toe, Sherise checked every inch. Her shoulder-length hair, just done yesterday, was placed nicely in a sharp "don't fuck with me" bun with just a few "I might be flirting with you" dark brown tendrils falling down. She liked to keep the men confused. It gave her an advantage and Sherise was all about getting the advantage. Her makeup was flawless, highlighting her high cheekbones and dark green eyes. It was spring, so her lipstick was a soft, flirtatious pink. Her golden caramel skin was glowing and it would wow when she took off the jacket of her black and white striped Nipon wide-legged pantsuit to reveal her white sleeveless Marc Jacobs business shirt. No one who saw her at the Executive Office Building today would forget.

"I'm back," she said in that sexy, raspy voice of hers. "Bitches better step aside."

"You're late," were the first words Justin Robinson said to his wife as she entered the European-style, contemporary designed kitchen only seconds later.

"I'm fine," Sherise answered as she rushed for the refrigerator. "I'm taking a cab."

"Ah! Ah!"

Sherise quickly closed the refrigerator door and rushed over to the little monster emitting those sounds. Her six-month-old baby girl, Cady, was the love of her life. She sat in her baby chair, her hands reaching out for her mommy with evidence of her breakfast all over her face, not to mention her bib. She was an adorable baby with soft, chocolate skin; nice and chunky with fat cheeks that Sherise couldn't get enough of.

"Sorry, baby!" Sherise leaned in for a quick kiss, but

didn't trust herself for more. She knew leaving Cady today would be hard enough. "Mama has to go."

"You should eat something." Justin put down the baby spoon and leaned back in his chair. He was looking at his wife with concern. "You don't want to go in there without your fuel."

"I'm grabbing something on the way." Sherise appreciated her husband's concern, but there was a part of her that was still a little angry with him for trying to pressure her to stay home for good.

Justin, thirty, was old fashioned and his upbringing had been very different from hers. Because Sherise grew up poor as dirt on the hard streets in Southeast DC with no father to be found and a mother who couldn't give a damn, she only knew how to fight. Justin was a lover, not a fighter. From Chicago, he grew up in a traditional middle-class black family with a stay-at-home mother, a doctor for a father, and all the safety cushions that came with such an upbringing. He was stable and reliable and represented what Sherise wanted to be, which was why she decided she was going to marry him the same night she met him four years ago when he was just a recent Georgetown Law grad. A reliable wage earner who was hot enough to be attractive, but not so hot that every other woman would want him, too. He was the kind of guy that would come home every night. Most of all, Justin, a six-figured salaried lobbyist on Capitol Hill, had the connections that Sherise's never-ending ambition could use to get ahead.

But Justin put a wrench in her ambition game when he suggested Sherise be a stay-at-home mom after Cady was born. They had agreed to a regular twelve-week maternity leave, knowing that Sherise had plans of moving beyond her position as Assistant Director of Communications for the White House Domestic Policy Council. She was hungry for power and her ultimate dream was to make it from the Executive Office Building across the street to the West Wing of the White House. After endless fighting, Sherise went the route that had always served her well: refusing affection until she got her way. While she loved Justin, he did not overwhelm her, which made him a good husband candidate for her. She could control the way her body reacted to him, thus control the power he had over her.

It wasn't as if he wasn't attractive. He was six feet tall and while he had an extra 10 lbs, he wore it well. He was a sexy dark brown with beautiful light brown eyes and a sturdy face. He wore preppie boardroom glasses that made him look distinguished and was always looking sharp in his expensive business suits. The point was, while she found him perfect husband and father material, Justin had never gotten Sherise to lose control of herself. She could resist him, but he couldn't resist her. She played her games and made certain he couldn't resist, which resulted in a quick marriage proposal. This control over him was why her compromise of a six-month leave was quickly accepted and rewarded with access to affection again.

Sherise felt a pull in her gut as Cady called for her again, but she fought it and went to check her briefcase. It made her want to cry, but she wasn't a stay-at-home mom type. She was too ambitious; too greedy. Did that make her a bad mother? She didn't know. She only knew that she would be miserable without the challenge of a career. It made her feel strong, safe and allowed her to do what she did best: power play and win.

"I filled up her bag." Sherise's back was to her husband and child as she organized the items in her briefcase on the French villa designed dining room table. "So all you have to do is grab it and walk her over to the day-care center."

Sherise almost jumped when she felt Justin's hand on her shoulder. She turned to face him and was comforted by the compassion in his eyes.

"I know this is hard for you, baby." He leaned forward

and kissed her on her forehead. "You don't have to pretend."

"Please," she begged. "Don't do that. You'll make me cry. I can't walk in there with red eyes."

"You know that you'll be back in the swing of things before noon," he said. "Don't sweat it, baby. Cady will be fine at day-care. I'll drop her off on my way to work and you can pick up her up on your way home."

"And you don't hate me?" she asked.

Justin smiled his usual charming smile. "I couldn't if I tried."

She knew that. She could always rely on Justin to be a supportive husband and a fully involved father. Which made her feel all the worse knowing that Cady might not even be his child.

Billie Hass felt her stomach getting tighter and tighter as every second passed. Her petite fingers gripped the coffee cup in her hand as she stood at the counter and looked out the window facing the street. The building where she was starting her new job on K Street was right in front of her. She didn't look much different than any of the expensively suited lawyers that walked inside, but she knew she was different.

Growing up in southeast DC Billie had witnessed the injustices against the poor first-hand. A father she watched accused of a crime he didn't commit and railroaded by the system and a mother who died trying to fight the power of health insurance companies had molded her opinion of power. She knew two things. She had to get out of poverty and she had to fight for those who couldn't fight for themselves. This was why she fought against the odds and made her way to law school always with the objective of fighting for the little man.

She graduated four years ago, at age twenty-five, and began her career as a public defender in DC. She was chided for not shooting for Big Law and six-figure salaries, but was planning for something better. Billie intended to run for office one day and use her power to fight for legislation that spoke for the voiceless. The young men who were guilty until proven guilty and poor women who the system shepherded toward dependency. She had met with a lot of obstacles but was winning more than losing. That was until Porter Hass happened.

Billie met Porter at Georgetown Law School. He was four years older than she having spent time in the navy before coming to school so she found him to know a bit more than the average brother she dealt with every day. They had so much in common. While Billie had grown up in the tough streets of Southeast DC, Porter had struggled to survive in the dangerous Highland Park neighborhood of Detroit. Seeing his brother shot dead by cops at the age of ten and get away with it, Porter had many of the same plans to fight the power when he started law school.

But something changed. One of the other things Porter and Billie had in common was a desire to live a better life than they had known as kids; to escape the ghetto mentality that bad was good and there was no way to succeed so why bother. They wanted to escape always being on the wrong end of . . . well, everything. But unlike Billie, who only wanted to get rid of the bad, Porter began to desire an escape from all of it. Billie didn't want to forget everything about the Hood, but Porter did and at some point during law school, he decided he wanted to be the power that they were supposed to want to fight.

She still married him because she loved him and he had a lot of good qualities. He was smart and sexy and he was a great father to his now fourteen-year old daughter, Tara. While he was still in law school, Porter fought for custody of Tara when her mother, Shawn, got too deep into drugs to care for her properly. Porter and Shawn were teenagers when she got pregnant, and while Porter fought his way out of it all, Shawn never bothered. He never turned his back on Tara and for that, Billie loved him. That, and the fact that he set her body on fire every time he touched her. She had never felt the passion for a man that she had for Porter. Their sexual chemistry blew her mind.

But while it blew her mind, it wasn't enough to save their marriage. Billie could handle Porter's negative comments about the people she defended and even his digs at what he called her "ghetto tendencies," but if it wasn't clear they were moving in different directions, his affair with the blond, perky twenty-three-year-old associate at his law firm, Claire Flannigan, was as clear as rain. The heartbreak was followed by the divorce where Porter's expertise and connections gave him the upper hand over Billie. It all put her in a position where, financially, she could no longer afford to work for a pittance. She had six-figure student loans, new bills, and Porter had taken everything in the divorce.

Now, here she was on the corner of K Street and 18th in northwest DC, barely visible above the morning crowd in her petite five foot three inch frame. She had the skills to get a high-paying job in Big Law white-collar criminal defense. Her money problems were taken care of, but starting her life over, divorced and single at twenty-nine, was not what she had imagined.

Feeling her phone vibrate in her pants pocket gave Billie an excuse to wait just a few more minutes before entering the building and leaving the career she loved behind. The fact that it was Tara was just icing on the cake.

"Hey, sweetheart," Billie said, holding her finger to her free ear to drown out the crowd noise. "What's up?"

"I hate that bitch!"

"Whoa, Tara. What is going on?" Billie knew her step-daughter had a short temper just like her father. She got angry over anything. "What's wrong?"

"Claire," Tara said with a voice that sounded a lot younger than fourteen. "Billie, you just don't know what I deal with."

"What did she do now?" While Claire was the last person Billie wanted to talk about, she would never turn Tara away. Porter was making it hard enough for her to spend time with the girl now that they were divorced. She loved Tara and missed her terribly, which Porter knew.

"She's moving in," Tara answered.

Billie felt her chest tighten at the words. She tried to control her emotions. Their divorce had only been final three months. "Well, she is your father's girlfriend."

"She's his jump off," Tara corrected. "You don't marry the side piece."

"He's not marrying her." Billie shuddered at the thought. "At least not yet."

"He married you after you moved in," she countered. "Only I liked you. This stuck-up Barbie is not going to be my new stepmother."

Billie sighed. "Tara, I can't really tell you how to be with her. You know I'm compromised on this."

"You hate her," Tara said. "Just like me. She's selfish and stupid and had the nerve to try and tell me what to do this morning."

"You really need to talk to your father about this." Billie's instinct was to advise Tara to tell Claire to go fuck herself, but she knew that wasn't right. Tara didn't need to be put in the middle of this more than she already was. "You're gonna have to sit down and . . ."

"Billie?"

Billie didn't even need a second to recognize the voice of her ex-husband. Porter had a deep, mesmerizing voice that pulled at something inside of her even when he was mad, like now.

"Billie," he repeated. "Is that you?"

"Yes, it is." Billie could hear Tara complaining in the background. "Look, Porter, I was just . . ."

"You're not allowed to talk to my daughter without my permission!"

"Since when?" Billie asked.

"Since I said." His voice was cold and short. "You're not her stepmother anymore."

"But you know I love her and she loves me," Billie said. "We were just talking."

"You're trying to turn her against Claire," Porter accused. "And I'm not gonna let you do it."

He hung up before Billie could defend herself. Not that it would have made a difference. While he had promised to give Claire up once Billie found out, he never had. And when she made it clear a divorce was what she wanted, he made it clear that Claire was what he wanted. Ever since, Billie only saw the ugly side of the man she used to love. He had humiliated her and betrayed her and now he was going to try and keep her from Tara, the closest thing she ever had to a child of her own.

Which made it all the more insane to Billie that she was still sleeping with him.